LAURA THALASSA

D1707680

the
Damned

BURNING EMBER PRESS

A Burning Ember Book
Published in the United States by Burning Ember Press, an imprint of Lavabrook Publishing Group.

THE DAMNED. Copyright © 2015 by Laura Thalassa
www.laurathalassa.blogspot.com

To all my readers,

This one's for you

PROLOGUE

Eons and eons ago, the fates decided to fashion a woman for an untamable god. One saw it as a gift to honor his greatness. Another saw it as a curse to bring destruction on his house. The third saw it as a chance for the world to evolve.

They planned and plotted the woman's birth and death and spoke of her far before she breathed life.

And the god, he was intrigued.

The eons came and eons went, and the world forgot. But the god didn't.

And when the time came, Nona spun his intended into existence. Whether by accident or by plan, the fate grabbed the thread of the god's undying creation—a vampire—along with the dark god's own, and she twined both cords to that of his betrothed.

All three forever to be bound.

The god's intended and his creation found each other, for a time, and the thread that bound them pulled tight. Then their time ended, and another began.

And so the woman became the dark god's and the dark god became hers. Heaven and earth revolted, and now hell will pay.

CHAPTER 1

Gabrielle

"WELCOME TO HELL, my queen."

The roar of the crowd was thunderous. Their moans, their screams, their exultations blended with the crackle of fire. I couldn't even say what emotion rode the hordes that stared back at us. Excitement seemed too pleasant a word. Blood-hunger seemed better—the kind of fervor that fueled mobs. It stared back at me. It wanted to devour me.

I stood outside on a castle balcony, the devil at my side. Scorching flames rose all around us, as far as the eye could see, yet I felt none of the inferno's heat.

My hand shook in the devil's, and his thumb began rubbing circles on my skin. Perhaps it was meant to relax me. It did the opposite.

"Enough," he said to his subjects.

Hades, I corrected myself, *I have to think of him as Hades*.

He hadn't raised his voice, but the crowd quieted. If you could call it that. Out there, in the land of eternal suffering, nothing was quiet.

"Meet my consort, Gabrielle Fiori, Regina Inferna, Queen of Hell."

Gabrielle Fiori, a thousand different beings whispered, testing my name on their tongues. I could hear them even over the shrieks of the burning souls, and I could feel their intrigue brush against my skin.

Demons. Demons whispered my name.

"You are to give her the respect a queen deserves. Anything less will be met with ..." the devil paused for effect, "severe punishment." He didn't need to smile to alert every single being in that room that he'd love nothing more than doling out more pain.

On that sobering note, he tugged on my hand. "Come, consort. We have much to discuss."

MY PALM SWEATED as he led me back up the stairs.

I am in hell. I am in hell. I am in hell.

"Yes, you are," Hades said, answering my thoughts. Our footsteps echoed ominously in the abandoned castle. "Finally, you're here with me. The centuries I have waited for this. And now the waiting is over."

So this was how it all ended. Here in this damned realm that felt so crowded yet so lonely, and me trapped by this man's eyes and our bond. I should've known the first time I saw him, standing amidst the flames of my burning house, that this would be how it ended—in another house of flames.

"There are two areas of hell you must know about," the devil said. "The inside and the outside—the palace and the fields. We are, as you might've guessed, currently on the inside, and you have glimpsed what is on the outside.

"The palace is where you'll be staying for most of the time."

I looked up at the ceiling, feeling the walls of this place close in on me. Stuck here, confined to a palace. It might be large, it might be vast, but it was still a prison.

The devil must've read my thoughts for he said, "Of course, if you wish to join me in punishing the damned, you are always welcome outside."

As he led me through the castle, he gestured to some of the doors we passed. "Torture chamber. Torture chamber. Conference room. Torture chamber."

"I'm noticing a theme here," I said.

The devil smirked but said nothing. His shoes clicked against the stone floor. I'd come to hate the sound of them.

The walls here, made out of the same dark stone as the rest of the castle, were carved with faces of gargoyles and demons, and if I stared long enough, I could swear those faces moved.

We halted when we came to an elaborately carved door. Hades pushed it open and stepped aside so I could enter.

The room was hexagonal, just like the one I woke up in, and, like the rest of the palace I'd seen so far, it was decked out in black. On the far side of the room, the walls opened up to an opulent balcony. And in the center of the room was a canopy bed. Gauzy swaths of semi-transparent material hung from each post.

"Another torture chamber?" I asked.

He stepped in close behind me, his lips a breath away from my ear. "Not quite. This is one of our bedrooms."

My stomach dropped at his words while my connection ... my connection flared to life.

"What've you done?" I whispered.

He came around to face me. As he did so, our connection throbbed. The devil's—shit, *Hades*—and mine. "Many things, little bird. Elucidate me on which you're accusing me of."

I edged away from him and clutched my heart, which thumped beneath my hand. I had no time to marvel over the fact that I once again had a heartbeat. "Why do I feel you here?" I asked.

He took another step forward. "You were made for me."

Not an answer.

"But, Andre—"

"Do not speak the vampire's name to me," the devil hissed.

How could this happen? Making a deal with the devil, coming to hell, that was one thing. But to be bonded to this man, to have a part of me joined with him ...

Sickness rose within me. My body had betrayed me in the most fundamental way.

"Come, my queen."

"No."

He took my hand without asking and our surroundings disappeared, only to be replaced with those of a grand dining room.

Hades led me to an intricately wrought chair. I sat, thinking he would take his own seat, but instead he knelt in front of me.

"I will take care of you and cherish you the same way I do my power," he said.

I searched his eyes. They were beautiful, just like the rest of his features. Beautiful, foreign and frightening.

"Why?" I asked. The devil wasn't supposed to have a caring side. He was sadness and despair and loneliness and anger and violence and—

He sighed. "I can burn away a soul but apparently not your human misconceptions. You think I'm incapable of anything but hate and pain."

You are.

"I am everything and nothing," he continued. "Cultures have never agreed on a definition of me because I exceed language and logic. But, know this, Gabrielle: I am not the devil. Not with you."

"Then what are you?"

"Your soulmate."

That word implied so many things. I sorted out which ones I thought the devil meant and which he probably didn't. The result left me cold.

"I know what you want from me," I said.

The subarctic temperature of the room warmed. Literally. The devil's eyebrows rose. "I'm no human man, but yes. I would take your flesh along with your heart and soul."

He saw my terror, and I swear it looked like someone slapped him before he recovered his composure. Then the expression was gone as fast as it appeared, leaving me wondering if my eyes had played tricks on me.

"What do I call you?" I asked, pretending to go along with his declaration that I had things all terribly wrong.

Our connection throbbed. His face gave nothing away, but I realized as I stared at him that the pulse came from satisfaction. His. He liked that I asked, that I wanted his opinion on something.

"When we are alone, you may call me 'Asiri.'"

I'd never heard of that name. "Did you just make that up?"

He laughed, and the sound rose the hairs on my arms. More disturbingly, it also seemed to caress me like soft velvet. I enjoyed the sound of his laugh.

This situation was so messed up.

"No, I did not. Men and women who lived and died thousands of years ago addressed me as such. They liked me better then. They liked you too—not as much, but we can't all be favorites."

That didn't even deserve a response.

"*Asiri.*" I tried out the word. It echoed in the cavernous room, and hot, phantom winds ruffled my hair, then resettled. In this realm, the word itself had power behind it.

I might call him this. So long as he didn't piss me off. Otherwise, it was back to the usual gauntlet of names. Only I'd find which one annoyed him most, and I'd use that one over and over again.

The devil—Asiri—smiled at me, whether from my thoughts, which he sometimes heard, or my saying this archaic name.

There was something intimate about the name he gave me. Asiri. A name no longer spoken by humans. It was mine and his alone. My heart beat faster. I knew he could hear it because he reached up and covered the skin over it with his hand.

"Are you nervous?"

Staring at this beautiful, evil thing? This ageless god who shared a secret name with me?

"I'm petrified."

He smiled, not unkindly, and kept his hand on my chest until the thump of my heart went back to normal.

"Better?" he asked.

"No. Your hand is still touching me."

"It is."

I could feel the heat from his palm seeping into me. Our bond tugged at us, beckoning us closer. Before, when the cord connected me with Andre, my soulmate had fought to keep his physical distance, fearing that if he didn't, he'd rush me and I'd regret it.

Now that my bond had somehow attached itself to the devil, I found myself pulling away, fighting this force of nature that tried to eliminate the distance between us.

I could tell as the devil leaned forward, something wondrous and hungry in his eyes, that he'd never come across anything like this bond.

Just then, a woman—demon?—came in with a tray bearing two champagne glasses. Celebratory drinks.

I exhaled, my body relaxing at the distraction.

"Ah, here we are," Hades said, taking the flutes from the tray and handing one to me.

Mechanically, I wrapped my hand around it.

The woman bowed to Hades and left, leaving us alone once more.

"To us," he said. He clinked his glass to mine and took a sip. I watched him, fascinated. He drank ... champagne. So weird.

I glanced back down at my own glass, twirling the bubbly liquid. "Aren't I not supposed to eat or drink here?" In the myths, Persephone trapped herself in the Underworld after she ate the food. I may be dense when it came to these things, but imbibing anything seemed like a bad idea.

The devil brought his glass away from his lips and stared at me for a long moment. Then he threw back his head and laughed. "You're already here, consort. I'm not trying to entrap you. Just trying to get you drunk while I whisper sweet nothings in your ear in hopes that I might get lucky."

Ewwww.

I lowered my glass. "I'm too young."

"To drink? Or to bang?"

"'Bang'?" I couldn't stop my scowl.

"Forgive me—to make sweet tender love to your nubile body."

"Ugh, you can stick with bang."

I stared at my drink again, until the devil removed it from my gasp. "If you don't want to drink perfectly decent champagne, I'm not going to force you to."

"You won't?" The words slipped out before I could help myself. But seriously, the devil's M.O. had changed since we were last together.

Take it or leave it, Gabrielle. He's being decent when he could be bashing your skull in.

The devil's lips twitched. He had to have heard that thought.

I worked my throat. "What do I call you when we're not alone?" Which would be always if he kept looking at me like he was.

"Pluto or Hades is fine," he said, his eyes focusing on my mouth.

He'd avoided his Christian pseudonyms. Those were the especially depraved ones. Interesting.

"And what would you like me to call you in private?" he asked.

"Gabrielle is fine."

"Not ... 'soulmate'?" He'd clearly said the words to goad me, and damnit if the endearment didn't lance right through me.

"Do you even have a soul?" I asked.

He flashed me a secret smile, his eye glittering. "Maybe. Maybe not. It's a mystery I'll enjoy watching you unravel."

He rose and pulled me up with him. "Secret names and cordial conversations. It's not Rome, but it is a start."

I eyed him warily.

"Soon," he said, placing a finger at the hollow of my neck, "you'll crave the chance to say my name. To hear my opinion." He ran his finger down. There were holes in the webbed lace of the dress I woke up in, and I felt that finger slide over bare skin. "To feel my affection." His finger kept going, only stopping once it reached my navel. "And my touch."

Never. I'd never forget all the heinous things he'd done to me and those I loved.

"But until then, there is much you need to know. And while I'd enjoy watching you struggle to learn about your new powers and position, I cannot afford to have you look weak."

The power he spoke of thrummed beneath my skin. I'd acquired new abilities as the queen of the Underworld. I knew, for instance, how to place a new soul into hellfire and forge him into the devil's weapon, and I could command the devil's legions.

"Not, my sweet, without my approval."

My chest rose and fell, faster and faster. The devil—Lucifer—*Hades*, damnit—stepped closer, his eyes transfixed on my chest. Either my boobs or my fear pulled him in. Neither alternative made me feel better.

I stared down at my hands, as if they held the answers I sought. "What am I?"

"You're Gabrielle Fiori, queen of the Underworld."

"That's not what I'm asking."

"I know that's not what you're asking. You want an identity when there's none to give. You're Ereshkigal, the Mesopotamian queen of the great earth, goddess of the Underworld. You are Hel, the beautiful Norse goddess whose embrace men ran to their deaths for—though, if they were wise at all, they will think twice about that. I don't take kindly to interlopers." The way he looked at me when he said that made me feel like I needed another layer of clothes on. He took one of my hands. "You are Mania, the Roman goddess and mother of the dead. And, finally, you are Persephone, the woman I stole from earth and laid claim to.

"You are all of them and not quite any of them. You can cross worlds, drink blood, beguile men with your voice, and reign—second only to me—a legion of souls. You can do all that and more. The power you wield is near limitless because it is bonded to mine."

I narrowed my eyes at the devil. "You don't share your power. You've said so yourself."

"I am known as the Deceiver. I have said many things in the past that you should not believe, wife."

"I'm not your wife," I said sullenly.

Wrong thing to say.

His hand tightened on my own. "Yes," he agreed. "In the most archaic of terms, you are not. I am willing to rectify that, immediately."

I swallowed.

"Or—" he said, "you can agree with me and save the rectifying for a time you truly want it."

That would be never.

The devil suddenly looked beyond me, towards the door out of the dining room. "I need to go. Explore on your own. I'll be back later." And then he winked out of existence.

I SPENT THE next several hours—at least what felt like hours—wandering through the castle. It had great halls, cavernous rooms, and staggering towers, each area more oddly beautiful than the last, and each barren of life. From what I could tell, the palace was sprawling. It would take me weeks to learn this place.

The floors, walls and vaulted ceilings all appeared to be made out of obsidian—volcanic glass. The faces of gargoyles, screaming souls, and horned, snarling beasts all twisted their way up the walls, their faces pressed against the stone's surface as though they were trying to break free. I'd glance away for a moment, but when I'd look back at the wall, I'd swear those faces changed shape. The place seemed alive, and I got the distinct impression that these walls did in fact talk.

Now I stood halfway down a long hallway fitted with narrow windows that looked out over the kingdom of fire. I stepped up to one.

The flames began just beyond the wrought iron gate that circled the palace grounds. They stretched as far as the eye could see, popping and hissing as they burned through their human fuel.

My eyes darted up to avoid catching a glimpse of all those agonized souls. Thick, filmy smoke hung high in the air, hell's version of clouds. The firelight danced upon it. Beyond the smoke, all I saw was inky darkness.

While on earth, I'd never actually believed hell was below us. But right now it felt like I stood at the core of the earth, and the only thing that kept this place from being consumed entirely was the devil's magic.

Despite my best efforts, my eyes moved back to the flames. I caught glimpses of souls here and there, and then the fire would roar up and swallow their image once more. And all those screams, they came together like a symphony, something haunted and hypnotic.

Somewhere out there the devil stood among them, or maybe he'd gone to the land of the living to make deals with the desperate.

Either way, he'd left me here to molder, and I had no doubt it was intentional. After all, I couldn't spend an eternity cooped up in this building; I was barely managing a single day. Eventually, I'd seek him out.

Another frightening thought had me backing away from the window. I didn't feel hollow. I didn't feel like the wickedness of this place was trying to burrow under my skin. I could only guess that it had already claimed me.

My back bumped into the wall. The cold stone vibrated against my skin.

I was so fucked. So, so fucked.

My heart seized, as though it too realized the mess we were now in. I wheezed in a breath.

Not again. I thought I was done dying.

But it wasn't my body giving out. Power washed over me, and then the cord that connected me to the devil flared to life.

Hello, little bird.

I sagged against the wall. "What are you doing?"

Strengthening our bond.

That was what caused the pain in my heart?

"I thought I was dying." I rubbed the material covering

15

my chest.

Not until all memory of our existence is wiped from the world and all traces of us have been destroyed will you face annihilation. Only then should you worry.

How reassuring.

"Where are you?" I asked.

Everywhere there is sin. Are you speaking out loud to an empty room?

My cheeks pinkened ever so briefly at the realization that I was, in fact, doing just that. I touched my cheek. I could blush again.

I wish to see this.

In the next instant, the devil stood in front of me.

I startled.

He tilted his head as he studied my face, and I had to look away because he was too much. Even though I'd shed my mortal life—along with the last of my humanity—the perfection of his features still felt almost painful to gaze at.

"I don't like you inside my head," I said.

"You also don't like me inside your heart. Too bad for you, neither is going to change any time soon."

The connection between us felt like a livewire. I could sense him on the other end, his glee and his anger and, beneath it all, his contentment. I hadn't expected him to have human emotions, and I definitely hadn't expected them to be so ... normal.

"You make me feel human." He said this with a frown. Someone didn't like that fact.

Before I could react, he was gone again.

I breathed in and out through my nose, trying to control the cocktail of emotions welling up in me.

Hot damn, that man was unsettling.

CHAPTER 2

Gabrielle

I DIDN'T SEE the devil again until that evening. By then I'd discovered the castle's (only?) library—if you could even call it that. A single bookshelf stood amidst the room.

Still, it meant respite from the boredom quickly setting in. The shelf contained a whopping thirty-two books. I knew because I'd counted them all. And now I'd begun the tedious process of flipping through each one.

I heard leather crack as I opened the newest tome. I winced. I wouldn't think about the creature this leather came from. Nor would I think about the type of ink responsible for the brown pigment of each handwritten word.

I traced my finger over the letters. The language wasn't English, and I'd never seen this alphabet before.

But I could read it. And when I opened my mouth and spoke the words out loud, I understood what I was saying. This had to be the language of the Underworld, a language I inherited the moment I had been made queen.

I began to read about a demon known as Razael who liked to—surprise, surprise—torture people.

Come to me, consort. Hades' voice startled me from my reading.

No, I responded after I collected myself.

You used our connection. He smiled in my mind, and oh God, I needed a shower from the inside out.

I could help you with that. We could crack you ribcage open, disembowel you—

Ugh, stop it. That imagery ... I shuddered.

Water is a scarce commodity here, he continued, *but anything for my queen. I'd rinse you down then oh-so-tenderly put each bone and organ—*

Asiri, stop.

—back. Another smile into my mind. *You used my name.*

I ignored him, flipping to another page of demonic book number twelve.

Come to me.

I focused on the chicken scratch scribbled onto the paper. Seeing him would probably be more entertaining than trying to read these texts, but I also refused to establish a pattern where he called and I came.

Silence on the other end of our bond.

Ignoring him might've actually worked. Served him right, trying to bully the queen of hell.

I read Razael's account of how incubi got human wom-

19

en pregnant. Apparently, that whole myth about incubi fathering children—totally real. Only it was way more disturbing than I was led to believe.

Somewhere off in the castle, doors groaned. My head snapped up and I concentrated on listening to the sounds coming from that location. Throughout the day I hadn't come across any other beings lurking in the castle, save for a few shades, shadow-like creatures that scurried off as soon as they saw me.

But now I heard the huff of breath and the thump of feet.

I closed the book and cocked my head. The noise was getting louder, and it was heading my way.

I stood and slid the tome back onto the shelf I'd pulled it from. A second later, the doors to the library crashed open and two gray-skinned demons strode in.

They looked like gargoyles with their large jaws and sharp teeth. Their faces were more beast than human, but their bodies looked like those of linebackers. Freakishly large linebackers.

Did I mention they were naked? Painfully naked. At least I knew for sure now that these demons had genders.

Vomit in my mouth.

I backed up as they headed straight for me. So this was the devil's strategy—order me around, and when that didn't work, have his goons fetch me.

The demons grabbed my arms, their claws digging into my skin.

"Get your hands off of me!" I struggled against them. The action sliced my skin open where their nails dug in too deeply.

My fangs descended at the smell and the siren rose.

It just keeps going from bad to worse, I thought as I felt her unfurl beneath my skin. The last thing I needed was her to make an appearance.

The demons sniffed my glowing skin.

"Let me go," I said, the siren riding my voice.

Instead of doing just that, they began to walk, dragging me along with them.

Damn, doesn't work on Underworld creatures.

We left the library and wound our way down to the first story. Then down some more. Did I really ever think that Peel Academy's tunnels were creepy? They had nothing on the subterranean floors of the devil's castle. Here the air felt sick with evil. Fires burned in basins set into alcoves on either side of the hall. Even these gave off less light than the scones on the floors above.

"Please let me go." The siren still had full control of me, but she wasn't making much headway with these two.

I was met with silence.

"Do you even talk?"

Nothing.

"I'm just going to throw this out there: you two are no fun."

My little speech did nothing to loosen these demons up. They carted me down several hallways. My arms started to ache.

The demons finally stopped outside a set of black doors. My captors tilted their heads back and bellowed, raising the hair along my arms.

In response, the doors creaked open. I stared down a long room. I hadn't seen the throne room before this moment. An entire day wandering this place and I missed this room. Hell, I'd missed this whole floor. Not that I was complaining.

Unlike the rest of the castle, this room was packed with creatures—*demons*, I corrected myself. Some looked just like my captors. Others were more animal than man. But most looked entirely human.

At the far end, sitting in a large, onyx chair, was the devil. As soon as our eyes met, he smiled. "You will learn to follow my commands." He lifted a hand and gestured to my guards. "Bring her here."

My skin, which had been dimming, brightened as I passed the crowd of demons. Incubi watched me as they petted each other, their eyes drifting to my glowing skin. Others, beautiful men and women dressed in suits and gowns, stared at me with narrowed eyes and sinister smiles, their faces calculating.

I read about this particular group of demons earlier. They were part of the upper echelons of demons, the ones that probably started out as angels.

My eyes moved away from them and back to the devil.

My captors stopped at the foot of his throne and released me so suddenly I crumpled to the floor. Behind me, several demons laughed.

"You think that's funny?" Pluto's voice boomed.

The laughter cut out.

"You there and you," Pluto said. I glanced up in time to see him point to two demons in the crowd, "think twice before you laugh at my queen. Belial, take them to the dungeon and slice them open until they no longer have the voice to laugh."

Oh, crap.

I scrambled up to my feet in time to see Belial, one of the suit-clad men, nod to the devil. The demons slated for punishment began to beg, but Pluto ignored them, instead focusing his attention on me.

I had to force myself not to look away. The intensity of those dark eyes and the pull of our connection made me want to creep closer.

"Little bird, next time—" His voice cut off as he stared at my arms. Then, "Whose blood is on your skin?"

Beneath the fabric of my dress I could see smears of blood where the demons gripped me too tightly.

"It's mine."

"Did my guards do this to you?" he asked, his voice hypnotic.

My skin brightened as I realized where this was headed. I pressed my lips together instead of answering.

It didn't make a difference.

Hades beckoned another demon forward. "Take these guards away and remove appendages until you believe they've learned their lesson."

For a minute, the throne room was in an uproar as the detained demons screeched their outrage and others cheered and heckled.

The devil frowned. "Let it be known that if so much as a hair is out of place on my queen's head, I will make you wish you were trapped in hellfire."

A wave of vertigo hit me. This was my life.

"Now," Hades turned his attention back to me and patted his lap, "come here."

"I am not a dog," I said, my voice harmonizing with itself.

He stared me down with those almond eyes of his. The entire hall waited, the tension ratcheting up. Undermining him like this, among all his subjects, probably wasn't wise.

Just as I began weighing the benefits and drawbacks of defying him, a howling wind tore through the room. It lashed against me, dragging me up the dozen or so steps to the devil's throne and throwing me against his black leather boots—which smelled disturbingly human—before thrusting me up into his lap.

His arms came around me. I could feel dozens of eyes on us, assessing the situation. "Defying me will get you nowhere."

This monster had me locked in his embrace. He ran a hand up my still-glowing skin. It was putting off more light than any of the fires in this room. The siren hadn't resettled inside me, likely because I still felt as though my life was in danger.

"I must admit, you are lovely. You've captivated my entire audience." His eyes flicked to them. "Out."

He watched me as the demons exited. When the last one left, the doors thundered closed.

His hand continued to stroke the flesh that peeked out between the lace of my dress, up and down, up and down.

Despite my best efforts, I couldn't help but lean into

his hand. I fixated on his mouth. The siren wanted her pound of flesh, and she wanted it from her mate.

"Troubling, isn't it?" he said. "Reconciling two warring impulses."

I nodded, leaning towards his lips. But even as I leaned forward, I fought the siren. With her, a kiss was never just a kiss. She'd want to do more. I ripped my eyes from his mouth and pushed her down, down, down and locked her up. The light from my skin extinguished all at once.

"Shame," the devil commented, "she seemed to like me well enough."

I narrowed my eyes at him. "Why did you call me in?"

"Ah, yes, that."

He released me. When I didn't do anything immediately, he sighed. "You can get off my lap."

Wary of him, I did so. Were the last few minutes just some weird mind game? Maybe he really didn't like me all that much.

One glance at his eyes dispelled that possibility. They roved over me, looking hungry.

And there went that shred of hope.

My insides curdled. What happened a few seconds ago—that near kiss ... that wouldn't be the last of it. Between Pluto's sinful nature and my siren, they'd make sure of it.

That howling wind swept through the throne room again, tossing my hair about my face. The devil's, I noticed, barely fluttered.

He leaned his chin on his hand, studying me as the wind began to circle me. "I will miss you."

"Miss me?" As I spoke, I caught sight of my toes peaking out from under the hem of my dress just as they left the ground.

I balked. "Oh my Go—"

"Don't you *dare* utter his name," Pluto warned.

Oh my God, oh my God, oh my God!

Even in your head! the devil hissed.

"My feet aren't touching the ground!"

"Nor is the rest of you," he added helpfully.

"*Why?*"

The howling wind tightened its circuit around me.

"Don't you remember the myths, little bird? You only live here half the time."

The wind spun around me, a dark, shadowy cloud made up of thousands of lost souls. They brushed against me, and I could feel their torment.

The bottom of my dress disappeared, swallowed up by the screaming souls.

"Pluto, help me!"

"Help you?" He stood from his throne. "If I could, I would join you."

Why did I bother?

The tormented souls bushed against my skin, each one searing me until my entire body felt consumed by the same flames that had trapped all of the devil's other victims. They obscured my vision, until the man himself disappeared from view.

They dragged me up and up—and I wasn't just levitating.

I was flying.

Ohsweetbabyjesus no, no, no. I might no longer be

bound by the laws of physics in this realm, but some things should just not happen, regardless.

Bring me back a souvenir, Pluto whispered in my mind.

"Wait, seriously, what's happening to me?"

The souls that pressed in on me thickened until I couldn't see anything beyond them—until I had no choice but to breathe them into my lungs, swallowing their anguish as they swallowed me up.

You're returning to earth, and there, little bird, you will deliver my reckoning.

CHAPTER 3

Gabrielle

I TASTED EARTH in my mouth, felt it sift through my hair, rake down my face. It pressed against the crown of my head and my body.

Shadows, darkness, and magic. It all coursed through me. The brush of it felt foreign and tainted and powerful. Now I was a part of the darkness, and now the darkness was a part of me.

Faster and faster it rolled over me, pushing, pulling, forcing me up, up, up. I wanted to scream, but too much soil already filled my mouth, and I couldn't open my eyes.

This is hell. Everything else that came before now must've been a dying dream. This horrible sensation would last forever.

I needed to breathe. I wasn't blacking out from the lack

of air, but my lungs were spasming.

Just when I thought it would never end, the earth warmed and the texture changed. Looser soil.

The pressure at the crown of my head lessened. Then—

In one great burst, the earth purged me.

I coughed out the dirt and debris that weaseled their way into every orifice. My entire body hurt; I was just one giant bruise.

Distantly, I heard screams.

I stared down at the dusty soil, my fingers digging into the fine, dry dirt.

Get up, I commanded myself. I pushed to my feet.

The sky above me was dark, the moon hanging low in the sky.

Jeruselum, a voice whispered in my ear.

Holy ground had purged an unholy creature.

I shook off the dirt and brushed it out of my hair and off of the dress I wore. Only then did I realize I had an audience.

I'd gotten so used to the screams of the damned that I hadn't noticed that I was the cause of these particular ones until now. A crowd had formed around me, and as I met their eyes, they staggered back, watching me warily. A few of them held up smart phones—smart phones. It was that, more than any other detail that hit me square in the chest.

I'm back on earth.

Holy shit, I'm really back.

I stared at the crowd, shocked. The ground trembled again beneath my feet, shaking pebbles loose and scattering sand.

I'm ... free.

Power surged out of me at the realization and it rippled across the ground.

The screams intensified as the shockwave hit them and they lost their balance.

"*Excuuuse me. Yeah you, asshole.*" A head of ice blond hair bobbed through the panicked crowd, pushing his way forward.

My pulse hitched at the familiar face. A hand went to my mouth.

"Evening, sweets," Oliver said, stepping out of the crowd. He wore all white, and with his pale skin and light hair, he looked like some strange angel.

"Oliver ..." I had to be imagining things. "Am I ... really back?"

He gave me a kind smile when he stopped in front of me. "Yeah, sweets, you really are." He grabbed my wrist. "And now we've got to go."

I stared down at his arm. "Where are we going?"

"Away."

The crowd stirred, watching us uneasily. We made a pair—him in his white clothing, me a dress of dark cobwebbed lace. Darkness and light.

"Look at me, Gabrielle."

I glanced over at him.

"Time to let your siren out."

My siren? Even as I thought about her, she rushed to the surface, making my skin glow.

Gasps came from the crowd.

Next to me, Oliver's skin began to glitter. It didn't have the same effect as mine, but between the light emanating from my skin and the moonlight, he looked just as unearthly as I did.

Oliver stared at me strangely, then took a deep breath. He ran a hand behind my neck. My eyes widened as he leaned forward. And then Oliver was kissing me.

WE APPEARED IN the middle of the Braaid, the Isle of Man's stone circle.

Oliver tore himself away from me and began wiping his mouth with his forearms.

"Ugh, ew, you taste like death. I'm never kissing a girl ever again—siren or not."

I shivered, holding my arms tightly to my chest. A chill sank into my bones, a chill that had little to do with the cool evening air or my skimpy outfit. The last twelve hours …

I shouldn't be here.

"Of course you should," Oliver said.

I hadn't realized I'd spoken out loud. I dropped my arms and began walking away from my friend.

"Hey, ho-bag, where are you going?"

"Away." I didn't bother glancing behind me when I spoke.

Something was wrong with me. In the Underworld I had felt normal. Here I felt unnatural. Wrong.

"No, no, no, no—that's not how this works. I save your ass, so now you're in my debt. Fae bargain, get it?"

I ignored him as memories surged. Memories not of this world. My skin prickled, and I shivered. Would I ever be warm?

Maybe near hellfire, but not here.

The grass flattened away from me. Wherever my feet touched, the ground blackened, and the foliage died. My gown slithered behind me.

Oliver jogged to my side. "You are not leaving me, ho. Wherever you go, I'm going too."

I knew the first place I was going. "Fine. Take me to Castle Rushen."

"And what's at Castle Rushen?"

My revenge.

"It doesn't matter," I said to him. "Will you take me there?"

Oliver sighed. "What about Andre?"

I stopped, my knees threatening to buckle. "Don't say his name." If the devil's name had power to conjure phantom winds, then Andre's had the power to crush the last of my soul.

"You should visit him, show him that you're okay."

My gaze snapped to Oliver. "I am not okay."

I was the Queen of the Underworld.

I was a monster.

Andre

WAKEFULNESS CAME IN a short, shuddering burst. Andre let out a low moan. He was empty, absolutely empty.

She's gone. Oh, God, she's gone.

He bellowed out his anguish. The vampires that had pinned him to the ground woke at his cry, their hands reflexively tightening on him.

"Damn you all, let me go!" He could feel cool wetness on his cheeks where fresh, bloody tears replaced old ones.

"We can't," Vicca said. Her voice sounded like an apology. He didn't want an apology, he wanted *away*.

His blackened heart was shredded to pieces.

He couldn't say how fast the time passed. It could've been minutes since he awoke. It could've been hours.

A shape blurred into the room, stopping near his feet. "Sire," the vampire said, breathless.

Andre ignored the man. "*Kill me, I beg of you,*" he pleaded to those that held him down. He never used to plead, but now—God, what he wouldn't do to end this torment. Hell had to be kinder than this.

"Sire," the vampire repeated.

Andre thrashed. "Let. Me. Go!" He felt his hair ruffle, but that was it. He could no longer conjure his power.

Because I've given up.

"*Is this what you want?*" Andre roared at his vampires. "An existence bound to me? Holding me down?"

His coven had already started to drain him of blood. They would have to weaken him until he was a desiccated husk. Then they'd chain him inside a coffin and bury it so deep in the ground that the earth would convince him he was really a dead thing. Then perhaps he could sleep and they could live.

It wasn't a good enough option. He needed death. That was the only way he could be near enough to her.

"*Sire!*" the vampire shouted, finally drawing Andre's attention. "Gabrielle is alive."

Gabrielle

"WHY DID YOU kiss me?" I asked. We sat in the back of a taxi that headed towards Castletown.

Oliver's lips curled. "Ugh, don't remind me. I was giving the people of Jerusalem a show. Leanne mentioned that this would be all over the news in a few hours. They're going to call us the 'Angels of Jerusalem.'"

"FYI—angels don't kiss."

"If they're as hot as we are, they do."

I cracked a smile at that. "Where's Leanne?" I asked, looking at the scenery that flew past the window.

"She's preparing for the evening. If you don't diverge too much from her visions, then we should be seeing her soon."

I nodded at that, pressing my lips together.

"What ... what did he do to you, Sabertooth?" I could feel Oliver peering at me.

"I hate that nickname."

Oliver took my hand. I stared down at our entwined fingers, then up at him. His eyes were somber. It was a rare day when Oliver was serious.

"What happened?" he asked.

I pulled my hand away from his. He'd never know, never understand what it was like to be there even for a day. All those burning souls, all those demons ... all that attention from the devil. I'd come back to earth, but I'd come back corrupted, and now something wicked brewed within me. Now it whispered things of vengeance.

I shook my head. "Nothing worth discussing."

The taxi came to a stop in front of the castle, the Politia's headquarters. This place had taken me in and, for months, trained me.

"Sabertooth, you know I love the shit you get yourself into, but whatever business you have here—" Oliver eyed the castle, "you should really reconsider it."

Revenge swam like a poison through my veins. I finally understood Andre's need for vengeance.

Cut down the enemy. Right some wrongs.

And oh were there wrongs to right. One in particular I was especially looking forward to.

I opened the car door and slid out. Oliver made a grab for my wrist. "Seriously, Gabrielle. They'll shoot you on sight."

I turned back to him. "Leave this place while you can. I don't want you hurt."

"Gabri—"

I shut the door and crossed the road, heading for the building I used to work in.

Caleb might be in there, and he also might not. I'd find him either way. At this point, my anger wasn't limited to him.

The entire organization had kept me under their thumb, training me, pretending to care about me, allowing me to believe I was one of their own. How quickly they all turned their backs.

My gown dragged along the ground, the spider silk

sounding like scales over sand as I moved. Night had just fallen here.

My senses had expanded since I claimed my title as queen of the Underworld. I could feel magic, could sense spells and curses.

But more than that, I could feel a goodness to the world and my own corruption.

I didn't belong here.

When I stepped up to the castle's door, I could feel the protective spell that barred me from entering. An enchantment against dark beings. For the first time since arriving back here, I laughed.

Like they could keep me out.

I lifted my hands and forced my power out. The spell flared up, trying to blast me back. I braced my legs and pushed against it. As soon as I did so, an alarm went off inside.

Guess they now know I'm here.

I felt my hair ripple and shift. I shoved against the door, coaxing my supernatural strength to break the enchantment. Power continued to rise within me, the magnitude of it staggering. I funneled it into the wood all at once.

The spell shattered, and the door exploded inward, its metal hinges tearing out stone as they ripped away from the castle walls. A shockwave fanned through the air, throwing some of the officers in the lobby to the ground.

Did not know that would happen.

I stepped inside the castle as dust and rubble settled. Once upon a time, I had good memories here. This was where Caleb and I worked on cases together, where we brought bad guys to justice. Only now, *I* was the bad guy.

"Freeze!" Inspector Maggie Comfry, my former boss, stepped into the lobby. Both hands gripped the gun aimed at me.

"No." My power snapped out, yanking the gun from her hand and throwing her against the wall. The energy coursing through me was terrible, addicting. The more I used it, the more I hungered for it.

My gaze moved over the other people in the room. Just like Maggie, I ripped their weapons away from them and thrust their bodies back with my power.

Papers scattered in the melee, and I could see the surface of someone's cup of coffee ripple from the sheer force of the energy I wielded. I couldn't contain it all. It filled me and spilled out into the earth around me, shaking the floor. The angrier I got, the stronger I became.

And boy was I angry. Scratch that, I was *pissed*.

These people lied to me. They never wanted a vampire on their force; they wanted to watch their enemy closely. And in the end, they wanted to kill me. They almost had too, the devil just beat them to it.

Rage pulsed through my veins. I would make each and every one of them regret that decision.

I strode over to Maggie's prone body and lifted her up by the collar. "Where is Caleb?"

Her eyes flicked to the hall that branched to the right of the lobby. That was all I needed. The training rooms were in that direction.

I let go of her shirt. "I trusted you."

"You are an abomination," she hissed.

"I am the monster you fed. You made me your enemy when I needed an ally. Now you and everyone else here must reap what you sow." Even my words carried power; they boomed out of me and shook the walls.

I left the room with all the officers still pinned to the back of it, not bothering to release them. Let someone else's magic bring them down.

Death had not tempered my supernatural sense of smell, and in the Politia's busy headquarters, that wasn't exactly a blessing. The scent of human filth—blood, sweat, vomit, feces, urine—was embedded into the very building itself. It mixed poorly with the wet, mildewy smell of the stone castle. Overlaying it all was the tang of magic.

This last one I'd never been able to detect when I was simply Gabrielle the hybrid. None of my previous abilities had allowed me to sense magic.

Now, however, the scent of it coated my mouth, tasting somewhat bitter, somewhat sweet. Eventually—hopefully—I'd be able to understand the nuances of this new ability. For now I just had to endure it, along with everything else.

The training rooms were located belowground—conveniently close to the Politia's cellblock. As I got closer to them, I heard fists smack leather. Grunts accompanied the sound, and when I scented the air, I caught a whiff of Caleb's sweat.

Here he was, not twenty-four hours after he shot me point blank in the heart, working out like the whole thing never happened. How could he continue on as though my death didn't affect him?

That cut deep.

The florescent overhead lights flickered with my anguish and my anger.

The room fell silent, punctuated only by the sound of heavy breathing. "Who's there?" Caleb called. "Maggie?"

I wasn't trying to be quiet, but in human form, Caleb couldn't sense my approach. After a few moments, he resumed his workout. The smell of blood increased the closer I got. Shapeshifter blood.

Someone had propped open the door to the training room, and I slipped inside. The room was full of all the fixings of a regular gym. Weight racks, machines, workout benches, mats, and free weights.

On the far end, Caleb slammed his fists into a punching bag. He hadn't bothered wrapping his hands or wearing gloves, and his knuckles were bloody. The sight and the smell triggered some primal part of me. My fangs dropped.

Had I been mostly human yesterday? Now I felt far from it. I saw Caleb's blood, and I thought, *food*.

I took the rest of him in. I'd been wrong. My death *had* affected him. I could see it in the sickly pallor of his skin and the smell of bile that lingered on him.

When he caught sight of me, he stumbled away from the punching bag.

"*Gabrielle?*" Shock and hope and despair all rolled into that single word.

I thought maybe the smell and sight of his anguish would soothe my anger. It worsened it.

The lights went out.

A vampire wouldn't be able to see in total darkness, but I was the queen of the Underworld. I could see even in the darkest corners of this world and the next.

The scent of Caleb's magic flooded the air. He thought he could shift. He thought wrong.

I grabbed him just as he changed into a tiger. Grabbing the beast's muzzle, I slammed his head into the ground, and his body went limp. I assumed that perhaps unconscious he'd return to natural form, but nope. Still a tiger.

I gripped the feline by the scruff and dragged him out of the gym. As I passed by a bin of fresh towels, I grabbed one. From here I could hear the mayhem at the front of the building. Someone had discovered the officers.

I hauled Caleb to the prison block of the castle. Called "neutralization tanks" for the deep enchantments woven into them, each cell stripped certain supernaturals of their powers. Not all beings could be stripped of their powers; for some it was too innate. Imprisoning them was the same as death.

I wasn't surprised to find this place empty. The Politia had proven time and again that they preferred to kill rather than contain the guilty.

As I headed down the prison block's walkway, the overhead lights began to flicker. Off. On. Off. On-off-on.

I threw a giant, furry Caleb and the towel into one of the enchanted cells and slammed the door shut. As soon as the lock clicked, the magic began taking effect.

Caleb's eyes snapped open as his back arched. Fur forcibly sank back into skin, and claws dulled to fingernails. His entire body shrank, tan skin replacing orange and black stripes.

When the transition completed itself, he groaned and rubbed his head. His previously bloody knuckles were now scabbed over. Caleb had once mentioned that changing form could accelerate healing. Now I'd seen it for myself.

He lifted his head and met my gaze. "How are you alive?" he asked from where he crouched. His eyes searched mine. I could smell his disbelief and his relief. But regret wouldn't undo the fact that he mortally wounded me last night.

"What makes you think that I am?" My voice came out calmer than it should've. The florescent lights continued to flicker and pause.

Caleb wrapped the towel around his waist. "Are you a vampire now?"

"I was always a vampire."

He covered his eyes with a shaky hand, then let it slide down his face. "I–I'm sorry, alright?" He said it like I'd already accused him. "There aren't words to describe just how much I am. But I warned you I couldn't be trusted. And you were considered the anti-Christ, for God's sake. You knew where things stood."

"So this is my fault."

Say it, I dared him. *Say it and allow me to unleash my anger here*. I'd do more than level this place. I'd wipe it from existence.

He padded towards me. "Of course it's not. You didn't choose to be the devil's consort. But you are. When I joined the Politia, I swore an oath to protect supernaturals. That means setting aside my feelings for you and protecting the innocent."

"From me," I filled in.

His mouth formed a grim line.

"You were my friend," I said. The overhead lights flickered faster and faster.

He glanced at them but said nothing.

"You were my friend and I trusted you when I needed you most. You betrayed that trust. You betrayed me."

He shook and goosebumps sprouted along his arms. "I know, Gabrielle, I know, and I'll never forgive myself. I did my job, but now I can't seem to live with the person I now am."

So this was still about him.

"Four months ago, I saved you. I carried your body out of a burning house. The same one you returned to, to kill me."

"I know," he breathed. "That wasn't lost on me. I came to kill you. I pulled that trigger and watched one of my closest friends die—" His voice caught, and his eyes swept over me anew. "But I didn't kill you," he breathed. "You're not dead." Wonder lit up his eyes.

I wrapped my hands around the cell's iron bars. "I'm worse than dead. I wasn't the anti-Christ when you shot me, but now I am."

CHAPTER 4

Andre

"The news captured footage of her in Jerusalem earlier this evening," the vampire explained, talking as they headed down Bishopcourt's hallway.

Impossible. Andre would've felt it. That hollow ache inside him only worsened with every minute that ticked by. But damn his heart; even the shredded remains of it seized on the possibility of Gabrielle being alive.

Andre strode into Bishopcourt's conference room, where the television had been set up. The sound had been muted, but footage from a camera phone played out on the screen.

Andre staggered at the sight, bracing his hand against the conference table, his eyes transfixed.

There she was. His soulmate. His queen.

Clad in some dark dress that shimmered even under all that dirt. Her startled eyes swept over the camera as she stared out at the crowd.

"*Dios mio*," he whispered. A tear leaked out.

His mouth had gone dry. He reached out and touched the screen. "Gabrielle."

Even newly risen from the ground, she was the most beautiful thing he'd ever laid eyes on.

Absently he rubbed his heart as he watched Oliver—*Oliver?*—step up to her and—

Kiss her?

I'm going to remove that fairy's organs and slowly feed them to him.

Then the two disappeared.

Andre let out a gasping noise. She was gone once more.

He read the banner at the bottom of the screen.

Angels of Jerusalem.

The news looped the footage again. Of the earth shaking, rolling, rising. Of it giving a final heave and pushing Gabrielle out from it. Dirt fell from her, not like it would a normal living thing. It fell off completely. As though it wanted to get away from her.

This wasn't a supernatural news channel. Mortals had witnessed the spectacle. The Politia would be stepping in. They'd have to.

Andre watched the kiss and her subsequent disappearance all over again, anger then anguish rising in him once more.

Somehow Oliver had known where to retrieve her, and he'd whisked her away via ley line. Which meant she could be anywhere in the world.

Behind him, several vampires and the head of his security team entered.

"I want all personnel plugged into the media." Andre spoke to them without tearing his gaze away from the screen. "Find what you can about Gabrielle Fiori's whereabouts. Once you've located her, put together travel arrangements."

He was going to find his soulmate.

Gabrielle

A BLOODY TEAR snaked down my cheek. Normally, it would've horrified me to let someone see me cry. At the moment, however, I was high off of anger and power and retribution. Not even a tear could make me feel weak.

"After you fled last night, the devil came and claimed me. While you wallowed here on earth, I spent the day in hell."

"You spent the day ... in hell?" Horror bloomed on Caleb's face.

I tilted my head to the side. "Did you really think I wouldn't?"

"I thought I had saved you in time ..."

"*This is the Politia. Come out willingly and we won't kill you.*" The order boomed throughout the cellblock.

My tear slid off my chin, the drop of blood splattering against the floor.

I could go round and round, trying to understand why I deserved the fate I received. But that logic required the belief that life was fair when it wasn't.

It really wasn't.

Caleb wrapped his hands around the bars. "You need to leave."

I didn't want advice from him, my would-be killer. "They don't scare me."

Caleb stared into my eyes. "No, I guess they wouldn't. Why did you come?" he asked.

"I wanted to make you pay," I said. I caught the faint whiff of smoke as I stared into Caleb's eyes.

"And this is your revenge? Putting me in a cage?"

I backed away from him, the smell of smoke getting stronger.

"I expected worse," he said.

"I just wanted to remind you who the true monster is." The world might believe I was evil—and I felt thoroughly wicked at the moment—but feeling evil and doing evil were two very different things.

A wall of smoke rose in front of me, stretching and deepening by the second.

"What the—?" Caleb said.

It took on a humanoid shape before filling out, flesh replacing smoke.

Aw, crap.

I'd seen these fuckers before. In fact, I'd just spent an entire day with them.

"Holy shit. Is that what I think it is?" Caleb asked, his eyes wide.

"Probably." And it smelled like ash and my tainted blood.

There was only one reason why it would smell like me—somehow I had gone and given it life.

Naturally, the moment I went and made a point of being a better person, something like this had to happen.

"Gabrielle, are you armed?" Caleb asked.

"Do I look armed?" I said, as the demon's muscles filled out under his skin.

Burnished charcoal flesh stretched over corded muscles. Human feet and hands ended in curved claws. At the tips of his big toes and thumbs, the nail arced into deadly talons. Webbed wings sprouted from the demon's back.

Sharp, pointed teeth descended from his mouth, none so large as his inch-long canines. Those were teeth meant to rip out throats. Nasal slits bisected the demon's face, and red eyes with horizontal pupils glowed with unholy fire. Finally, wicked horns grew from his temples, twisting back from his face.

Once the demon was fully formed, the smell of sulfur and rot replaced my scent.

He knelt, bowing his head. "Azaelbub, my queen. I am yours to command." His voice rumbled in a pitch so low I was sure no creature of this world could mimic it.

"What are you doing here?" I didn't realize until after I finished speaking that the language we conversed in wasn't English. It was Demonic.

"Whatever it is you bid me to do." Azaelbub's voice was a growl.

Oh, screw that. I wanted nothing to do with this creature.

"Can you just go away?"

"Yes."

Caleb watched us with some combination of horror and fascination on his face.

"Err, then do so."

Azaelbub bowed his head and crouched. I don't know what I was expecting—maybe for him to just return to shadow—but that wasn't what happened.

He sprang up, throwing his body into the air, and blasted through the stone ceiling high above us. His wings, which appeared to be thin, membranous things, battered through stone and mortar.

I covered my head as debris rained down. A moment later, the walls of the castle shook as he exploded through the upper floors of Castle Rushen.

Fucking-A, that wasn't good.

Outside I heard the sound of shots fired, and then a demonic roar.

Nope, decidedly not good.

Once debris stopped falling, I stepped over to the hole in the ceiling and glanced up. Far above me I could see the night sky. Azaelbub had tunneled an exit through the roof.

"You just let a demon loose. First you imprison me and now you set that thing free."

I didn't bother answering Caleb. My job here was more than done.

I padded back down the hall.

"Wait!" Caleb shouted. "You're not seriously going to leave me here, are you?"

Ignoring him, I hooked a right out of the cellblock.

Most officers used the main entrance to head in and out of the building, but there was also a back entrance, one I used to take when I was late or didn't want to socialize. I decided to make use of that exit once more.

There'd be a fight waiting for me outside, regardless of what exit I chose. But after releasing a demon and confronting a former friend who tried to kill me, a few officers were child's play.

I braced myself at the back entrance, then pushed the door open. Under the bright light of the moon, officers had fanned out, their guns trained on the various windows and doors of the castle. Once they caught sight of me, their aim shifted.

Without warning, they began firing. When I was inside, they said that they wouldn't hurt me if I surrendered. I hadn't surrendered, but then, the Politia hadn't given me the chance. They hadn't planned on letting me live.

A dozen bullets took me all at once and goddammit, being queen of the damned hadn't taken away my ability to feel pain.

I staggered and fell to my knees, gasping for air. I raised my hand, and with a small wave, stopped the bullets.

Holy fuck, I really needed to stop getting shot.

Rather than weakening, my power surged and greedily lapped up my pain. My blood slid down my skin and dripped onto the ground. It bubbled and hissed as it met rock and earth. Acrid smoke rose from the boiling blood, and it grew and grew, fanning out around me.

Uh-oh. I think I now knew how baby demons were made.

The Politia was really going to regret shooting me.

The smoke deepened, the smell of sulfur filling the air. I'd seen something like this happen before I was taken. A necromancer cut himself and spilled his blood onto the earth. From it sprouted demons.

Apparently now I had the same ability.

Andre

"SHE'S AT CASTLE Rushen," Tybalt said over the phone.

Andre stalked out of his room already dressed and armed for battle, should it come to that.

"The Politia has taken her prisoner?" he asked. It wasn't like them. Anything that appeared as dangerous as Gabrielle would go on their kill list.

"No. Reports are saying that she's taken one of the officers hostage."

"Taken an officer hostage?" he said into his phone. "Which one, and why?" He knew Gabrielle had her vendettas, but this sounded out of character.

Not that he was in any position to throw stones.

Andre left his mansion and slid into the town car waiting for him. "Take me to Castle Rushen," he told his driver.

"*Shit.* Andre," Tybalt said from the other end of the line, "she's—" Shots echoed in the background.

Andre's grip on the phone tightened. "*What's happening?*"

"She's been shot."

I RAISED A hand, focusing on the officers' weapons. Triggers froze and barrels jammed as they tried and failed to fire their weapons. I could smell their rising fear, and it fueled my power.

As the shadows around me took shape, they began to splinter, and then those began to splinter. How many demons had my blood spawned?

Smoke transformed into silvery skin. It lengthened into claws and teeth and talons and beady red eyes. Wings and horns burst from their flesh, twisting and unfurling. If it wasn't so terrifying, it would have been beautiful, like watching a time-lapsed flower grow and bloom.

... A really fucked up flower, but still.

Shakily I rose to my feet. The officers hadn't fled yet, but none of their guns worked. Gunpowder and metal. Meant to tear and break and bleed. It was utterly useless against my magic.

Wasn't my death last night enough? What did they hope to accomplish by killing a girl that was already dead?

My wounds sealed up, the bullets clinking to the ground as my body purged them.

After the demons finished forming, I rose. "You do not want to fight me," I told the officers.

"Stand down!" Someone yelled over an intercom.

A blast of magic slammed into me, and I staggered back, only to be caught in the arms of a demon.

Low growls emanated from him and the others at my

back. They hadn't asked me for a command, but I sensed they wanted to protect me. That was only confirmed when, instead of letting me go, the demon that clutched me tightened his grip.

Ruh-roh.

The demon's muscles tensed. Then, like the first one I'd inadvertently created, he sprang into the air.

… Only this time, he was still holding me.

CHAPTER 5

Andre

ANDRE WAS OUT of the car before it came to a complete stop. He arrived just in time to see a demon rise into the air holding ...

"*Dios mio.*"

There she was. Alive, like all the news reports had mentioned.

He touched his heart. It still felt like one giant open wound, a vacuum bent on sucking up anything and everything it could to fill the hollowness of his mate's absence. Their bond hadn't reestablished itself.

But unless the woman soaring away into the night wasn't his Gabrielle—and there are only so many women that consorted with demons—she was in fact alive.

He almost sagged with relief. None of the shots he'd

heard earlier had killed her, and now he could breathe again.

Andre didn't let his mind linger on the fact that she hadn't come to find him first. Now was not the time for petty jealousy.

She was still in danger.

He headed back into his car. By the looks of Castle Rushen and the officers and demons that swarmed around it, there'd be much to learn from the events that transpired here. But right now he needed to find his soulmate and clasp her to him. Only then would his heart know relief. Only then would he believe she was real.

Gabrielle

I RAPIDLY ROSE into the sky, locked in this demon's embrace. I screamed and clutched at my captor's neck, and—ugh—demon breath.

"Put me down!" I yelled.

Probably not the smartest order to give a creature that relishes others' pain, but this one made no move to do as I commanded.

"I am your queen, and I am ordering you to put me down!"

"Boss told me to protect you," he growled.

My breath caught at his admission. That was so ... uncharacteristic of Hades.

And apparently, my commands couldn't trump the devil's. Big surprise.

Far below us, the rest of the demons rushed the officers. My body tensed as an eruption of magic and blood saturated the night air. Even this far away I could sense it.

I was partially responsible for whatever lives were lost, and I couldn't stop it. I wondered if that was part of the plan—to get me out of there before I could command the demons to cease.

Either way, it was too late to stop the carnage. Castletown, the city below us, was quickly becoming just a cluster of lights.

The wind howled, sweeping around me. I could feel the lost souls as they blew by me, some lifting my hair, some caressing my face. I could taste their sweet sorrow and ruin on my tongue. There was a whole procession of us evil things arcing across the night sky.

"Where are we going?" I yelled over the roar of the wind.

The demon either didn't hear me, or he chose to ignore me. I grimaced as his hot breath hit my skin.

Just when I thought my life couldn't get any more screwed up, it went and did just that. A good part of it was my fault. What was I thinking, going into the Politia's headquarters like that?

Way to kick the hornet's nest, Gabrielle.

Once we hit the outskirts of Castletown, the demon began to descend. He lowered us rapidly, aiming for what appeared to be a residential area. Little houses with pitched roofs sat close together. I breathed in the damp smell of wet asphalt. The rain had let up, but it would be back.

As we touched down, I eyed the homes around us. No fluttering curtains or strolling neighbors to witness a winged beast delivering a strange girl to the earth.

I turned and stared the demon in his red eyes. No joy lingered there. No happiness. Just a thirst for others' suffering. He nodded to me and tensed.

A moment later, he shot back into the air. I threw an arm over my face as his large wings whipped my hair around my head.

"Hey!" I yelled. "Where are you going? Don't leave me here!"

He had to have heard me, but he didn't once glance my way as he flew back into the night.

Motherfucking demons.

I brushed myself down, mostly to get the smell of sulfur off me. Several streets over, a car screeched as someone took a turn way too fast, then gunned its engine. From what I could hear, it sounded as though it was getting closer.

I began to walk, not sure where I was going because some idiot demon dropped me in the middle of nowhere.

For the first time all evening, I had a moment to think. What was I doing here? On earth? I'd hated hell, but I didn't want to be thrown right back into this melee.

Then end the fighting.

I started at the devil's voice. I hadn't expected to hear it this far away from him.

"This is larger than me," I said out loud.

Nothing is larger than you, save for me. The devil's voice rang in my ear. *Remind them with blood and violence and pain.*

"Go away."

Never, his voice whispered.

A car turned down the street, fishtailing as it did so. I squinted as headlights shined into my eyes. It screeched to a stop next to me, and the driver-side door banged open.

Leanne leaned out. "Hey stranger, long time no see."

"Leanne?" I began to smile at the sight of her before I remembered my situation. My eyes moved from her to Oliver, who sat next to her. "What are you guys—?"

"We've got thirty seconds to execute this, or else the future changes dramatically," Leanne said. "I love you, Gabrielle. Now please get in the fucking car."

"Damn girl," I heard Oliver say over her shoulder. "Just when I thought you had no attitude left."

Wise enough to heed her warning, I headed over to the car and slid into the back seat, my feet and long skirt dragging mud and grit in with me.

"You really did it this time, Sabertooth," Oliver said as Leanne maneuvered the car out of the neighborhood. "That was a lot of demons."

The only way he knew that was if he stayed to watch. "I thought I told you to leave Castletown."

"Because I follow orders so well." Oliver shook his head. "One day in hell and you've forgotten that your BBF is a fucking fairy."

"Speaking of fairies," Oliver leaned around his seat and lifted up an edge of my dress, "this looks fae made." He rubbed the lace together. "Why is this wet—?"

He squealed when he realized what the liquid was. "Ewww!" He wiped the blood off on the seats, then swore, staring at the stain for several seconds. When nothing happened, he relaxed. "Phew, thought I'd just released another hellspawn."

I scrubbed my face. "Why are you guys helping me?" I asked the car. I'd asked both friends this before, but then I'd still been human. Now there was no denying what I was—the queen of hell sent to earth.

"Because we're your friends, and when all is said and done, we will fall on the right side of history," Leanne said.

Slowly I lifted my head, my heart thumping like mad. "What have you seen?"

She met my eyes in the rearview mirror. "Nothing I can speak of in great detail."

Oliver coughed, "Copout," into his hand.

She glared at him. "Every detail I reveal can and will change the future, sometimes a little, sometimes a lot. If we want it to go our way, you'll both have to trust me."

"That's fine," I said. I was used to working with cryptic messages. "Where are we going?"

"We're meeting with Andre—I think."

Andre. The thought of him was a punch to the gut. I'd obviously not been myself because he should've—would've—been the first person I visited. It felt like a fog was lifting around my heart, my feelings for him rushed in. Suddenly, seeing him seemed paramount.

"What do you mean you think?" I asked.

"The seer's shroud is still in Andre's system, as it is in Oliver's and mine, so I can't foresee his future. Now that you've died, I can see yours, and in it we meet with someone whose future I can't see."

"So Andre knows I'm alive?"

Oliver snorted. "Footage of you is all over the news. He'd have to be blind, deaf, *and* dumb to miss it."

Or dead.

No, I couldn't think like that. Of course, telling myself this didn't stop my rising panic.

Focus on other things.

Focus—on—other—things.

"Who's car is this?" I asked running my hand over the seat's plush fabric.

"No one's," Leanne replied. "Paul conjured it." Paul was Oliver's roommate. In the past, he'd conjured clothes for us, but nothing close to a running vehicle.

"He was able to conjure an entire car?" I didn't attempt to hide my shock.

"My BBF is literally the mother of demons," Oliver said, "and she's surprised someone can conjure a car."

"But," I said, "he made a car *out of nothing.*"

"And you made demons out of a couple drops of blood," Oliver said, checking out his lilac fingernails. "You all are special snowflakes, m'kay? Hey, you know next time, when you spill some more blood, could you try calling up some incubi?"

"Oliver!" I shoved him lightly on the shoulder. "Those things want your soul."

"Not as much as they want my—"

I slapped a hand over his mouth. "Please, let's not," I said. "I can only handle so much trauma in one evening."

He began to pry my fingers away.

"Are you done?"

He held up three fingers—the scout's honor symbol.

Reluctantly, I let my hand fall.

"—big, glittery cock!"

I couldn't help it; my face flushed at his words. "Oli-*ver*, *ewwww*."

Oliver laughed. "Still such a prude." He swiveled in his seat to face me. When he saw my pink cheeks, he squealed. "And my baby can blush again! All is not lost after all."

Andre

HE'D LOST HER. The demon had landed somewhere in this neighborhood, and when he'd taken to the sky again, it was without Gabrielle. A quick search of the neighborhood hadn't turned up his soulmate.

Andre gnashed his teeth together. This would be so much easier if they still had their bond. Now he had to make a decision: search the neighborhood again or follow the demon. And with each second that ticked by, the creature moved farther and farther away from them.

He ran a hand through his hair and swore. "Follow the demon," he finally ordered his driver.

This had better work out.

Andre pulled a gun from the car's center console and leaned out the window. The creature soared a football field length ahead of them. Well within his range. He lined up the gun's sights and fired.

The bullet hit the creature just left of where his heart should be—if demons had them. Even from here he could hear the demon's shriek. Andre pulled the trigger twice more, clipping the creature's wings. It continued to fly, its movements jerky, but it was quickly losing altitude.

Andre shot it again, this time hitting a wing joint, and the creature crumpled in the sky, its body plummeting to earth.

"Move it," Andre said, not tearing his gaze away from the demon.

They tracked it down to an open field. Andre stepped out of the car and stalked over to his prey, the wind whipping his coat and hair. He still loosely held his gun, and he rubbed the trigger tenderly. It had been a very long evening, and without Gabrielle nestled in his heart, the humanity he'd slowly been reclaiming was now long gone.

As soon as the demon caught sight of him, it rose to its feet. Andre lifted the gun and shot the thing in the knee-cap. It screeched, falling back to the ground.

"If you try to fly away, I'll shoot your wing bones. Again." Not that the creature would necessarily be able to fly, considering how badly wounded he already was. But Andre had never been around one of these things long enough to know whether they regenerated.

"Fool," the demon said, its voice a low growl. "I will tell my master of this and he will punish you."

Andre laughed at that, closing the last few feet between the two of them. He placed his boot on the demon's throat. The creature reached up, its claws ready to sink into Andre's leg.

He pointed the gun. "We have the same enemies at the moment. If you cooperate, I will not send you back to hell."

The demon stopped struggling and eyed him warily.

"Where is Gabrielle?"

The creature smiled. "Can't say I know."

Andre's boot dug into the demon's neck and he cocked the gun. "Try again."

"She's on this island somewhere."

Still not good enough. He shifted his aim and shot the demon's other kneecap.

The thing screamed, the sound not of this world.

"Where is she?"

The demon began to laugh. Andre could smell its blood seeping out. The wounds weren't healing. It couldn't fly, it couldn't walk, it clearly felt pain, and yet it laughed at the prospect of more. "Beyond your reach, vampire."

Andre should've stayed in that neighborhood.

He shot the demon point blank in the forehead, and the creature dissolved into smoke and ash.

Another dead end.

How to find Gabrielle before the others did?

Of course.

Andre pulled out his phone. There was one seer out there who cared about his soulmate, and she was going to help him find her.

Gabrielle

THEIR CONJURED CAR careened down the highway, headed for the city of Douglas.

Leanne's phone buzzed. "About time," she muttered. She pulled it out of her pocket, the car swerving as she did so, and brought it to her ears. "She's safe and she wants to see you," Leanne answered.

A beat of silence passed before the caller spoke. "Gabrielle's with you?"

I stopped breathing at the sound of Andre's voice. Goosebumps broke out along my skin. And then oxygen was rushing into my lungs and it felt like I was coming up for air for the first time all evening.

"Let me talk to him," I said.

"*Gabrielle.*" Andre's voice changed at the sound of my own.

"Neither of you gets to talk to the other," Leanne said. "I'm not fucking with the future. Right now, Andre, you need to listen to me," she said. "We're heading to Douglas Cafe. Meet us there as soon as you can."

"Is my mate alright?" Andre growled. "At the very least, you can tell me that."

"She's fine."

"I'm trusting you with her life."

I didn't realize I'd been biting my lip until I tasted blood. I knew it was important to heed Leanne's advice, but that didn't make it easy. My surroundings all took on a rosy hue, and I blinked away the tears. It was wrong to love someone this much when they were no longer yours.

"I know," Leanne said, "and I know what you do to people who betray that trust."

"He eats them!" Oliver yelled oh-so-helpfully.

Andre sighed. I'd seeded that misconception—that vampires ate people—and Oliver had latched onto it with his normal enthusiasm.

Leanne pulled the phone away from her mouth. "Thanks for the visual, Oliver."

Into the receiver she said, "Douglas Café in twenty." Leanne clicked the phone off and blew out a breath, rumpling her hair. "I don't know how you deal with that man, Gabrielle. He's so ... "

"Overbearing?" Oliver piped in. "Ridiculously protective? Scarily possessive? It's okay, Leanne. We know he's too much man for you to handle. It's a good thing Gabrielle and I like strong men. And now that Sabertooth's hitched to the lord of the Underworld, that frees up her honeypie for me."

He was only joking, but my stomach flipped anyway because he was right. Andre was no longer mine, and there was nothing I could do about it.

CHAPTER 6

Gabrielle

LEANNE, OLIVER, AND I waited in line, and when I got weird looks for my blood-spattered, spider-web dress and bare feet, Oliver shook his head. "Sabertooth, you're stealing my thunder," he said, patting his ice blond hair self-consciously. "It's like ... I don't even exist next to your weird."

"Someone's going to recognize me," I said. I'd seen the news crews stationed across the street from Castle Rushen.

"No one will act on it," Leanne said, facing forward. "Guys, go sit down, I've got this."

She ended up buying us all hot chocolates, bringing them over to the table we'd chosen, one nestled close to the back entrance where we'd parked our car. Outside it had started raining again, and it splattered against the window

The whole thing was so ... normal, something I hadn't had in a very long time. I couldn't remember when exactly I had lost it.

"So," Leanne said, "Tell us about it."

"About what?" I looked at her, startled.

She lifted her hand and gestured to my getup. "The last time we saw you, the devil claimed you as his mate ... and then the two of you disappeared."

"Yeah, and then you show up tonight looking like you ran through a cobweb"—I narrowed my eyes at Oliver—"and you decide to go take on the Politia with nothing more than a vendetta—so very badass and so very unlike you."

"I wasn't fighting them. I was after Caleb."

"Caleb?" Oliver said, glancing at Leanne.

"Don't look at me," she said. "I know nothing about this."

"Why?" Oliver asked.

I traced the veins of the worn wooden table. "Last night? He was the one who shot me."

Oliver lifted his brows. "Wait, seriously? That fucker. I'm so going to hex him."

"I went to the Politia to pay him back," I said. I glanced out the window at the stormy night beyond. "I didn't kill him. Just threw him into a jail cell and left."

Oliver gave me a disapproving look. "You're the queen of the Underworld and you didn't even try to kill him?"

My lips thinned. "It didn't seem right."

"Hmph. I would've thought hell would have corrupted

you more. Have you at least sullied that?" Oliver asked.

"Sullied what?" I asked, cupping my drink.

"The guy you're now shacking up with."

"Oh. Ugh, Oliver," I winced. "Stop." No one wanted that visual.

"What? Soulless people need love too." He looked at me expectantly. "So ... ?"

Persistent fairy.

"No, Oliver, I didn't 'sully' that," I said, bringing the cup of hot chocolate to my lips. I really didn't want to upchuck the drink in the middle of this nice establishment like I had all other liquid for the past few days, but it smelled good and my stomach seemed settled. After hesitating for a second, I tried it.

"You mean to tell me that you spent an entire day in hell, and you and Satan didn't do the nasty?"

I closed my eyes for a second as that first sip went down. So good.

"—or were you too busy getting off on foodgasms?"

I gave him the bird as I took another gulp.

"Guys," Leanne said, scanning the room, "Andre should be here any minute. Unless you want him to hear about Gabrielle's time with the devil, I suggest you both shut up."

"Don't tell me to shut up," Oliver said testily, his voice rising. "I'm the queen bee-otch here, not you. You're just one of my bitchy ladies-in-waiting. And I'll talk about sex and foodgasms as often as I want to."

Leanne threw her hands up. "This is hopeless."

My back straightened when I felt it. Divinity.

Before I could think twice, I was out of my chair, my eyes locked on the man who entered the café.

It wasn't Andre.

He dressed like any other person. Jeans paired with a button down and a tweed coat on top of it all. But he didn't look like anyone else.

This man was beautiful in a way that wasn't of this world. But even if he'd masked his true appearance with spells, he wouldn't be able to hide his essence.

The holiness that poured off him in waves sparked two different, warring instincts. Half of me wanted to fall to his feet and bask in his presence. The other half of me, the half that spent the day in hell, wanted to attack him. My hands curled into fists, my nails biting into my palms.

"Fuck, fuck, fuckity-fuck." Leanne yanked on my wrist. "Sit down before he sees you."

Too late for that.

One moment our eyes locked, and in the next he was streaking across the room. Catching me around the waist, he plowed us through the window. Glass shattered and screams rang out from the coffee shop as we tumbled outside.

Night air blasted against me. My body reacted first, my fists pounding against any flesh I could reach. The angle proved too awkward, and we hit the ground before I got a good shot in. My attacker grunted as his shoulder took the brunt of the impact. We rolled over and over.

My blood sang for this. The confrontation, the promised violence. My skin glowed, the siren surging up, and my fangs dropped.

"Revenant," he hissed, "you should be back in the ground, where you belong."

My hands found his neck, but by then he had me pinned to the ground. He pressed his forearm to my windpipe as I squeezed.

I fought an inner battle. I wanted this being's help, but I also wanted to scratch his eyes out. *Really* wanted to scratch his eyes out.

So not normal.

Chill, Gabrielle, and let the scary man go.

Slowly, I released my hands from his neck and raised them where he could see them.

He jerked his head back, his lip curling, and I realized too late, he took it as a threat. In the supernatural world, showing your palms to someone could be considered a threat if you wielded magic. It hadn't been an issue for me before, but now it was.

One of his hands threaded into my hair. He yanked up, then brought my head down, slamming it into the street. I moaned as my vision dulled. "St-stop. Please."

But he didn't. Again and again he smashed my head into the ground until the skin ripped. My blood pooled around me, giving me a macabre halo. It boiled away and thick, oily smoke rose.

Demons were coming to my rescue.

This was so messed up.

His grip loosened on me as he watched the creatures take form. Abruptly, he released my hair to reach for a sword I hadn't seen a minute ago.

"Help me," I wheezed. "Please."

"I will *never* help you, nor will my brothers or sisters."

This was the second time someone had shot down my plea for help. Maybe I needed to work on my delivery.

His arm reared back, and I saw the glint of his sword. I could see in his eyes he'd like nothing better than to end me. What would happen if I died here? Would I cease to exist? A rulebook on what it meant to be queen of the Underworld would be nice.

Intrigued though I was, I wasn't going to wait for this guy to skewer me to find out. I closed my eyes and, steadying my breath, drew on my energy. I felt it rise, and with one great push, I slammed it into my assailant.

The man went flying back, his sword clattering against the cement as he hit the ground.

I rose to my feet and approached him before he recovered. Flakes of snow clung to my hair and eyelashes.

"I don't want to be your enemy," I said, even as my hands fisted and the need to destroy him surged through me.

"We will hunt you until you're wiped off the earth once and for all," he vowed, pushing to his feet and retrieving his sword. "Count your days, revenant."

His eyes flicked to the partially formed demons at my back.

His wings unfurled, nearly as bright as the sun. I shielded my eyes against his glory. He rose into the sky and hung up there for several seconds, sword held loosely in his hand, watching me and the beings behind me.

The demons made gurgling sounds that turned into growls as their windpipes formed. Once they finished filling out, they came to flank me. These ones stood seven, eight feet tall.

"You will lose," he said. "It is inevitable. Enjoy the reprieve from hell. Soon enough we will cast you back to the fires like all those other traitors, and there you will stay."

CHAPTER 7

Gabrielle

Right after my attacker's little speech, he shot up into the dense cloud cover. He even managed to make it look like he wasn't fleeing from the six fully formed demons that now surrounded me.

Probably heading straight to the big man upstairs to tattle on me.

The demons didn't wait for my orders. They leapt off the ground, their leathery wings stretching out incredible distances to carry their weight. Without a backwards glance, they flew into the night, trailing the celestial that had taken off before them.

I just fought an angel.

I prodded the back of my head, still dazed from the injury. It hurt the way poking a bruise hurt, but despite the lingering blood, the skin had sealed up.

Silver lining: I could heal fast again.

What a mess. I'd managed to make enemies of both earth and heaven all within a couple hours of arriving here. That had to be some sort of record.

"Hot damn, Sabertooth," Oliver said from behind me, "just when I think things can't get any freakier around you, you one up yourself."

I turned to see him and Leanne heading towards me. I glanced around my surroundings, noticing the onlookers for the first time. Most had their phones out, angled towards me.

"Go home," I told them, the siren riding my voice, "and forget what you've seen here and remove all record of it from your devices and your mind."

The crowd dispersed, and I used that time to catch my breath and allow my skin to dim.

"That meeting you foresaw wasn't with Andre, was it?" I said to Leanne once the siren was safely locked away.

She rubbed her face. "Apparently angels don't have clear futures." Her hands muffled her voice.

The fairy clucked his tongue. "That would have been helpful to know beforehand. Not that I minded the show. Fuck me, angels are *hot*. I wonder what his feathers would feel like ..."

"They'd burn you faster than they would Gabrielle," Leanne said.

"Hmph."

"I didn't realize angels could visit earth," I said, staring up at the sky. I mean, it made sense. Nephilim, after all, had to come from somewhere.

"They can, but they don't. At least, not often," Leanne said.

"What brought him here?" I asked.

"You."

I swiveled to face her. "So they know about me?"

"Oh, I'm sure they've known for a while." She didn't sound happy about it. "They've just decided to act on it now, I suppose."

I frowned. What kind of divine beings sought to murder a teenage girl?

I stared into the sky. I could no longer see the angel or my demons. My skin prickled. I'd set loose nearly twenty creatures since I'd arrived on earth, and they'd all made themselves scarce. That ... probably wasn't good.

"Can we go? It's colder than a witch's tit out here," Oliver complained.

"We're still waiting for Andre."

My heart sped up at the mention of him. I dreaded seeing him, dreaded revealing what I was—a being whose evil was second only to the devil's—dreaded exposing him to my situation. I could only give him more heartache.

But I was weak enough to want him anyway.

"Do we have to do this outside?" Oliver asked.

"For the future I've seen, yes, we do."

"Pfft. Is that the same future where Gabrielle took on an angel? Dropping the ball, Leanne."

"You think I haven't already spent hours pouring over how this should go?" Leanne asked. Her appearance was a testament to it. She looked worn. "I don't have the time and mental capacity to figure out the future in its entirety *and* live life in real-time."

I didn't know what Leanne had seen, but I now understood how this could go very wrong. She mistook an angel for Andre based on her inability to foresee either's future. And that small detail could've meant the difference between life and death.

A car door slammed. I swiveled towards the noise, and I swear the world went silent for a moment.

There.

He.

Was.

Andre strode towards me, the wind whipping his hair and coat. As soon as our eyes locked, all those images I'd seen when we first met swept through me. Me and him, laughing, crying, kissing, in formal attire, naked, in the sun, in the rain. Always touching, always together, forever and ever and ever and—

Severed.

The images ripped away from me violently. My heart clenched. It still had the muscle memory of a time when it held him inside it. I closed my eyes. He was a beautiful illusion that had come to destroy what little was left of my heart.

"Soulmate."

I opened my eyes. He hadn't disappeared.

Disbelief and the purest form of hope moved across his face. He took a step forward.

I should run, I should force him to keep his distance and allow him to grow to hate me the way nearly everyone else did. But in the end I couldn't.

I was moving and he was moving and I couldn't look away and my heart ached and ached and ached because he wasn't mine anymore.

He wasn't mine.

And then Andre swept me into his embrace and crushed me against him. My hands gripped his upper arms, and they couldn't decide whether to push him away or pull him closer. My mind and my heart were utterly conflicted.

"Andre." My voice came out broken.

His body shook. "I thought I'd lost you. *I thought I'd lost you.* Please never leave me again. *Please.*"

I couldn't make that promise before last night, and I definitely couldn't make it now. In another world and another life he and I were human, and worlds and bonds didn't separate us.

He didn't wait for my promise. His head dipped and his lips crashed into mine. That was the only way to describe it—crashing together, like some terrible train wreck.

I twined my arms around his neck, wishing I could melt into him. He tasted like I remembered—like home. Sharp tears pricked my eyelids. All I wanted to do was live in this moment and never go back. Just him and me and our lips and tongues and no distance between us. But the moment came and went and that little voice inside my head kept saying, *not mine, no longer mine.*

My emotions tangled together, and for the first time since I arrived back on earth, I felt human again.

"Andre, I'm sorry, I'm so, so sorry. I'm sorry, I'm sorry, I'm sorry." I couldn't stop saying it. Maybe if I repeated it enough, it would wipe away any suffering he went through.

"Shhh, it's okay," he said, running a hand over my hair. "It's going to be okay."

How to tell him it wasn't though?

The tears I tried to hold back now trickled down my cheeks.

He brushed them away with his thumbs. "You still cry blood," he said, his tone laced with ... relief? Satisfaction that I hadn't wholly changed?

My bloody tears glimmered on his hand, and ... oh my God.

I caught his wrist. "Don't let it touch the ground."

"I wasn't going to." He brought his hand—and mine along with it—to his lips.

Even worse.

I jerked Andre's hand away. "Stop. Don't—it's unholy."

That ... sounded crazier than it should've.

He paused, then carefully brushed his hand off on his shirt. "Better?" he said.

I swallowed and nodded.

"You still have your fangs," he said, wonder filling his voice.

"I do."

"And your glamour," he said, touching my cheek as my skin dimmed.

A crazy laugh wanted out. I clamped my jaw shut. I was an unholy, taint-of-the-earth badass. I needed to start acting like one.

Something pained entered Andre's features. "I can't

feel you."

I should've known this would come up immediately. I looked away, staring out at the dark night. "That's because I'm bonded to something else." A shiver worked its way up my spine.

Andre went rigid. His eyes flashed, and his hair lifted. "Who are you bonded to?"

"You already know," I whispered quietly, finally meeting his gaze.

Bad idea.

God, don't cry again.

I was hurting him all over.

His power flared out. I felt it pass through me, rippling the air and earth as it moved outwards.

"Has he hurt you?" Even without our connection I could feel Andre's power building on itself.

I shook my head. "I'm fine."

Andre's nostrils flared as he scented the lie. I wasn't fine. I'd been in hell for a day.

The sound of engines distracted us. A line of cars were approaching from the direction of Castletown. It didn't take a genius to guess that the Politia had somehow caught wind of my presence in Douglas.

"We need to go," Andre said.

He tugged at my arm, but I resisted.

"Just leave me," I whispered. I was no good to him like this.

"You must've hit your head when you came back. I will *never* leave you, soulmate."

That endearment killed me. He still considered me his.

He glanced away from me, and I followed his gaze. Only then did I realize we had an audience. Oliver, Leanne, and Andre's driver all watched us.

Andre refocused his attention on me. "We need to get you and your friends to safety," he said.

Leanne stepped up to us. "We do need to get going, Gabrielle, and yes, Andre—we'd love to."

Andre nodded to them, even as I flashed him a strange look. He caught my gaze and gave me a small smile. "I was about to ask them if they wanted a place to stay."

Ah.

Oliver squealed. "Sleepover at the vampire castle! Love!"

"You've both risked your lives and futures to help my mate," Andre said to Leanne and Oliver. "You have my protection as long as you need it. Now, do you guys need a ride?"

Leanne shook her head. "We'll be fine," she said. "We have our own car."

"Then we'll meet you back at Bishopcourt."

He took my hand and led me to his car.

I worried my lower lip. "How badly have I ruined their lives?"

Andre gave my hand a squeeze. "Your friends will be fine. Money and power talk, soulmate, and I have plenty of both. I will make sure Leanne and Oliver are taken care of."

That, I believed without a doubt. As much as Andre punished those who'd wronged him—or me—he rewarded those who helped us. And right now, allies were in short supply.

Still, the possibility that my friends wouldn't be able to go back to Peel Academy broke my heart. They'd given up so much to help me. If nothing else, I had to remedy the situation for them.

"Did I mention that I like the dress?" Andre said, lightening the mood. His eyes strayed to those holes between the spider silk where he caught peeks of my skin.

"Oh, it's the dress you like?" I asked.

He tugged me a little closer so that his mouth pressed flush against my ear. "And everything beneath it."

He pulled away, only to catch sight of my bare feet. "Why aren't you wearing any shoes?"

Before I had a chance to respond, I was up in the air and then cradled in his arms. I let out a small squeal and wrapped my arms around his neck.

"Never mind," he said. "We will be remedying the situation soon enough. And this gives me an excuse to be close to you."

"Andre, I'm fine. Put me down."

Surprise, surprise, he didn't.

Punk.

Even once we were situated inside his town car, he didn't let me go. Instead, he clasped me closer and ordered his driver to turn up the heat.

I buried my head in Andre's chest. How long would I get him before the fairytale was up?

Then I'd be back in the devil's lair. The thought sent my pulse spiking.

"You have a heartbeat, soulmate." Surprise coated Andre's words. "And I can smell your fear. What are you frightened of?" Absently he rubbed my leg, trying to warm me up.

"So many things," I said. "But losing you, most of all."

"You will never lose me," he said, his expression intense. "We'll figure this out." He was determined, just like all those other times he'd been sure he could save me.

I wanted desperately to believe him. But could things ever go back to the way they were? My hope had long since run out.

"Each day it's going to get worse," I whispered. "I'll lose a bit more of my humanity each night, until you no longer recognize me. You won't want to be with me then."

He let my leg go to cup my jaw. "I will always want to be with you, Gabrielle. Always."

"And I will always want to be with you," I whispered. "But that doesn't change things." I swallowed, this next part hard to say. "I really am his soulmate."

Andre's eyes stormed, hurt and anguish rolling through them.

"I really am," I repeated. "It's impossible, but it's true. And I can't stay away from him. I don't know how."

CHAPTER 8

Gabrielle

I COULD SENSE Andre's anger and his thirst for violence. In the cramped space of the car, I practically choked on it.

One guess where his thoughts were.

He stared out the window, his hand absently stroking the inner skin of my arm. I still sat on his lap, but we might as well have been worlds apart. From what I could see of his profile, a muscle in his jaw feathered.

I got the impression he had only the barest of holds on his normally tight control.

Leave him be, the practical part of my mind instructed. The illogical, cursed part of me refused to let him continue to brood.

I reached up and turned his head to face me. For the barest of moments I caught sight of the heady anger consuming him from the inside out. But as soon as his eyes landed on mine, his expression gentled.

His hold tightened. "You are mine." Possessive.

"And you are mine," I said.

He inclined his head in agreement, and I pressed myself in closer.

Andre rested his chin on my head.

"How have you been?" I asked. I always thought of this man as a force of nature, but right now he seemed vulnerable. And so tired.

He laughed gruffly, the action shaking me. "I lived an eternity every second you were gone, and I died countless times in each." He pulled me tighter to him. "It's a strange thing, having a bond break. Strange and excruciating. A part of me is gone.

"Stranger still to sit here next to you and have it throb like an open wound. But when I'm near you, it aches less, and the will to die—I can think through it. But this isn't natural. My body believes you're gone and it wants to follow you. It can't bear to be apart."

My blood ran cold. "You ... want to die?" An uncomfortable heat followed the chill that passed through me. I hadn't felt this type of fear. Ever.

"Soulmate, this isn't the first time. When you've lived as long as I have, death crosses your mind many times."

I brought my fingers to his lips. "Stop it." I didn't want to hear this, didn't want to know that my situation might well and truly kill my soulmate.

That couldn't happen.

That *wouldn't* happen. Earth and heaven and hell be

damned. I'd defy everyone and everything to keep this man safe.

Andre wrapped his hand around mine and removed it from his mouth.

"You promised me you'd stay strong and not give up," I reminded him.

"Soulmate, you survived hell to end up in my arms. I'm as far as you can be from giving up."

Something awfully close to a sob caught in my throat. I cleared it. "Good."

And that was about when the last of my control snapped.

Suddenly, I was kissing him and he was kissing me. My hands were in his hair, and his ran possessively over my back and down my hips. Our mouths didn't separate as I hiked up my dress so I could straddle his lap. The only air I wanted to breathe was his, and the only taste I wanted to drink up was his essence.

At some point the car came to a stop. Andre managed to open the door without us completely spilling onto the pavement, and I wrapped my legs around him as he stepped out of the vehicle.

I didn't notice Bishopcourt, or the people that witnessed our class act. There were only two things in my world—Andre and I—and soon there'd be only one.

If this was just fairytale, then I would make the most of it.

I didn't remember the journey from the steps of Bishopcourt to Andre's bedroom, but suddenly we were in there. Andre kicked the door closed and then we were ripping at each other's clothes. Buttons popped as I tore Andre's shirt open. He knelt, gathering the skirt of my dress and pulling it up and over my head in one fluid movement.

At the back of my mind I realized he'd probably done this thousands of times with thousands of different women over the thousands of months of his very long life. But none of that mattered. He could've been with them and I might be with the devil and none of it meant anything. I knew this as surely as I breathed.

This time, we didn't ask permission. We didn't fumble. Didn't hesitate. His chest touched mine and I wrapped my legs around his waist. His lips met mine.

In one smooth stroke he entered me.

I gasped, my skin brightening. He leaned his forehead against mine, and our gazes locked. This close to him, I could see all the hues that made up his irises. And I wanted to look into those eyes for the rest of my immortal life.

"This close to you, it doesn't hurt," Andre said between kisses.

He was going to make me cry, and I really didn't want to cry. I wanted to obliterate every thought beyond this moment. Thinking of the future was when things got messy, and really, this was all very simple. He was my one and only. I was his. No bond could create or destroy this. It had a life of its own.

Andre moved, and air hissed out from between my teeth. He thrust back into me, his eyes locked on mine. There they stayed.

"I will *always* be yours." He went about saying those words like he did everything. Fiercely. Deliberately.

"And I will always be yours."

He moved against me and my fingers sunk into his back. After that, we let our bodies do the talking.

Andre

Andre held Gabrielle tighter than was necessary. But if he had it his way, they'd still be joined completely. Instead, he had to deal with this restlessness.

Bonded to another man.

One far more monstrous than Andre, and that was saying something. The delicate skin he now stroked—would the devil touch it with the same reverence Andre did? The situation might be more bearable if the dark god were capable of kindness.

In all his seven hundred years, he'd never heard stories of the devil's compassion.

He rubbed his mouth. What would the lord of the Underworld do to Gabrielle once he found out Andre had been with her?

He'd been a selfish bastard, not considering this until the deed was done and it was too late. She might have to suffer the consequences alone. And there were bound to be consequences.

He dragged Gabrielle closer and pressed a rough kiss to her mouth.

Her brows furrowed. "What are you thinking about?" she asked after the kiss ended.

"What am I ever thinking about, soulmate? You." And he smiled at her because she was his sun.

As if to prove his point, her skin brightened. She stretched out along him, and he all but groaned. Yes, if he were a better person, he'd keep some distance between them for her sake. But he wasn't a decent person. Gabrielle had given him his humanity only to take it with her to hell.

And he wouldn't apologize to anyone about it—not even the devil himself.

Gabrielle

I THREADED MY fingers in Andre's hair as he rained kisses down my neck. We'd been in his bed for well over an hour and it felt ... ephemeral, this happiness. Which made me more hesitant to leave. Because as soon as I did, I'd have to stop pretending my life was normal.

"Andre."

He must've heard something in my voice because he raised his head.

Now that I was coming back down from my earlier high, I'd begun to shake. "Something's wrong with me."

He cupped my face, brushing away several stray strands of hair. "Nothing's wrong with you."

He noticed my body trembling. "You're working yourself up for no reason."

"My blood gives life to demons—just like that necromancer."

Andre didn't so much as bat an eyelash, which probably meant that he'd already learned about this ability or figured it out on his own.

"That doesn't mean anything's wrong with *you*."

"It's unnatural."

"That's a word the Politia uses to damn anything they deem evil," he said.

"But Andre, I *am* evil. I'm the queen of the Underworld."

He pulled back. "That does not make you evil."

"Then what does?"

"Your heart, your actions."

I couldn't meet his gaze. Instead I chewed on the inside of my cheek.

"I hurt Caleb," I admitted. "After what he did last night, I wanted to destroy him."

"What happened last night ... ?" Andre repeated. His face darkened as he put the pieces together. "He was the one that shot you." A muscle in Andre's cheek feathered. "And you returned to Castle Rushen to punish him."

I nodded.

"Good." His voice roughened with renewed anger. "The boy should be thankful I haven't had the chance to punish him myself. I doubt he'd survive it."

Last night felt like an eon ago. I closed my eyes and remembered Caleb's expression, his shaking hand. He'd gone through with it—fired the bullet that nearly killed me. It might've too, had the devil not claimed me before my life could expire on its own.

I sat up and brought the sheets along with me. "I wanted to hurt him," I said. "That was my first thought. It should've been you. When Oliver led me back to the Isle of Man, I should've pulled him into a hug and then insisted we find you."

Finally I found the courage to meet Andre's eyes.

He was frowning.

"I'm ... not quite myself," I continued, "and I'm worried that the Politia's right to try to get rid of me."

"Soulmate," he slid a hand along my jaw and cupped my face, "I understand. I do. You've seen me destroy an entire branch of my coven when my anger took me. Men and women whose company I'd cherished for hundreds of years. All gone in an instant because the need for vengeance rode me too hard.

"So you were angry, and you hunted down Caleb. What happened once you found him?"

I chewed on my lower lip. "I threw him into a cell to rot."

"You threw him into a cell." Andre's lips twitched.

I gave his shoulder a light shove. "It's not funny."

Andre's expression sobered. "No, it's not. A boy tried to destroy my queen, and he still breathes."

Er, ... not the direction I was hoping to take this conversation.

"You will not feel bad about what happened," Andre said, bossy as ever.

When I didn't nod, he gave me a slight shake. "You will not. The world thinks badly of you. The world is wrong. Don't let their misconceptions cloud your judgment."

"But—"

"You can keep your guilt, but you cannot let it consume you," he said. "Now, you still look far too thin. Hungry?"

I knew what he was doing. Trying to distract me from

my thoughts. It was such a little thing, this kindness, but it made me smile.

"Famished."

I FOLLOWED ANDRE through his house, towards the kitchen, wearing a robe Andre had bought for me at some point. I ran my fingers over the silky material. If he had it his way, his closet would be filled with my clothes. Already, bits and pieces intended for me—such as this robe—were making their way into his home.

The thought had me pressing my lips tightly together. If I could have a do-over, I would give it all to him. I'd let him fill his house to his heart's content with knickknacks meant for me, and I swear I would never fight it again.

Anything to make this man smile because I couldn't bear his pain.

As we crossed the foyer, I saw that Bishopcourt's windows, which had blown inwards last night, were intact once more. Kind of embarrassing that I hadn't noticed it when I first entered.

"How are they all ... ?"

Andre came to my side. "Someone in my coven fixed it, but I don't know who or when."

Andre, the control freak, in the dark about his home? I took a good look at him. He hid it well, but sorrow tugged at his features, and beneath that, pain.

"What happened after I left?" My voice came out as a whisper, because things that scared you shouldn't be said too loudly lest you give them power.

"Dark times, soulmate," Andre said, taking my hand. "I would rather not speak of them."

I nodded, trying not to worry over the past.

"Come," Andre said, ushering me forward.

For the most part, the mansion appeared untouched by the horrors of the previous night. Someone had swept the floor, righted the furniture, and removed or magically repaired the broken items in the room.

A twisted part of me wanted to venture into the bathroom where I'd been shot, just to see if any of my blood still stained the floor. I already knew I'd smell myself embedded into the cracks. The alluring scent of the siren, the sickness that clung to me, the taint from the devil's premature claim, and the ancient curse that rode through it all. A darkness still clung to this place, a darkness that called to me. You couldn't wash away evil with cleaning supplies or a simple spell.

Andre led me to a table. "Blood or food?"

"Um ... " I rolled my lips inward. "Either?"

He gave me a nod and ordered the chef to prepare both blood and a plate of fettuccine alfredo, my favorite dish.

He took my hand and played with my fingers. "You still haven't told me about the twelve hours that preceded this."

"And you haven't told me of the time after I left."

His lips tilted up, but there was no mirth to his smile. "After you left, there was nothing but pain and anguish. My coven had to hold me down out of fear that I would kill myself."

I breathed through my nose to keep myself together.

"They began to drain me of blood, hoping that if they weakened me enough my body would go into stasis—a type of sleep—and I could remain like that indefinitely so that they could live."

"That's so ... cruel." Anger rose at the thought of anyone hurting Andre. That emotion quickly morphed into a sharp ache—*I'd* hurt him far greater than any of his coven could.

"It was their only option," he said, scenting my emotions. "Don't begrudge them their actions. I would've done the same had I been in their shoes. Now," he said, squeezing my hand, "what happened to you?"

I was still digesting his words. So much pain I'd left him with. Enough to force his coven into incapacitating him. If things remained as they were, that pain of his would continue to grow. That didn't sit well with me.

"Love?"

I blinked several times, refocusing my attention. "At the center of hell, there's a castle. The devil took me there."

Andre squeezed my hand tighter.

"He showed me around the place, tried to get under my skin,"—and succeeded—"and introduced me to his a demon horde, but for most of the day he left me alone."

"He left you alone?" Andre clearly didn't believe it.

I shrugged. "I got the impression that he's a busy guy."

"Indeed," Andre said quietly.

A moment later, my food came, saving me from having to detail the horrible intimacy that had developed between the dark god and me.

The pasta smelled heavenly, and when I took my first

bite, I groaned. It tasted even better.

"I take it this means you got your appetite back?" Andre's lips twitched.

"Mmmhm."

God, I'd missed food.

I tried the blood next. Two weeks ago I might've had a hissy over drinking the liquid. At this point, I was simply thankful that I was hungry at all. Bringing the glass of it to my lips, I tipped it back and took a swallow.

That awkward moment when blood tastes delicious.

"My mate enjoys both blood and food," Andre stated, reading me like a book. He glanced up to the ceiling. "Thank the heavens."

Once I polished off the meal, Andre took my hand again. "I'll have a shower started for you, and one of my servants will bring you clothing," he said. He led me back to his room. And I let him.

This temporary calm couldn't last. For one thing, my blood thrummed for carnage and chaos. For another, I would return to hell soon enough and face another day in the devil's company. But I'd enjoy this while I still could.

Andre didn't let me go until after he started the shower. Then he backed away. "I'll leave you to it."

I fiddled with the ties of my robe. "You don't have to go," I said, somewhat shyly, my earlier courage now nowhere to be seen.

Andre's expression was tormented. "God, soulmate, I would love nothing more. But I can't."

"Why?"

Regret swam in his eyes. "Because I cannot know how

the devil will punish you for it."

The thought had crossed my mind, but I didn't care then, and I didn't care now.

"Once he might forgive, but if you continuously betrayed him—I won't risk it."

"Andre—"

"No, soulmate, on this I won't budge."

When I realized he was being dead serious, I bit out, "Fine."

I undid the ties of my robe, and let the garment slide off my shoulders, not bothering to cover myself.

His jaw clenched. "Don't tempt me. My good intentions only go so far."

"Then leave." I tried to sound confident, but the words came out full of hurt. I stood naked and bared for him, and I felt spurned.

My voice was the cue he waited for.

He pushed me against the wall, his hands in my hair and his lips on my mouth. I gasped, and Andre took advantage of the action, his tongue pushing its way against mine.

So much for him not budging.

I returned the kiss, mussing his hair as I wrapped myself up in him. He groaned into my mouth, and all my momentary insecurities vanished.

With reluctance, he pulled away from me. "I can't, soulmate," he said against my lips, breathing heavily. "As much as I want to, I can't have you incur the devil's wrath even more than you already have. Please don't force the issue."

I swallowed and nodded.

"Thank you." He pressed a soft kiss to my lips. Then he bowed his head and left me to my shower.

Andre

ONLY WHEN HE was far away from Gabrielle did Andre allow himself to slam his fist into the wall. At this point, he wasn't even sure what he was pissed about. The devil's new claim to her? The very real possibility that the man might punish her for sleeping with Andre? Or turning Gabrielle down when neither knew how much time they had together?

The anger dissipated into steely resolve, and he continued down the hall. One of his men intercepted him.

"Sire," he said, "the Politia just arrived outside our gates."

In spite of himself, Andre's lips curved up. They picked the perfect time to come knocking.

"They're demanding we turn over Gabrielle."

"That's not going to happen. Prepare the men and alert the coven members that remain. I will meet with the Politia and let them know what I think about their demands," he said darkly.

His man nodded and split off to see to his orders.

Andre headed for his room, where his fondest weapons were kept. At the back of his closet rested a timeworn chest. Crouching in front of it, he ran a hand over the wood.

The modern world was usually tame. But thanks to his

bond with Gabrielle, he'd seen more violence in the last several months than he had in the last century. And the predator in him was pleased.

He unlatched the chest's bindings and swung it open. Inside, his favorite swords and daggers rested.

Andre strapped the swords to his back, his movements jerky due to his agitation. That gaping maw he still felt in his soul, it was real. Worse, there was the very real threat that his soulmate could transfer her affections from Andre to the devil through the god's trickery.

He wouldn't let that happen. Whatever it took to win her over, he'd do it. The connection wasn't everything. People fell in love all the time without the aid of a bond. And if the bond was all there ever was to his relationship, well then, severing it should've released him, not imprisoned him more than ever.

He clenched his jaw, an angry smile stretching across his face as he threaded a belt around his waist. He'd love nothing more than tearing into her enemies.

The shower still ran. He'd let his soulmate be—for now.

He stalked back down the hall. It was time to remind the Politia why he was someone you didn't cross.

BOOM.

Bishopcourt shook as something powerful blasted against it.

Those bastards hadn't even waited for him to tell them to shove their orders up their asses. They'd gone straight to declarations of war.

Andre pulled his twin blades out from his back, rolling his wrists and swinging the swords lightly. The last time he'd wielded these, it had been to deliver Gabrielle's retribution. A grim sort of satisfaction spread through him at the thought that he'd use these blades once again on her behalf.

Tonight he would be her champion in earnest.

CHAPTER 9

Gabrielle

I RELAXED UNDER the spray of the shower. Water pelted my skin, and after hours in that hollow underworld, the sensation felt indescribably good.

I leaned against the wall. So screwed. I was so, so screwed.

BOOM!

The explosion threw me to the floor of the shower stall.

Typical. The moment I got naked, shit would hit the fan.

I reached up and turned off the lever. An eerie silence descended. The lack of noise raised the hairs along my arm.

The Politia had found me once again. They still thought that antagonizing me would get them somewhere. All it did was piss me off.

The mosaic saints in Andre's bathroom pleaded with their eyes as I toweled off. What they wanted me to do, however, was a mystery.

A set of clothing rested on Andre's bed.

Hurriedly, I pulled on the items, sighing out my relief at the shirt and pants. Now I looked less like Elvira and more like ... Buffy.

Whatever, I looked better.

I stalked out the door, passing several faded paintings of various individuals, and that saint's relic. Vampires and their old-ass trinkets.

Andre's coven gathered in the entryway. When they saw me striding out, one after another dropped to a knee.

My steps faltered. Even now, after I was taken, they still showed their allegiance. Or maybe it was because I was taken.

"You can't have her. Not today, not tomorrow, not ever." I could hear the cold determination in Andre's voice. He was already outside, facing down whatever had come for me.

I nodded to the vampires who rose. They stepped aside as I passed through, regarding me with respect—and probably wondering what, exactly, I was.

One of Andre's men intercepted me. "Miss, you should stay inside. Andre has asked us to protect you the best we can."

"Andre, she is no longer your soulmate. She's the devil's tool," a much fainter voice drifted in.

In the distance I could hear the blades of a chopper

slicing through air. Whatever was out there had brought in massive reinforcements, and Andre was taking them on alone.

"I'm not going to sit by and have him fight my battles," I said, sidestepping the man.

"But miss—" He made a grab for my hand. A mistake. I blasted him back with my power.

Around me I heard gasps from Andre's men and his coven, but no one else tried to stop me.

I didn't bother picking up my pace. I knew Andre well enough to understand that out of all those supernaturals, the seven hundred year old vampire king was the most dangerous being out there.

At least, until I arrived.

The siren rose to the surface. She no longer felt like a different, dangerous being that resided under my skin, though I still referred to her as such. More like another facet of my personality, one that came to my aid when I needed help. Her presence threw a little more sway into my hips.

I passed through the entrance and got my first glimpse of the standoff outside. At least a dozen cars fanned out along the circular drive, and—

Was that a tank?

Odd to think that a supernatural police force needed something so mundane. Odder to think that the tank was meant for me.

The Politia had come to Bishopcourt armed for war. All to stop little ol' me.

In addition to all the manpower, mounted halogen

lights shined on us. God, did they burn.

As soon as I strode out the front door, the officers tensed. I could smell their mounting fear, and I drank it in.

Having over two dozen weapons trained on me should've been cause for worry. Instead, the siren purred, welcoming the potential bloodbath.

They can't kill you, consort.

I turned, and for the barest of moments, the devil stood to my left.

Show them what happens to people that cross you.

His form dissipated, and he was gone once more.

I shouldn't listen to that sick, insidious voice, but it lured me like mine did men.

"Hands behind your back!" one of the officers shouted.

Only then did my soulmate turn. His eyes flashed as they caught sight of me, clearly displeased that I had joined him.

"If you come quietly, we will leave this place without drawing blood. No one has to get hurt," the officer continued.

He should've stopped talking a long time ago.

My fangs dropped, my skin glowed brighter. I was a far cry from the innocent school girl that had come to this island all those months ago.

The Politia had made a similar promise mere hours ago. They'd lied. They then chose—unwisely—to barge onto Andre's property with all the trappings of war. Another mistake.

I was a shark that scented blood. The fight that had

come to my doorstep called to the darkness in me. There'd be no stopping me now.

I flicked my gaze to each mounted halogen light, and one by one the bulbs burst. I didn't stop there. I burned out every single bulb within range. Plastic cracked as car lights flickered out. Screams came from inside as lights popped and burned out. The chopper circling the estate went dark. Lamps that lined the drive dimmed to darkness one by one. I drove the light out until I was the brightest thing out here.

The entire time the Politia did nothing. Their reasons weren't lost on me. Back at Castle Rushen they'd seen what happened when I was wounded. For all their weapons, they weren't willing to spill my blood.

"You really thought you could coerce me?" I asked conversationally, sauntering down the steps. The entire time I was acutely aware of Andre. He clenched his swords in his hands, but he made no move to attack or divert attention away from me.

The Politia had forced their way onto Andre's property, disregarding their treaty with vampires—a treaty I'd risked my life and soul for only a few months ago. They had already bombed Bishopcourt, firing the first proverbial shot. But most of all, they'd threatened Andre.

Fury boiled beneath my skin, building by the second.

Threatening my mate, bond or no bond, was a line you just didn't cross. And they crossed it.

Ho, was I pissed.

My kinsmen hovered along the periphery, nothing more than shadows. Waiting, waiting. They wouldn't have to wait much longer.

Yes.

I smiled, lifting a hand to the sky.

The ground trembled, my hair swishing.

Mete out your revenge! my power screamed.

A gun went off from one of the officers positioned behind his car. The bullet tore through the flesh of my side. I gasped as I clutched the wound, and Andre roared.

The maelstrom only grew from my pain. Another gun went off, slicing into my thigh. I let out a defiant shriek, and the wind kicked up.

My gut wound closed, but not before blood covered my hand. It seeped between my fingers, trickling down them and beading along the edge of my hand.

And then it dripped.

The blood hissed as it came into contact with the earth. Shouts rose from officers as the devil's minions took shape.

Andre's blurred form moved from person to person. I could hear the wet slice of his swords as he cut down anyone in his path.

Lightning cracked overhead, illuminating the night. Men and women scrambled to their cars. They looked like spooked horses, the whites of their eyes large and visible.

The demons finished forming around me, and they charged the officers.

I threw my power out, lashing it across the tank. The metal armor of it groaned as it dented inwards. I needed to work this anger out of my system, but the more power I released, the angrier I became. I feared that the next time I used it, it would be to hurt someone. As much as a part of me craved that, a smaller part—the part I admired—wanted to retain what little humanity I had left.

Luckily, before I had a chance to test the limits of my self-restraint, the Politia retreated.

"I don't want you risking yourself like that again," Andre said, stalking back to me. He bent to wipe his swords off on the grass. Behind him, several men and women lay unmoving on the ground.

I lifted my chin. "This goes two ways, you know. You don't just get to protect me."

The storm raging in his eyes calmed at my response. When he reached me, he brought my forehead to his. "Soulmate, you can't know the effect your words have on me." He squeezed the back of my neck. "That still doesn't change my mind."

Andre stepped away at the sound of footsteps. I swiveled to see his guards and several vampires heading towards us. Beyond them, I caught a glimpse of a wide-eyed Oliver and Leanne.

"I need five good men to deal with the bodies," Andre said. "And someone needs to start lighting candles for those who don't have night vision. Jon," he called to one of his men, "get what spare bulbs you can from the basement."

It took some time for Andre to organize his people. As he did so, I stared off at the horizon, where the Politia members had fled.

They'd be back, possibly during the day, when Andre would be sleeping. My being here endangered him—endangered everyone. Andre, our coven, my friends, even those that wished to do me harm. Blood would spill in the coming days, and it would be my fault.

Andre came over to me and wrapped me in his arms. He pressed his nose against the thin column of my neck. "I can smell your guilt," he said.

I found his hands and gripped them tightly. "Promise me you'll stay safe."

He pulled away enough to meet my eyes and pushed the hair away from my face. "I have not survived seven centuries on luck alone, nor do I intend to die when my mate needs me most."

"Promise?"

"On my life."

No other attacks came in the hours that followed, not that this made us any less tense. People wanted me dead. If they weren't actively attacking me, then they were planning on it.

As the evening came to an end, Andre kept me by his side. It became a thing, keeping me close. Neither of us knew when, where, or how I would disappear. And as the hours tick by, and I remained on earth, I became almost ... optimistic.

Maybe I wasn't going back.

We stood on the steps of Andre's home to see off the cars carrying the bodies of the fallen. Andre was delivering them back to the Politia.

"Even in war there are ethics. One gives honor to the

dead," he said now, by way of explanation.

This was one of Andre's medieval beliefs.

"I didn't realize we were at war," I said.

He glanced down at me. "Soulmate, if there was ever a time or a cause for war, this would be it."

That … wasn't reassuring.

Andre placed a hand on the small my back and began to walk, steering me along. Instead of heading back inside, he led me to the gardens around his mansion. I bit my lip when I noticed the grass shriveling beneath my feet. And when we passed the first of the hedges, they leaned away.

I'd seen this before; this was what plants did in the presence of the devil. And now they were doing it to me.

"It's safe to say that heaven and much of the earth wants to get rid of you," Andre said, interrupting my thoughts.

I could already tell this was going to be a fun conversation.

Not.

"What I want to know," he continued, "is what hell wants."

Oddly enough, I never thought of it that way. But if anyone had motives, it would be the devil.

He stopped us in the middle of Bishopcourt's rose garden and turned to me. "More importantly, I want to know what role you have in all this."

Beneath my feet, I swear I felt the earth shift. I didn't bother looking down for fear that I'd see the plant life taking more drastic measures to get away from me.

Andre touched my cheek. "I want you safe."

I leaned into his touch, knowing what he said would be

impossible.

The ground shifted again, more forceful this time, and I grabbed Andre's arm to stabilize myself. He wrapped his hands around my waist to steady me.

"What was that?" I asked.

He furrowed his brows. "I thought that was *you*."

I shook my head. "It wasn't me."

The earth began to rumble, and my feet shook as grass and dirt shifted.

My eyes met Andre's and a sick sort of realization passed between us: I was going back.

"Gabrielle," Andre said, as fear flooded his features, "*run*."

Grabbing Andre's hand, we tore out of the gardens.

The earth beneath my feet began to fall away.

Roots sprouted on either side of me. They grew unnaturally fast. Unlike other foliage, these grew towards me, reaching for my feet.

Bishopcourt's back door was just ahead of us. We could make it.

And then what?

I pushed the thought away as a vine latched onto my foot, jerking me back.

Andre's hold tightened. "Stay with me, soulmate!"

"Trying!" I said, ripping the vine away.

I'd barely gotten it off when another latched onto me. And then another. And another. They twisted around my ankles, pinning me in place.

This was what the myths meant when they called me the daughter of Demeter. Demeter was just the personification of nature. And just as the earth bore me each evening, it claimed me at the end of it.

Andre, whom the vines had avoided, stopped to wrap his arms around my waist. He yanked me forward, and several of the shoots ripped. But now they were growing faster and faster, and dozens of them extended towards me, grasping my feet and legs. It took only seconds for them to cover my lower half completely. The vines twined around my waist like a python. They weren't constricting, but they held me firm. And they were steadily pulling me down to earth.

I wasn't going to win this fight.

My eyes fell heavily on Andre. "You need to let me go."

"Never."

The shoots slid up my torso, now covering Andre's hands as well as my stomach. I didn't know if the vines would take him too if he refused to let me go. And if they did, then he would come to hell with me.

I couldn't let that happen.

"I'm sorry," I whispered. I threw my power out.

It slammed into him, ripping him from me and sending him flying back twenty feet.

"No!" I heard him bellow.

The ground dipped as it began to suck me under. The vines wrapped around my arms, pinning them in place. They crawled up my neck and into my hair. Ugh, what a way to go.

I caught one last glimpse of Andre, pushing himself up to his feet. And then the vines slid over my eyes and pulled me under completely.

CHAPTER 10

Gabrielle

THE JOURNEY DOWN felt much, much worse than the one up. The roots that sucked me into the earth now squeezed me tightly, cutting off my air and circulation. The devil lied; I wasn't immortal, and I was going to die.

Just as true panic set in, I felt something inside myself release. My body seemed to lose form until I was nothing more than consciousness falling farther and farther from everything that I knew and loved. I cried out, not from pain, but from the terrible emptiness that filled me.

After what felt like ages, my feet finally made contact with solid ground, and I was whole once more.

I dropped to my knees, staring at the onyx floor. I knew where I was before I glanced up. I could smell the brimstone and ash ... and the fear, and the despair.

Back to this wasteland.

Shoes clicked against the polished floor.

"Barvo, bravo, consort." The devil clapped a couple times, the sound echoing in the cavernous room. He stopped a foot away from me.

"You did well—for your first day," he said, staring down at me, and those unnerving eyes of his seemed to see into my soul. "Destroyed law and order, spilled blood, brought my servants to Earth."

"You knew that would happen?" I asked. "That my blood would create them?"

"Mmm. They're there to guard you and do my bidding."

Months ago, the devil wouldn't have thought to have his demons guard me. Since then, something had changed. Even the fact that he mentioned protecting me before he mentioned the other ways his demons served him ... it said something about where I stood in his mind. Had he noticed the change?

I rose to my feet and fought the urge to take a step back. He was dangerous enough when he simply wanted to kill me. I didn't know what to do now that I could see hints of a conscience.

He stepped forward and I backed up. "You've been a naughty little siren." His tone changed, and I could feel the heat of his wrath. "I know you've been with Andre since you went topside." He crowded me until my back hit an obsidian wall.

Here comes my punishment. I was ready for it.

Pluto's arms came up, trapping me between them. "You insolent little thing. My wife doesn't get to fuck other men. Even here in hell we have standards."

"I wasn't *here in hell*."

His hand shot to my neck. "*Don't* try to play me at my own game." He squeezed lightly, his face contemplative. "Perhaps it's time I show you what happens to my vampires."

I reached up to dislodge his grip, but it might as well have been a shackle. Behind him, the room dissolved away, and then we stood outside his palace, right where the flames began.

A line of fire spit and crackled in front of me, the light from it dancing along my skin.

Pluto released my neck. "Follow me." He turned and strode right into those flames. It reminded me of the first time I'd seen him, my childhood home going up in smoke. Even then he watched me. Even then he knew.

My feet refused to move.

"Don't make me come and get you, consort. You won't like it."

"I'm not going in there." Repercussions be damned.

A moment later, the fire blasted out at me, engulfing my body in flame.

Well, that was one way to end the stand-off.

I screamed.

He wants to trap me here like the rest of his prisoners.

But as the seconds ticked by, I realized that the fire didn't scorch me. In fact, if anything, it felt cool.

Hellfire doesn't burn me.

That couldn't possibly be good.

A hand clamped around my own, and the devil loomed

over me, looking far too handsome for a monster. His hair swept back from his face and his eyes glittered. Inside them the flames danced, and I realized this fire was just as much a part of him as the siren was a part of me.

"Stop being melodramatic and come, my queen." My skin crawled at the title. Not just a queen, but his.

My gaze bored into his back as he led me through the fire. He was being nice to me again—or at least not overtly hostile. Even his grip on my hand was gentle. It made my heart pound. I knew the devil, being the devil, would punish me for sleeping with Andre. It was an insult to him to have his mate stray. If there was one person who wouldn't tolerate that, it was him.

So why the unnecessary kindness?

Like usual, I couldn't figure him out.

We traveled for what felt like an eternity. I couldn't see anything beyond the flames, but the devil must've because he never once hesitated as he led us forward.

Right in the thick of the flames, the screams of the damned vibrated against my skin. I flinched as I felt someone's hot breath. I swiveled to see a wisp of a man—nothing more than a shadow, really—writhe in the flames. He was almost completely gone, all but his voice. I had a feeling that was the last thing that went.

What happened to a person once there was nothing left?

"They become the fire." Pluto answered my unspoken question.

So the tormented turned into the tormentors.

"And ash," he continued. "Some become the earth

and walls of this place. And some become demons. It all depends." I sensed a rising giddiness coming off of him. That and a flash of something else, something I didn't have a name for.

Suddenly, he stopped. "Here we are."

The devil stepped aside, releasing my hand, and I finally got a good look at what he'd been so eager to show me.

Another screaming soul. But not just any soul.

My knees went weak as I stared at the man who raised me and then saved me the night he lost his life ... and his soul.

Santiago Fiori, my father.

"D-DAD," I SAID, stumbling forward.

He didn't react. His eyes were wild, moving over me as his body contorted. He screamed and screamed, and the sound sliced through me.

I reached for him. I needed to save him from this; I couldn't bear to see another second of his pain.

"Ah ah ah," the devil said, stepping in front of me. "I can't let you do that."

"Let him go!" I had to avert my eyes He'd endured this for over ten years. *Over ten years.* I couldn't even imagine.

This is what happens to those that try to help me.

"And what do you propose I do with him once that happens?" the devil asked, coming up behind me.

I turned to him and gripped his arms. "Free him," I begged.

The devil pulled my hands away from him and cupped

them in his own. "His soul will either crumble to dust, or if it's rotted enough and he's wicked enough, he will become a demon."

I shook my head vigorously. "I don't believe you." I sucked in my lower lip, my eyes watering. My father continued to shriek, the sound unbearable.

"And why would I lie about this?"

"Because you don't want to help me."

"You're right," he admitted. "I don't feel very moved to lessen your father's suffering after you spent the evening with another man. I'm sure even to measly humans that's a fair enough reaction. And I do lie—when it serves a purpose. This doesn't."

"*Please*," I begged, my tears dripped down my cheeks only to evaporate in the infernal heat. "You are the devil, you can save him!"

"I'm not the deity that saves things. I'm the one that punishes them."

"Please," I repeated, even though I knew it was useless.

"Take a good look at your father, consort. This is what will happen to your beloved Andre when he dies. Should you choose to screw the vampire again, I'll make sure his death is swift and soon, and I will make him suffer like none of my souls have suffered—and I will make you watch."

Heaven help me, I believed him.

I stared at my father. His screams blended with those of other damned souls. It would break me, watching Andre burn. Watching this was already breaking me.

Before I was aware of my actions, I reached for my father once more.

Pluto caught my wrist. "*What* are you doing?"

I couldn't take my eyes off of Santiago. "Saving him myself."

"*No*," he said.

"I'm not asking your permission," I snapped, tearing my gaze away.

Our surroundings changed so suddenly I stumbled. A split-second ago I stood amidst flames, and now I was back in the obsidian palace, in our bedroom.

The devil pushed me back. "You dare much, challenging me like that," he said, his eyes flashing. "I didn't bring you there to free your father. I brought you there to snuff out whatever foolish ideas you have about the vampire king."

He stepped in close. "And if you don't, it would give me great pleasure to prove to you just how ruthless I can be. I promise you, the stories don't do me justice.

"Are we understood?"

I worked my jaw. After a second, I nodded.

"Good." Hades lifted a strand of my hair and rubbed it between his fingers. "Now, you will change out of your clothes and dine with me—and you *will* eat."

I scowled at him, telling him wordlessly how much I hated him.

He tugged on the lock of hair he held captive. "Little bird, give me your hate. It makes me strong. And once I use it all up, we'll see what lies buried beneath it in that heart of yours."

I THOUGHT HE would leave while I changed out of the clothes Andre had given me.

He didn't.

Instead, his hands dropped to the buttons of his shirt. He began undoing them one by one.

I cleared my throat, and he raised an eyebrow. "Yes?"

"You wanted me to change."

He looked me up and down. "I still do, and you're not moving fast enough."

I backed up as those hands of his continued to unbutton his shirt. "Yeah, but I want a little privacy."

"You are my wife. We will not hide our bodies from each other." To punctuate the thought, he shrugged his shirt off, and I saw way too much pale, muscled skin. On earth, Hades appeared thin. But here, where he didn't bother masking his true appearance, he had far more muscle.

I backed up until I'd plastered myself against the far wall.

He sat down on a side chair by the window and sighed as he unlaced his shoes. "You still aren't changing. I think someone wants me to remove her clothes for her."

"I'm not going to change when you're in the room."

He glanced up at me as he pulled off a shoe. "Little bird, your skittishness is bringing out the predator in me. If I were you, I wouldn't show any signs of weakness. Then again," he continued to assess me, "I like hunting tricky souls."

Hades had given me plenty of warning. I might not like the current situation, but the devil didn't make idle threats either. I needed to change, or he'd do it for me.

"Where's the clothing I should change into?" I asked.

He nodded to an armoire. I headed over to it and opened it up.

The entire thing was filled with those same gowns. "I'm beginning to sense a pattern here."

"Your wardrobe will change when I decide it will."

Right.

I yanked a random dress from the rack and threw it on the bed. Time to get this over with.

Grabbing the edges of my shirt, I lifted it over my head.

His eyes smoldered, and I swear the flames in them brightened as he watched me. "And the bra," he said.

"This isn't a strip tease."

His lips curved up, but he didn't argue with me, so I didn't bother removing the bra. If he really wanted me to remove the garment, then we'd just have to duke it out.

Despite my words, this felt exactly like a strip tease. I could feel the touch of his gaze the entire time I changed. Only once I'd tugged the dress over my head did he resume undressing himself.

He pulled off his socks. "You might as well get comfortable changing in front of me. We'll be doing a lot more than just that very, very soon."

I bit back my fear. He hadn't tried anything yet, but he was the devil, the lord of the Underworld. Give him enough time and he would.

He turned away from me to retrieve a new shirt from a dresser adjacent to my own.

I sucked in a breath.

His back was the only part of him that lacked any sort of perfection. Two painful looking scars sliced down either side of his spine.

Where wings once were. This *thing* had once been an angel.

The flesh was stained a burgundy color, and it didn't lay flat. Broken bone and scar tissue rested beneath it.

Without meaning to, I crossed the room and reached out.

"Don't."

I ignored him—never a wise move—and ran my fingertips over the lumpy, discolored tissue. He shuddered but didn't stop me.

Vulnerable. He was definitely being vulnerable, and it was doing strange things to our connection, like urging me even closer.

"These look like they still hurt," I said.

"Sometimes they do."

I ran my palm over them, and whether unconsciously or not, the devil tilted his head back under my touch, his hair brushing against my face.

He swiveled and caught my hand. Bringing it up to his nose, he breathed in my scent.

"Why are you being nice to me?" I asked, staring at our entwined hands.

"What makes you think I'm being nice?" At his words, the atmosphere in the room changed completely. Now he felt like a threat.

I pulled my hand from his grip and backed away.

Faster than I could react, he grabbed my chin, squeezing it tightly.

He stared at me long enough for me to squirm. Long enough for me to realize that he was the devil, and my soulmate, and I was trapped in a room with him.

Our connection throbbed. I'd felt that familiar pulse before, I knew that what usually followed was something physical. In this, I was more knowledgeable than the devil.

I closed my eyes and swallowed. A moment later, I felt his lips brush mine. I could only barely taste the brimstone on them.

His free hand angled my head towards him.

"Kiss me back, my queen," he said, his lips moving against mine.

I shook my head.

"You think I won't punish your vampire for more than just your infidelity? The moment you displease me, I swear to you I will."

A shudder worked its way through my body.

So that was how it was going to be.

If Andre were here, he would've told me to fight the devil, no matter what might happen to him. That was what soulmates did, they protected each other. And I'd always protect him, regardless of the personal cost.

My stomach churned as my lips began to move against the devil's.

Wrong, wrong, wrong! my mind screamed, but my connection seemed to approve. As did the siren.

Traitorous bitch.

The devil's hold on my chin softened. The kiss lasted far too long, and I felt dirty from the inside out.

Finally he broke away, and I gasped out a breath as his lips left mine. He looked breathtaking, which only made me feel more conflicted. His face was one you should trust, one that you wanted to forgive of any wrongdoing because he appeared incapable of it. It would be so easy to give in to that pull, and if I lived here long enough, without anyone but the devil and his demons to keep me company, it might happen.

No. Fight for your humanity, Gabrielle. Don't let him have that last part of you.

"You've given me human urges, consort. They're weaknesses, but I can't say I regret them." His thumb skimmed over my lower lip. "Not at all."

CHAPTER 11

Gabrielle

Ten minutes later we entered the dining room. Two place settings had been set out at the end of the table, along with trays full of an assortment of breakfast items. It'd been over twenty-four hours since the devil took me. In all that time, I hadn't slept. The urge to had disappeared along with my mortality.

The urge to eat, however, had not. I hungered more now than I ever had—for food, for blood, for violence, for power. It was just one more twisted aspect of who I now was.

Our chairs had been angled so that we could face each other while we ate. I slid into my chair. A plate of French toast had already been placed in front of my seat. Hades also had a plate of steak and eggs waiting for him.

Not what I was expecting.

"Were you hoping for a rotting corpse?" he asked, clearly listening in to my thoughts. "Sorry to disappoint. I only eat corpses on Wednesdays."

"Ha-ha."

"Oh, she laughs!" he said. "You'd almost had me convinced you were incapable of it."

"*Me* incapable ... ?" I asked incredulously. "*You're* the one who doesn't feel the full spectrum of emotions."

"Careful," he warned me, all playfulness gone from his voice.

The devil picked up a gold chalice, twirling it while he watched me. "Eat," he commanded.

I lifted the fork and knife and stared at the French toast. Did I dare?

"*Eat.*"

Again, I found myself out of options. I cut into the toast, dipped it into the cup of syrup left next to it, and brought it to my mouth.

This better not screw me over.

I ate it, surprised to find it tasted just as good as the French toast I'd had on earth.

"Well?" he said, lifting an eyebrow.

"Well what?" I asked, my voice snarkier than it should be when talking to the king of the damned.

"You can be so tedious," he muttered. "How is it?"

I took another bite by way of answer. After I swallowed, I added, "It's good."

The devil leaned back in his seat and sipped his drink, smiling over the rim of it. "This pleases me."

I'll bet it did.

Thinking about my own damnation made me think about my father's agony. Poking at my food, I couldn't dispel a thought that'd taken hold ever since I'd seen him.

"What is it?"

I glanced up at him sharply.

He studied me. "Go ahead, get whatever it is off your chest."

I took a deep breath. He was just going to lie to me.

He covered the hand that held my fork. *Let us set aside deception for the moment, wife.*

My throat worked. I set down my utensils. "Is my biological mother—Celeste—down here?"

The devil held my gaze. His hand tightened over mine. "No, she isn't."

"You swear?" I whispered, blinking back moisture from my eyes.

"I swear on my immortal life, she is not."

My breath left me in a shudder. I gave him a tight smile and nodded. It was as good an answer as I was going to get from him, and oddly, I believed him. Something in me loosened at the realization that Celeste's soul was free of hell's torment.

We ate in silence. Every so often Pluto's leg would brush against mine, and I'd tense as our bond flared up. Pretty soon those touches and the tug of our bond were all I could concentrate on, and they were driving me insane.

I needed to distract myself.

I forked another bite of French toast, studying it as I spoke. "When were you first aware of my existence?" I asked.

He put down his knife and fork. "You wish to know more about me? About us?"

I nodded. The truth was, at the moment, I could hardly think of anything outside the two of us.

He leaned back in his chair, scrutinizing me. "I first learned of your existence thousands upon thousands of years ago."

When he saw my shocked expression, his lips turned up.

"You thought that because you weren't born, you hadn't existed?" He touched my nose endearingly. "You still have a thing or two to learn about gods."

"And the first time you saw me?"

"Before or after you were born?"

"'Before'?" I asked. "Before what?"

He opened his mouth to reply, some strange mixture of emotions dancing in his eyes.

I shook my head. "*After*. Tell me about after."

He kicked his heels up on the table, crossing them at the ankle. "I was there the moment you were born."

"You were?" What was that odd emotion I felt? Unease? Disbelief? Something far kinder?

"I have never left your side. Not really."

There was something oddly touching and vastly disturbing about that.

"Out of all the things I have done, *that* disturbs you?" he said. He swung his legs off the table and leaned forward. "You were my fated mate; do you really think I wouldn't keep an eye on you? I am not where I am today by luck alone. There's a reason only one fallen angel rules hell when many reside here."

I discreetly swallowed. "*Are* you an angel?"

"You've seen my scars. What do you think?"

"The fates refer to you as Pluto."

"They do," he agreed.

"So, which is it?"

His pinched his lower lip, scrutinizing me. "Are you familiar with ancient Egyptian mythology?"

"Not really," I said. And by *not really*, I meant *not at all*.

"The ancient Egyptians knew something that your modern culture doesn't."

"And what's that?" I hated to admit that I was actually intrigued.

"Contradictory myths can coexist. The Egyptians had multiple beings and multiple myths for the same deity, and they had many neighbors who believed in still more deities with more myths to accompany them. They believed these were all aspects of the same gods. I am Pluto, and Hades, and the devil, and Osiris, and many, many other gods.

"I am whatever people believe me to be, and my image adjusts as such. That's why Morta told you to think of me as Pluto."

When he saw my face, he smirked. "What? You didn't think I knew about that? Or that you've been chanting it to yourself almost constantly since I took you?"

It didn't escape my notice that the devil openly admitted to taking me, and he didn't show an ounce of regret over the matter.

The devil leaned back in his seat once more, his face smug. "So you wanted to know all about my fascination with you."

"That's not what—"

"Ask away."

I huffed. My mind was still reeling from all that he'd just admitted. I breathed in deeply, pulling myself together. I did want to know more about the devil. If I was going to be stuck down here, I needed to know the enemy.

"I'm not the enemy."

"Stop that!"

"Reading your mind? Then stop throwing objectionable thoughts out there."

Oh my Go—

The devil hissed his displeasure.

—odness. Oh my goodness.

"Have you ever cared about me?" I asked.

"What an absurd question, little bird. Of course I cared for you, and I continue to. If I didn't, you wouldn't be sitting across from me, asking your inane questions."

"You know what?" I pushed out of my chair. "Forget this." I didn't need to sit here with the devil as he lobbed insults my way.

The devil stood up with me, and faster than I could follow, he was in front of me, pushing me back into my chair.

I sank back into my seat, glaring at him as I did so.

"You are not to leave until this discussion is over, and it is *not* over." He flicked his wrist, and his chair dragged itself over. He sat down, so close that he trapped my knees between his.

He captured my hand and threaded his fingers between mine. I was holding hands with the devil. *I was holding hands with the devil.*

"And you like it," he said. "Now, should I tell you about the time that hateful girl, Sarah Boffington, tried to steal the necklace I gave you?"

I recognized the name and the instance he was referring to. There was only one problem.

"The necklace *you* gave me?"

Back in junior high, a certain Sarah Boffington returned a birthday gift of mine that went missing, but so far as I could remember, she hadn't tried to steal it and the devil hadn't given it to me.

"The locket with the rose," he said.

"I know which one you were talking about," I said. "My mother bought it for me."

"You really think your mother could afford a necklace like that?"

Before I had a chance to answer, he continued. "She couldn't. Not at that time. She barely had enough money to pay her mortgage and the bills that month."

I stilled. "What?" He couldn't be speaking the truth.

"Your mom had been laid off months before, and she was running low on money."

I squinted at him. "How did you know ... ?"

"Because, little bird, I watched you, and I intervened when she couldn't fully provide for my future queen. And on your birthday that year, she really couldn't."

What he was telling me was absurd. It had to be a lie. The devil wasn't like this. He wasn't thoughtful.

"I protect what's mine," he said, playing with my hand. "And I wanted you to treasure something I'd given you. So I stepped in and left the present for your mother. By then she was very aware of my anonymous donations."

"She was used to you paying for me?" What he was saying blew my mind. It called into question my entire perception of my childhood.

"Oh yes," he said. "Now that we've cleared that up, back to the story: Sarah took the necklace from your locker."

I'd lost it during gym class. I'd taken it off and placed it in my locker. I'd assumed it'd fallen between the grates, or that it got caught on something and dragged out. I'd searched our school's Lost and Found and talked to the janitors. I was broken up over losing it.

Sarah had been my friend, and she'd known my lock combination. And I'd never suspected.

"I had someone talk her into returning it to you," he said.

My stomach dropped. "What did your men do to her?"

"Nothing you should worry about, consort."

Riight.

But I couldn't concentrate on Sarah in the midst of this huge revelation. Before I'd even decided to come to Peel, before vampires and soulmates and magic, there'd still been this other side to my life, a secret world where the devil moved his players and pawns around to accommodate me.

My mind was officially blown.

"I ended up losing the necklace a year ago when I went swimming in the ocean," I said absently.

"And I retrieved it." The devil lifted a fisted hand. He tilted it to the side, and out slid my locket.

My lips parted as I stared down at it. The obsidian rose set into it was identical to my memory of it. I withdrew my fingers from Pluto's other hand so that I could turn the locket over and over. It was the same piece of jewelry, down to a nick on the back of it.

With shaky hands, I opened it. Inside, the pictures had changed. Instead of my mother and me, there were two new photos. One was of me and the other was of the man in front of me. Our faces were tilted towards each other's so that it looked like we gazed at one another, and we were smiling. I couldn't even fathom where or when he got the photos.

My connection throbbed at the sight.

I closed my eyes. "Why?"

When I opened them, I found him studying me.

"Perhaps I will share a story with you every morning," he said. "Maybe then that look in your eyes will stay."

Crap, I had a look in my eyes?

He rose. "Here," he said, "let me put it on you."

Before I had a chance to object, he took the necklace from my hand, and then he was behind me. Light fingers brushed the hair away from the nape of my neck. I swear they lingered longer than necessary, long enough for me to reach out and scoop my hair up from his grasp.

I heard the soft scrap of metal as the necklace latched. Then his hands fell to my shoulders and his lips brushed my ear. "I imagined doing this many times, fastening my locket around your pretty neck."

I shivered, and his fingers trailed over the gooseflesh.

A demon entered the room through the open archway, interrupting the moment. Judging by his beauty and his stern features, this was one of the fallen. "There's a matter that requires your attention," he said, addressing Pluto.

The devil's lips returned to my ear. "I imagined this moment, and I imagined it ending differently."

Oh *shit*.

The devil's hands released me, and he straightened. "We will speak again later, consort. Until then, continue to familiarize yourself with your land.

I grabbed his wrist as he turned to leave, and he looked back to me.

"Thank you," I told him, because it needed to be said, "for returning my locket." *And for all those other times you helped me and my mother.*

I couldn't read the expression he leveled at me. Eventually he gave me a slight nod. His gaze dropped to my lips, but he didn't step forward. "Until later," he said, and then he was gone.

I drew in a rough breath. The evilest being in existence provided for me when my mother couldn't. He'd even gone to the trouble of buying me a birthday present.

I glanced at the ruby ring Andre had given me. It had survived the transition from earth to the Underworld, and now I wore two pieces of jewelry, one from each of my soulmates.

What in the hell was I going to do?

AFTER I FINISHED breakfast—because, hey, even the queen of the damned has got to eat—I returned to our bedroom. Only, when I entered, I found that I had guests, a whole slumber party's worth of them.

"Whoa," I said, still clutching the doorknob. That was the only response my mouth could form.

Shirtless incubi stretched out on the bed. Those that couldn't fit on it leaned against it. There was so much skin, so little material, and so many roving hands, it took a second for my eyes to process it all.

At the sound of my voice, their attention snapped to me.

"Welcome, consort," said an incubus that was in the middle of the dogpile on the bed.

"Uh ..." Seriously, the world needed to prepare you for situations like this because I had no clue what I was supposed to do. I only knew that I was a few hot seconds away from losing my ever-loving shit.

I began to back up and close the door when I bumped into someone behind me. I swiveled around and—

Aww, crap. There was another one herding me in. He nudged me inside the room and closed the door behind us.

"Now," the man at my back said, "we can finally give the queen a proper welcome."

A proper welcome? I already knew I wasn't going to like this.

The one closest to me took my hand and attempted to lead me to the bed. He didn't get very far.

I snatched my hand back. "I'm, um, not interested."

"Not interested?" the incubus cocked his head. The others peered up from the bed where they reclined.

Oh God, oh God, oh God. Seriously, what was I supposed to do? It was easy enough to kick them out of my bed when I knew I'd wake up and they'd disappear. But here in hell, they weren't going to just vanish.

I heard one of the incubi on the bed whisper. "Perhaps she only wants one of us at a time?"

Seriously, this place was whacked.

"Do you not like our forms?" another asked.

God, this really was the nightmare that never ended.

"What? No, they're fi—"

Before I could complete my thought, they changed en masse to women. And there were suddenly boobs *everywhere*.

I couldn't help it, I shrieked. "Oh my God!" They winced at the name. "That's not natural!"

"Her skin lit up at the change," one said to the others. When they refocused on me, the succubi became incubi once more.

I let out a small noise, and damnit, my skin did flicker with my surprise. One approached me and reached out. I slapped away his hand. "Don't touch me."

"You are not pleased? We live to please."

I was backing up into a corner of the room, and the incubi crept closer.

"Listen, I already have two men in my life, and that's one too many."

"Then women it is." Their forms shifted again.

"Will you *please* stop that?" I begged the room as a

whole. They came even closer.

"The devil will hurt all of you if you so much as lay another hand on me," I said.

"It can be our secret."

"He can read my mind." Why was I trying to reason with them?

For the first time since I entered, they looked uncertain.

"And even if he didn't, I don't want any of you." I should've just ordered them out right from the get go, but to be honest, these demons didn't seem malicious, just a bit ... horny. Also, it would be nice to not make enemies on day two. I bet in hell, enemies were very bad thing. I also bet these were the nicest demons here.

"Truly?" one replied.

"Truly," I said.

"If the queen does not want us," one said to the rest, "then we should leave."

The others murmured their agreement, and they filed out of the bedroom. I practically sagged against the wall once they were gone.

Fuck my afterlife.

"DINNER," GROWLED A winged, red-eyed demon, entering the library where I was tucked away. Of all the types of demons I'd seen, this one appeared to be the most common. They were the devil's lackeys and the only ones that formed from my blood.

"Not hungry," I said, returning my attention to my

book, not that it was much more interesting than the creature in front of me. Hell needed to upgrade its reading material. This demonic stuff got old after a while. There were only so many ways you could describe torturing a person, and though I'd definitely give some of these guys an "A" for originality, the subject was getting repetitive.

I'd just flipped the page when the demon yanked me up by the arm.

"Hey!" I protested, the book falling out of my hands.

He began dragging me out of the room.

We'd already done this jig before, and I was noticing a habit forming here, one where I got pushed around. I needed to set some boundaries, stat.

"I said I wasn't hungry. Now, let go." I tugged against his uncompromising hold.

It was as though I hadn't spoken. The demon's stride didn't even slow and his grip didn't lighten.

My power rose, building like a storm beneath my skin. I could taste it at the back of my throat.

I thrust my hand against the demon's ashen chest and shoved the energy out, blasting him backwards. He hit the wall, shards of obsidian chipping off at the impact.

He slid to the floor, and I heard him growl. Then he was back up on his feet, stalking towards me, his expression murderous. I could see plainly that he was no longer interested in quietly dragging me off to the devil. He wanted my blood on his hands.

A series of daggers lined the walls of the library. Lifting my hand, I called one to me, using my power to pull it from its post across the room and into my hand. Andre's training came back to me, and I relaxed my muscles as the demon charged at me.

I stood my ground as he closed the distance. At the last minute I ducked and slammed the dagger beneath the demon's ribs, shoving it up with my considerable strength. It cut through flesh and bone and hit his heart.

Above me the demon choked. Weakly he swiped at me, his claws slicing across my skin. Ignoring the pain, I shoved the knife farther into him. He swayed, and then his body slid to the side, collapsing next to me.

I rose, wiping the black blood onto my dress and scowling down at the demon.

"Well done, consort."

My head snapped up. A moment ago, the creature and I had been alone. Now, however, the devil stood in front of me, a legion of demons at his back. They filled the room, watching me curiously.

Pluto turned his head to the side, addressing the beings behind him, "Look at how fierce my queen is," he said. If I didn't know better, I'd say he was bragging. "Take note—this is how she deals with dissent, and I will not stand in her way as she metes out justice."

I narrowed my eyes at him. Convenient how he showed up *after* the fight was over.

His lips quirked.

The demons at his back scrutinized me, some appreciatively, others apprehensively.

"Now," he said to our audience, "leave us."

In the next several seconds they dissipated into wisps of smoke, and then they were gone completely, leaving behind only the smell of sulfur.

Sliding his hands into his pockets, the devil strode over to the felled demon. A pool of black blood grew beneath the creature.

"Is he dead?" I asked.

"No, but after his impending stay in the dungeons, he will wish he was."

I cocked my head. "You set this all up, didn't you?"

"My dear," the devil said, turning his attention to me, "even I can't predict how a demon will act. I only knew that this one right here didn't much like women."

"And, knowing this, you decided to have him serve me."

He studied me, his hands still in his pockets. "You think I am cruel."

I gave an empty laugh. "I *know* you are."

The devil's heels clicked ominously as he crossed the room, stopping only a hair's breadth away from me. "The Underworld is the most dangerous of all the realms. It's built on power, and that power is derived from pain. Who gives it, who receives it. You are a teenage girl fresh from earth with one of the purest souls hell has ever seen.

"So, yes, I arranged this. I waited, and I watched, and I made sure when you delivered justice, other demons were here to witness it. You need to be seen as strong independent of me or else no one will respect you."

What he said made a frightening amount of sense.

He held out his hand. "Now, dinner?"

"I already told your servant, I'm not hungry."

"Perhaps you mistook that for a request. It was an order. Now, dinner."

When I didn't immediately take the devil's hand, he grabbed mine, and the room dissolved around us, replaced with the dark dining room.

So much for me asserting my will.

I sighed. I needed to pick my battles better.

Place settings now covered the entire length of the table, but the platters of food rested only near the two chairs at the head of it.

"Do other demons eat here?" I asked, eyeing the table.

"Sometimes," the devil said, leading me to my chair.

I tried and failed to imagine anything as civilized as demons eating together.

After I sat, he took his own seat, once again angling it towards me. He stared at me for several seconds, a small smile playing on his face.

"What?" I said.

"You sit at my table, reside in my palace, and will soon warm my bed." My cheeks heated at that. "After all my waiting and after so many tried to stop me," he pulled a grape from one of the platters and rolled it between his fingers, "I am gloating." He popped the piece of fruit into his mouth.

"That's what you call being a sore winner," I said.

"All talk of soreness and winning should involve my bed and less clothes."

I looked to the ceiling and silently beseeched it for deliverance.

He watched me as he chewed. "Speaking of beds, you didn't let the incubi seduce you."

I raised my eyebrows, though by now I shouldn't have

been surprised. This was his realm. Even if he hadn't grabbed the thought from my mind, he likely had eyes everywhere in this place. And he'd already admitted to watching me.

I swallowed. I couldn't trust anyone here, not even myself. And there were things I knew, sensitive things. If he learned of them ...

I stopped that thought in its tracks.

"You've pleased me greatly," he continued. "You've only been here little more than a day, and already you've punished a demon who sought to control you and disarmed a band of incubi bent on seducing you."

"I live to please," I said.

His sharp eyes caught mine. "Do not speak falsehoods."

I couldn't look away from him, but the more I stared, the stronger our connection pulsed. "I didn't think you of all people would mind a lie."

"Do you want me to be that man? The Deceiver? Just tell me and I can be every horrible version of myself."

I couldn't answer that, not when his mesmerizing eyes drew me in. Who was this god, who could be so awful and still have another side to him, one that lured me in?

He must've felt the shift in my emotions, must've sensed how weak I was in that moment. He leaned forward, closing the distance between us.

Before our lips could meet, that howling wind blew through the dining room, knocking over place setting after place setting. Glass and porcelain shattered as cups and plates hit the walls and floors. The screaming souls circled me.

"The worst timing ..." he muttered. "We'll resume this later," he promised. "Be good," he said. "Don't fuck any vampires."

In what world was telling someone that normal?

"In hell," he answered, winking at me as the wind lifted me into the air.

He stood and gave me a salute with his wine glass. "Remember, don't do anything I wouldn't do. And last, but not least—happy hunting."

CHAPTER 12

Andre

THE MOMENT HE awoke, Andre nearly choked on the pain in his heart.

Gabrielle's gone once more, and she's siphoning my soul away along with hers.

His last vision of her had been frightening. Those corded vines wrapped around her, sucking her under.

He rubbed his sternum, pinching his eyes shut. The bond soulmates shared might be made of nothing more than magic, but its absence physically hurt. Centuries of violence had taught him to handle pain, but ... there was no preparing for this.

He forced himself off his bed, pushing past the vampires that had hauled him inside yesterday, after Gabrielle was dragged back to hell.

Gabrielle.

If this evening was anything like the previous one, then she'd be back on earth, wreaking havoc on the righteous. He straightened his posture and strode down the hall. He could only hope history repeated itself.

He found his human servants clustered in his conference room. They'd dragged some additional screens inside, and each played a different news clip. Unfortunately, none of them were of his soulmate.

"Any sign of her?"

"None since you went to sleep."

Not surprising, but damn him and his illogical hope. He'd gotten so used to being around her that every second that ticked by without her was one he lamented.

My mate was right to be worried, Andre thought as he watched the news. Mortal news. For the last several centuries, the supernatural world had done a decent job cloaking itself from regular humans. But now it'd spilled over.

On the screen, demons set fire to buildings, dragged people out of their cars and high into the air only to drop them. Some had attacked leaders and important political figures. And what they weren't doing, their human servants were. Organized crime had apparently ballooned within the last day.

Andre stroked his lower lip as he watched, his brows furrowed. Something larger than Gabrielle was going on, something she may or may not know about.

"The seer and the fairy?" he asked one of his men.

"They left hours ago."

Andre turned to him. "Where did they go?"

"Sir, we don't know."

"What do you mean 'you don't know'?" Andre's voice had gone quiet.

The man flinched, hearing the promise of violence in it. He opened his mouth but nothing came out.

Andre helped him. "The next time those two leave without a tail, I will hold you personally accountable."

Andre's phone rang. His mouth tightened when he saw who was calling.

"Where is she?" he answered.

"In a half hour, I'll have instructions for you," Leanne said. "If you want to ensure Gabrielle's safety, I'll need you to follow them to the letter. Until then, stay at Bishopcourt." The line died before he could demand answers. He dialed her number only to be sent straight to voicemail.

My God, did no one fear him anymore?

Andre squeezed the phone tightly, then threw it across the room. It hit the wall, shattering into bits of plastic and metal. He threaded his hands over his head and stalked back and forth.

How dare she ask him to just wait. He stormed out of there. He needed to kill someone.

Gabrielle

HEAT SCORCHED ME as my body forced its way up, my cold skin drinking it in greedily. Magic and power vibrated through me.

Since I'd arrived in hell, I'd wondered what exactly I

was—not quite a vampire, not quite a siren or a human.

I understood now. My existence was a twist on the myth of Persephone, who supposedly came to earth for half the year. Instead of half the year, I came for half the day. I bet if I timed it too, it would be near twelve hours exactly.

Damp earth pushed me out, and I gasped in a lungful of air. Beneath me the ground shuddered, as though it wanted to throw me off its back. My hands dug into grass and soggy soil as I hunched over and caught my breath. The place smelled like old bones and rot and ... my friends.

"Took you long enough, Corpse Bride," Oliver said.

I looked up to see him leaning against a large tombstone.

He eyed me and whistled. "Girl, you put the *ho* in *hobo*."

"Knock it off Oliver," Leanne said. She knelt off to the side, tarot cards spread out before her, the knees of her jeans already soaked from kneeling for too long.

"What? I'm just making an honest observation."

From my surroundings, it looked like we popped up in a cemetery. I shivered, and not from the early evening chill.

The sense of not belonging was worse today. I hated that I felt more like myself in the pits of hell than I did here.

I bowed my head, letting my hair curtain in front of me as my face crumbled. The need for violence called to me. I knew it was tied up in the devil and the sick bond between us, a bond that even after only two days I was tired of fighting.

"Gabrielle?" Oliver called, the sassiness gone from his

voice.

"Give her a moment," Leanne said.

I removed my hands from the dirt, noticing that the grass near them flattened out. A wave of rage swept through me at that, and I breathed in and out through my nose, trying to control the dark emotions flooding me. After several seconds the anger dissipated.

"Where are we?" I cleared my voice after I spoke, my voice hoarse.

"Saint Keverne's Cemetery, Oldcastle, Ireland," Oliver answered. "Seems as though you like to show up along Otherworld entrances."

That made some sick sort of sense. Otherworld entrances were those areas where realms overlapped, points on ley lines where creatures could travel between worlds and within one.

"And what does the mother of demons want to do tonight?" Oliver asked. "Imprison more Politia members, create more little demon babies? Go get drunk and yell at random people—that's my personal choice."

I focused on Oliver. Yesterday I'd run around, first meting out vengeance, and then returning to my soulmate—

A guttural sob rose up my throat, and I forced it back down.

I can't go back to him. Not unless I wanted him to incur the devil's wrath any more than he already had. And yet each day he died a little more, now that our bond had broken, and each day my humanity stripped away a little more.

We'd made promises to each other not to give up. He

kept on living despite his deep desire to join me in hell.

I could fight whatever it was I felt for the devil. And I would, not just because I made Andre a promise. He was my soulmate, and all the best parts of me loved all the best parts of him. And we embraced all the terrible aspects of both of us because those, too, made us who we were.

I drew in a shuddering breath and wiped my hands off.

I might have to avoid Andre for now, but I wouldn't fall quietly into this fate, no matter how easy that would be, and no matter how badly certain parts of me wanted it.

And the first step was getting some answers.

Leanne made a noise. "Peel Academy, Gabrielle? Really?" she said, reading my immediate future in the cards. "That's one of the least safe places for you to be."

"I need to get inside," I said.

There were two people I'd wanted to meet with, and the first was there.

"SERIOUSLY, THIS IS your worst idea ever—and not one of the fun ones, either," Oliver said as we walked past the storefronts that faced the shore. Ahead of us, Peel Castle jutted out into the water, looking decrepit.

"Ignore him," Leanne said. "He's just bummed that he won't get to hang with you this evening." Next to me, Oliver grumbled.

Leanne had dropped that little tidbit shortly after I'd made my plans known. According to her visions, I wouldn't be seeing my friends again until tomorrow evening.

Probably for the best. I still grappled with my violent emotions. I didn't want them to have to see me like this, or worse, be the victim of one of these moods.

When we came to the end of the street, where we were to split up, we stopped.

Oliver wrapped me in a hug. "I'm still pissed at you," he muttered as he held me close. "Just do me a favor and stay safe so that I can be annoyed with you without feeling like an asshole."

I huffed out a laugh. "I'll try."

He let me go, and I gave Leanne a tight hug. The affection soothed some of the hollowness in me.

I stepped away from her.

"We'll see your skanky ass tomorrow," Oliver said.

I nodded and turned to go.

Leanne caught my hand. "Wait." She opened her mouth, searching for the right words before she spoke again. She gripped my hand tightly. "Please trust me when I tell you that I'm doing everything I can to help you."

I nodded, giving her a tight smile. My eyes had begun to water—bleed—*whatever*. "I know."

"I need you to hold that knowledge tight, even when things seem senseless."

"I can do that," I said softly.

She gave my hand a final squeeze. "Good," she said, her own eyes watery. She let me go and grabbed Oliver's arm. "We'll see you tomorrow then."

I watched them walk away, the mist rolling in behind then, before I resumed my trek up to Peel Academy.

As I headed towards the front gates, the enchantments

of the place brushed up against my skin. Most of them were meant to keep me and other dark beings out. At first it felt like gentle resistance, but as I got closer it felt as though I slogged through water, and when I closed in on the castle grounds, it felt like moving through molasses.

The gates at the front of the school were closed. On the other side of them professors had gathered. Someone or something had alerted them of my presence.

"Back away, Gabrielle," Professor Nightingale warned.

I was the bad guy. I got that. But seeing and hearing an old teacher of mine stand against me still cut deep.

I kept setting myself up for disappointment.

"I need to get inside. There's someone a need to speak with," I said, fighting to keep my calm demeanor. Already I was awash with anger that anyone would stand against me.

Behind the teachers, some students had gathered. Among them I saw Doris, an old nemesis of mine. She leaned in to speak with the group of girls, her eyes glued to me. An adult came by then and shooed her and the other lingering students inside.

"You're not coming in here, sweetheart," Professor Nightingale said. "Not without a fight. Turn around now before anyone gets hurt."

The ground beneath me began to rumble. I couldn't control it, this rage. It was too big for my body. It built and built beneath my skin. I lifted my arms, and the professors began to shout.

The ground trembled, pebbles tinkling away from me. High overhead, the clouds rolled in, and all around us I could hear the surf crashing into the cliffs surrounding the academy, the force of it growing with each wave.

The professors yelled at me to stop, but I was much, much too far gone to stop now.

I closed my eyes, my jaw clenching as the power became a physical pain inside me. It needed an exit.

All at once, I released it.

For a split second, the night was quiet. Then my power blasted against the metal gates, the boom as loud as thunder. With a crack, the gates split apart like overripe fruit, and the enchantment dissolved into the air.

The wicked part of me wanted to revel, but the part that was still human simply passed through. My thoughts were on other things.

Fate. Redemption. Salvation. Controlling this unnatural anger bubbling through my veins.

A good several seconds went by as professors recovered from the shock of seeing their main defense ripped away. Once they recovered, their attention turned to me.

"Don't." That was the only word I could bite out against the torrent of anger and bloodlust riding me.

They didn't listen.

The hits came from several directions. I couldn't tell who was responsible for each, but it didn't matter. My fury didn't have a specific target. It lashed out like some great unseen hand, sweeping them off their feet. I didn't want to stop there. I wanted to tear and rent and rip—

I forced the rage back and instead pinned the professors to the dewy grass so they wouldn't follow me.

Just like the main entrance, the doors to the library

gave me grief. Briefly. I was thankful that I could focus my unbridled rage on an inanimate object. My energy poured out, ripping the doors and hinges, and stripping the building of its enchantments.

"Well you certainly know how to make an entrance," Lydia Thyme, better known as the fate Decima, greeted me when I stepped inside. Peel's head librarian and the middle of the three fates sat on one of the couches scattered throughout the room.

She assessed the doors behind me. "It's going to take me hours to put those enchantments back in place."

My limbs were jittery with the need to use my power again, and my skin glowed as the siren stuck close to the surface. Without looking, I forced the broken doors back into place and used my power to seal the entrance shut.

I sat on the seat across from her, and it was an effort to even appear relaxed.

"You want answers," she said.

"I do." *I need them, badly.* "I don't want to be this way," I admitted.

"What way?" she asked.

"Dead. Evil. Immortal. *His.*"

Decima shook her head. "Those are dangerous words. He could be listening even now."

I sucked in a shaky breath through my nose. "So you know how much I'm risking by being here and telling you these things."

"Mmmm," she agreed. "What if I told you that what you want is impossible? What if I told you that there was no way out of your situation?"

"I would find someone else who would tell me something different."

"Dangerous, dangerous words," she muttered. And then, in the silence of the library, Decima began reciting the familiar riddle. "*Daughter of wheat and grain, betrothed to soil and stain, your lifeblood drips, the scales tip, but will it be in vain?*

"*Child of penance and pain, dealer of beauty and bane, a coin's been flipped, the scales tipped, nothing will be the same.*"

Hearing the words spoken unnerved me more than they had when I first read them.

"That poem is about you," she said. She leaned forward in her chair. "You know there is one more stanza, don't you?" Behind her the candlelight flickered.

I shook my head.

She began to recite once more. "*Queen of souls of slain, prisoner of ash and flame, heaven dips, the world rips, the future is yours to claim.*"

This time, the back of my neck prickled, like unseen eyes watched me. "So I have a choice after all?" I asked, hoping I interpreted that last bit of the poem correctly.

"You do," she said. "I am not Nona. I will not steer you away from Pluto. But nor am I Morta, who would steer you towards him. I can give you council, but not much else."

"Then tell me what I need to do," I said.

"You already know what you need to do," she replied.

My anger slipped its muzzle briefly. I wanted to scream. Or throttle her. My fingers started curled inwards.

So, so messed up.

Decima sighed. "You remember Jericho," she stated.

"I was going to meet with him next." He'd been the second person I wanted to speak with.

She leaned back against the couch. "Unlike me, he has an agenda."

Well, that was nothing new. "Everyone has an agenda."

She smiled. "True." She studied me for a second. "You know, Nona, Morta, and I made you for him."

We were no longer talking about Jericho.

"A thousand upon a thousand years ago we crafted you from the threads of time. *You were made for him.* And he was meant to please you."

I didn't say anything to that. I didn't even bother thinking on it. I knew where I stood on that front.

"As unlikely as it all seems, he was always your intended. The vampire was the mistake."

"Andre was *not* a mistake."

She pinched her lips together but didn't contradict me. *BOOM!*

My head snapped around just in time to see the doors ricocheting from the aftereffects of a magical hit. Reinforcements had arrived.

My blood sang the thought of another brawl.

"Go. Jericho will help you," Decima said, pulling my attention back to her.

"That's not the only reason why I came here."

A spark of understanding flashed in her eyes. "I thought you wanted nothing to do with him."

"Can I borrow a computer?" I asked her.

By way of answer, she gestured to a row of them that

lined the wall. "I'm not going to hold off the authorities," she said as I moved over to one of the computers, "and I don't know how much longer that spell of yours will hold," she said, eyeing the door.

I'd woven a spell?

"It'll hold," I reassured her.

I slid into the seat and shook the mouse. The home screen was already up. I clicked onto the Internet and typed a single name into the search bar.

Asiri.

"If you wanted information on Asiri, you should've just asked."

"Stop reading over my shoulder," I said, not looking away from the screen.

"I'm not," she said to my back, and I could hear the amusement in her voice.

Fate, my mind whispered. She could see my future better than Leanne did. I searched and searched, but all that came up were links to nonsense.

Lydia handed a book over my shoulder. "This you'll find more helpful."

"Thanks," I muttered.

The Book of Forgotten Names, Vol. XXVII

BOOM!

The broken doors shook again, and I funneled a bit more of my power to them.

The book was thin and clothbound, the color a washed-out black. I thumbed through the yellow pages and skimmed the table of contents for what I was looking for.

There it was, third chapter. *Asiri.*

I flipped to it and read the first paragraph: Asiri *was an ancient Egyptian name for Osiris, the god of the Underworld. Aside from his proper name, the god was also referred to as "Lord of Love," "He Who is Permanently Benign and Youthful," and "Lord of Silence."*

I reared back from the text. "'Lord of Love'?"

"That is why I remain undecided," Lydia said quietly.

I glanced up at her.

"There once was virtuousness in him. Apparently, there still is. That he shared this name with you is a good sign. Every time you invoke it, you lend it power, restorative power."

"What are you getting at?" I tightly clenched the book. Two sentences was all it took to unbalance me completely.

"Even gods are malleable. Bad to good, good to bad, they strengthen and weaken based on our belief in them. And," she cupped my chin, "your belief in him is especially important because he will rise or fall to it."

Just like what Morta said all those weeks ago.

I held her gaze for several seconds. "You mean he really is capable of good?"

"Yes."

"And what happens if he ... changes?"

"That is what the world is holding its breath to find out. 'The future is yours to claim.'"

CHAPTER 13

Gabrielle

I WAS SO, so troubled.

Leaving a monster, that was one thing, but leaving a being so capable of good he was once considered the Lord of Love? And I might have the power to coax that love out of him?

I'd seen hints of this side of him, I just hadn't trusted them. Should I trust them now? What would it mean for the world to have a god like Osiris reigning hell?

I ran a hand through my hair and drew in a shuddering breath. I pushed all thoughts of him away as I dropped my spell and the broken doors of Peel's library collapsed.

Outside, supernaturals were losing their ever-loving shit.

Someone had released the professors I'd pinned to the

earth, and since I'd visited Decima, the number of men and women waiting for me had tripled.

Helicopters hovered overhead, circling and circling, their search lights directed on the school's lawn. The patrol cars and tanks had returned. The Politia was back. Apparently they were gluttons for punishment.

Gingerly, I stepped over the splintered wood.

A spell slammed into me, knocking me back into the doorframe. Another followed on its heels, and another. My eyes fluttered at the onslaughts, and I gripped the doorframe until wood splinted.

I could taste magic in my mouth, bitter and acrid, and feel it sizzle against my skin. They'd upped their game this time, adding spells against me.

I was going down. They'd finally found a way to incapacitate me. I drew in a raspy breath when something changed.

Like flipping a switch, the pain that assaulted my body turned into a current, and the current became power. I clenched my jaw as I pushed myself up, ignoring the sharp burn I felt on the pads of my fingers when I cut myself on a jagged edge of the debris.

Surge after surge of power flowed through me, each one headier than the last. I glared at the swarm of supernaturals pitted against me. They backed up as I stood, some lifting their hands threateningly and others tightening their grips on their weapons.

Spells continued to smash into me, and I braced myself against the force of each. My body greedily sucked up the pain, fueling my power. They were strengthening me. I didn't understand how or why I could now do this, but I did know that this was decidedly bad for my enemies.

I steadied my breathing and focused on the silence inside myself. All those faces staring back at me, twisted with hate and fear. And beyond them, the faces of students who peered through their dorm windows, watching with horror and curiosity. I wanted to end each and every one of their lives.

I dug deeper within myself, beyond the seductive power that whispered into my ear.

Remember who you are. Hate would never end hate.

My power continued to build inside my veins, and it felt like I was sinking deeper and deeper, the pressure pushing me in from all sides.

Break the cycle.

Closing my eyes, I listened to the air moving in and out of my lungs. I didn't want them to die. I just wanted to end this.

Inhale.

The power was going to crush me.

Exhale.

Like a damn breaking, it flowed out of me. That howling wind that consumed me back in hell now blew past me, knocking supernaturals over like dominos.

"You will not harm me," I commanded. My voice projected over the wind, and guns and bare hands lowered. "Now, you will sleep, and you will not wake up for another hour. And once you do, you will realize that I didn't harm you when I could've."

One by one, their bodies swayed as their eyes closed.

Knees crumpled and bodies collapsed onto the soft grass of Peel Academy's lawn.

I sauntered past them, making a point not to rush. Deep inside the buildings, I could hear students running down the halls, descending down stairs. Probably eager to avenge the adults that protected them.

I waved my hand and barred the doors and windows. I hadn't put dozens of supernaturals to sleep only to face another wave of them.

Behind me, I heard the flap of wings. I'd forgotten all about cutting myself. While I'd been distracted, another demon had taken form.

I turned in time to see it rocket into the sky and head straight for one of the prone supernaturals.

"No," I commanded, my skin flaring. "They are not to be harmed."

He hovered in the air. "Everyone not with us is to be harmed," the creature said, speaking in Demonic.

"If you lay a hand on them, I will kill you and send you back to hell."

"I take my orders from the Boss," the demon said, his voice unnaturally low and gravelly. He resumed flying towards the sleeping supernaturals.

Now I did allow myself to relish my fury.

I threw a short burst of energy out. It slammed into him, knocking him off course. Bending down to the nearest officer, I picked up the man's gun, belatedly noticing the blond hair. I caught sight of the smooth expanse of cheek peeking out beneath the familiar mop of hair.

Oh, Caleb ...

We both made our beds, and now we had to lie in them.

The gun that Caleb had trained on me I now trained on the demon. "Last chance," I warned.

"Fuck off," the creature said, not scared in the slightest. He should be.

I aimed and pulled the trigger, and I didn't stop firing until I'd emptied the entire clip into him.

He screeched, stumbling first to his knees and then to his stomach. I headed over to him, picking up an abandoned knife along the way.

I stood over him, watching him choke on his own fluids.

His spit black blood at my feet. "The Boss won't be pleased that you stopped me," he said.

"He won't be pleased that you didn't listen to my order."

The demon gave a thick, choked laugh. "You're just his consort. Once he gets what he wants from you, he'll cast you aside. Then you will be at our mercy."

My tenuous hold on my anger slipped. Quick as lightning, I stepped behind him, grabbed his head, and dragged the knife across his neck.

I released him and stood up, a grimace on my face. His body turned to smoke and ash, the black blood evaporating away.

"You have made enemies of the minor demons." Decima's voice came from far behind me. She stood outside the door the library. "It was kind of you to spare the supernaturals. Kind, and telling. The demons know you are rebelling against your nature. I fear this does not bode well. Not at all."

CHAPTER 14

Gabrielle

I LEFT PEEL Academy, unnerved by Decima's final warning.

It shouldn't have surprised me that a taxi idled a little ways outside the school grounds. Leanne had likely coordinated this too. I walked up to it, and sure enough, the window rolled down and the taxi driver asked, "You the girl that called for a ride to Douglas?"

I nodded.

He eyed my dress and bare feet. He shook his head and said, "Get in."

Half an hour later he pulled up to Jericho's Emporium. I got out, realizing then that I didn't have money to pay for the fare or the driver's tip. But as soon as I slammed the passenger side door shut, the taxi took off.

I guess Leanne had paid for it too. I'd need to thank

her when I saw her next.

The streets of Douglas were utterly abandoned. It was late at night, but in the past there'd always been people milling about. I eyed the streets nervously before I realized that I was the most dangerous thing out here.

I walked up to the store both excited and nervous about what came next. Jericho would have more answers for me, but that was not the only reason I was here. Over fifteen years ago my mother had bought me my salvation in the form of a quill, and she paid for it with her life. I was finally here to collect.

But as soon as my hand curled around the doorknob, power blasted me back. I flew through the air. My teeth clicked together painfully when I crashed into the street. My body skidded along the rough asphalt, tearing open skin like tissue paper. Blood seeped onto the ground, and I heard the telltale sizzle of it burning. In a few short seconds a demon would rise from the ground, a demon who'd know exactly where I was.

If these creatures knew who and what Jericho was, then celestial quill or no, the devil would figure out what I was up to.

I'd need to kill the creatures, but if I did so, it would still look suspicious.

Damned if I do, damned if I don't.

Just damned. Period.

This needed to be fast. I turned my attention back to the building. Now that I stopped to really pay attention, I could sense the enchantments. The place was steeped with them. I probed them with my power only to be met with ironclad resistance. Unlike the Politia and Peel Academy, these weren't the kind my magic could break.

"Jericho!" I shouted. "Let me in!"

Nothing stirred. I couldn't sense the man even now. Perhaps he legitimately wasn't there. I still needed that quill.

Consort, what are you doing here?

Well, crap.

I could hear the beat of wings in the distance.

What. Are. You. Doing. Here?

I ignored the voice. I didn't dare think about my plans.

Jericho is the enemy.

So he did know who and what Jericho was, and he knew that he owned this shop.

He's your *enemy*, I clarified.

That was the wrong answer, he said ominously, his voice curling itself around me.

I realized then that he hadn't known that I was here seeking out Jericho's help. I could've been here to destroy him.

But now the devil knew that wasn't the case.

Double crap.

The wingbeats sounded closer. I glanced above me.

A mistake.

Three demons descended from the sky, heading right for yours truly. Another had just finished forming where I'd last spilled blood.

I turned back to the building. "Jericho!" I shouted. "Let me in!"

Nothing.

"*Jericho!*" I came all this way, and he wasn't even here.

Me and my terrible luck.

The demons grabbed me then, their claws digging into my skin. I threw my power out, knocking them off.

Four demons coming for me not even a minute after I spoke with the devil? That wasn't a coincidence. This was the devil's doing.

The four regrouped and began circling me. Before I could so much as devise a strategy to take them out, I heard the slick sound of swords unsheathing.

I rotated just as the demon at my back shrieked. Twin blades glinted in the moonlight. Then they were gone, and the demon's body slid apart. A second later it dissolved completely.

I'd barely made sense of this first death when I heard the growls and shrieks of the others. Their attacker's form was a blur, but I didn't need to make out his shape to know just who it was.

The last of the demons melted away to smoke, and behind them Andre stood, breathing heavily.

He lowered his swords to his sides. "Soulmate," he said, "I'm fine chasing you, but you have to let me catch you a time or two." He said this all playfully enough, but the hardness in his eyes told a different story.

"How did you find me?" I asked.

Shit, shit, shit.

He shouldn't be here, and I shouldn't be talking with him. Dangerous enough to be two-timing the devil. But to be near him at all after the devil's warning ...

In one smooth movement Andre slid his swords back

into their sheaths. "Leanne told me you'd be here." He sauntered forward. "She also told me you were avoiding me."

That narc.

"Are you, soulmate?" He peered down at me.

I couldn't lie to him. "Yes," I said softly, the word catching in my throat.

"*Christo.*" He looked away, running an agitated hand through his hair. "Why?" he asked, glancing back at me. He tried to mask the hurt in his voice, and had we not once shared a bond, I might've missed it. But I knew him almost as well as he knew himself. Andre was having a rare moment of insecurity.

My throat worked. It took several seconds to gain control of my emotions enough to speak. "Because the devil threatened to kill you."

Andre's eyes softened. "Soulmate, he does not have the power to do so himself, and no creature on this planet has both the balls and the ability to face me down."

He came forward, and I backed up. At the action, he frowned. It wasn't often that I moved away from him.

The softness fled from his eyes, and something hard and scary entered them. Something a whole lot like determination.

"You insist on protecting me, but you won't let me protect you," I said.

"This is not protecting me," he said, indicating the space between us. "This is destroying us from the inside out. You think you do me any favors by staying away?" he asked, his voice dropping dangerously low.

"Of course I do."

"No, my love," he shook his head. "You're putting distance and apathy between us."

"Andre, I need to protect you while I try to get myself out of this situation. And if I can't …"

"If you can't, then you're planning on resigning yourself to an eternity by the devil's side instead of mine," he answered for me.

Had that been my plan?

He nodded to himself. "I suppose you think that I'm going to be hurt enough to leave you here alone with your guilt and despair."

"Stop it," I whispered. He knew me too well.

He took a step closer, our chests brushing, and cupped the side of my face. "I am not some fair weather lover," he said. "You gave me your body, and you gave me your heart." His eyes gleamed as he spoke, and if I didn't know better, I'd say he was trying to captivate me.

"What's more," he tipped up my head. "I gave you mine."

He shook me gently. "We do this, over and over and over. You push me away when you need me the most. You fight my overprotectiveness—and I get that it's an issue. I'm working on it." He flashed me a rueful smile. "But this cycle? It ends tonight. Right now. This time, you and I are going to do things differently."

"But the devil—"

"The devil has wanted my soul and all those connected to me for a very long time, and I'm still here. He's had seven hundred years to claim it, yet he hasn't. Don't be fooled by any pretty lies he's spun, soulmate."

Damnit, he had a point.

"The worst has already happened," he continued. "You're trapped in hell for half of every day, and it's breaking you."

I opened my mouth, but he spoke over me.

"It *is*," he said. "I can see it on your face, I watched it play out on the news, I can hear it in your voice, I can even smell it in your lies and your guilt. The person we need to worry about most is you."

He took my hands in his. "Now, this is what's going to happen: You are going to stop running from me and stop protecting me. You're going to yell at me when I infuriate you and I'm going to rage. And then we're going to make up and continue on because that's what soulmates do. We're going to figure this out together. And so long as you love me, you are going to greedily—selfishly—accept my love. Even if that means putting me in the devil's line of fire."

I pinched my eyes shut. I wanted to protect him—desperately so. But I was also trying to protect my heart from something so powerful that if I lost it, I might never recover.

Before I could object, his lips were on mine.

It wasn't a question whether or not I was going to kiss him back. My mouth moved against his, and he pulled me against him, clutching me tightly. I almost cried out my relief. I had resigned myself to not having him so long as I was the devil's, and I'd felt the ache of his absence every hour since.

Clearly our bond wasn't everything; it hadn't stopped either of us from trying to protect the other. My bones ached from his absence inside of me. Having him at my side was a close alternative.

"I'm not giving you up, soulmate," he said when the kiss ended. He still held me in his arms. "I will never give up on you. I'm just hoping that one of these days you'll realize that I am more stubborn than you are."

For the first time that night, I smiled, and the action caused him to smile, the corners of his eyes crinkling as he did so.

A strange lightness took root in my chest and it bubbled up my throat. I tilted my head back in Andre's arms and laughed for the first time since I'd been taken. Had I ever wondered why people fell in love? This was why.

"Ah, that laugh. Soulmate, it makes me believe all things are possible."

ANDRE AND I were so wrapped up in each other, neither of us registered the heartbeat until it was too late. One moment it wasn't there, the next it was.

A hand fisted in my hair, jerking my head back. A metal blade pressed against my neck. It happened so fast that I hadn't realized that someone wanted to slit my throat until after the knife sliced across my skin.

"For my son," the man hissed, and then he was gone, along with that heartbeat of his.

Had I been in any position to think on it, I would've recognized that voice as Byron Jennings'. But I only had eyes for Andre. His shocked expression must've mirrored my own.

I grabbed at my neck, only to feel it slick with blood. The liquid drenched my hand in a matter of seconds as my arteries pumped it out. It dripped down my hands and into my clothes, and I heard it hiss as it hit the ground.

"*No.*" Andre lunged for me just as my legs gave out.

He cradled me in his arms as my blood continued to spill. My wound hadn't healed. It should've. Weakly I reached for Andre's hand. I caught it, only for it to slip away, so slick my hands were with blood. Pain should've assaulted me—and distantly I could feel it—but I think I was in shock.

Andre rocked us. "Stay with me, love."

I reached for his hand again.

My vision was fading, and I couldn't speak. I tried forming words on my lips anyway. *Keep fighting. I–love–you ... soulmate.*

CHAPTER 15

Andre

THE MOMENT HE was sure her spirit had fled, Andre curled his body over hers, and he began to weep. He'd gone from one of the highest highs since she'd returned to … this.

Hopelessness.

His body shook with the force of his sobs as he crushed her to him. Her arms hung limply at her sides. So much had been asked of her—of them both. He let himself be weak now that she was gone. Taken. This time by a mortal hand.

Around him dozens upon dozens of demons formed. He stayed there rocking her body in his arms long enough for several rounds of them to rise from the ground. He ignored them and they ignored him. One by one, they flew off into the night to torment the innocent.

He didn't care. His bloody tears dripped onto her skin.

All I want to do is join you, soulmate. Fighting that impulse took more work than he'd let on earlier.

The earth shifted beneath him. Andre thought nothing of it until the first vines sprouted between cracks in the asphalt. They grew fast, deepening the fissures in the street as they did so.

"You can't have her." Andre's hair began to lift. If he lost control now, he might never regain it. The thought appealed to him.

The ground shifted some more, splitting the street open. The vines grew and stretched, and Andre tightened his grip. He didn't want to let her body go. There were people out there, people who could coax life back into the newly dead. Pay or threaten them enough and they'd do it.

The plants slid over Gabrielle's body, avoiding him entirely. Andre attempted to rip them off only to have more sprout and tether her to the earth. He yanked his soulmate away from the unnatural plants, and to his great horror, rather than breaking, the vines sliced into his soulmate's skin.

Skin he'd spent months memorizing. He could trace each and every contour of her body. He knew all her angles and the shape of her smile. He'd committed to memory how she felt in his arms and precisely how they fit together.

Letting out an anguished cry, Andre stopped trying to free her and simply stared down at her body cradled in his arms.

"This was never how it was supposed to be between us, my love," he whispered. Her dying over and over again and taking bits of him with her. Maybe that was how he was destined to enter hell—little chunks at a time.

He knew death, had seen it claim mortals over and over again. None of it could've prepared him for hers.

The earth opened up and vines tugged his mate's body out of his arms. He pulled a knife strapped to his belt and slashed at the roots. He fought the vines to the bitter end. It didn't change anything. The earth still claimed her. It sucked her down and the ground resettled.

Andre placed a fist to his mouth to stifle the sobs shaking his body.

There was no one here to witness this. No one save for him. This girl that no one could stand to look at. Her end shouldn't be like this—murdered on some abandoned street. Just like her mother. Killed and discarded like someone's trash.

Andre had to shut his mind against these thoughts before they destroyed him.

He now had another face to add to her list of enemies, a face he'd seen before. The man was a Politia officer and a shapeshifter. It had to be Caleb's father, based on his features and what he'd said.

The loose bits of asphalt vibrated against the street. He'd hunt down both Caleb and his father, then he'd kill the man's son before his eyes.

Pieces of the broken street had lifted off the ground.

Only once he knew the pain of losing what he most loved would Andre kill him—or maybe he wouldn't. Right about now death seemed like a godsend.

"Andre?" An old man hobbled out of the store he knelt in front of.

He almost didn't react to his name. Not until he smelled the divinity of the being.

The fury he'd nurtured had found a target.

He swiveled to face the man. "You coordinated this." Andre's hair lifted, and the bits of gravel and loose asphalt lifted higher, beginning to swirl around him.

"I assure you, I did not," a weak, raspy voice replied. "I do, however, want to rectify the situation."

"You cannot, old man," he said, his eyes returning to the disturbed earth. All at once his power abated and the rocks and asphalt fell to the ground. "No one can."

"Yes, it does appear you lost this particular battle. But you and I are angling to win a war, not a battle."

Andre stood, a severe frown on his face. The impulse to follow his mate into the ground was nearly impossible to drown out.

She is immortal. She will come back. She must.

"The devil is trying to seduce your mate," the man said. "What is worse, his efforts are sincere."

"Who are you?" Andre asked.

"An ally."

"Gabrielle has no allies." None except for him and her two friends.

Andre took a step forward. "You have told me who you are to Gabrielle," Andre said, "but I still don't know your name, and thus, who you are to *me*."

"Jericho Aquinas, the owner of this store," he pointed

to the dusty storefront behind him, "and the keeper of a valuable object that belongs to Gabrielle."

Andre's eyes narrowed on him. The name rang no bells, and it should've. He made it his business to know powerful beings.

"If you will please come in," the man said, motioning to the door. "And hurry." He looked up and down the block. "Our business needs to go unnoticed by all parties."

"If this is a trap, I won't hesitate to cut you in two, angel." As it was, Andre's unholy power had a tight grip on him, and it wasn't letting up.

"Messenger," the man corrected. "Angels are the sword of God. I am the mouth. I do not wish to be compared to them."

Andre wasn't yet convinced the distinction had any merit. But Gabrielle had also faced off angels and still been intent on coming here, to Jericho's Emporium.

Andre inclined his head. "Lead on."

The man wheezed a laugh and clapped him on the shoulder. "You aren't half bad, for a damned thing." He turned on his heel and headed inside, his joints stiff from age—or so he'd like others to assume. The scent of holiness poured off of him.

"Why trap yourself in such a withered body?" Andre asked, following him inside.

"Perspective." The man's voice was a husk of what it should've been. "There is no vanity to distract me from my purpose here."

"And what is that purpose?"

The man gave a shrug but said nothing.

Andre took in the grimoires that lined one of the store's walls. Rows and rows of seemingly benign knick-knacks lined the room. But the dusty looking glass to his right was actually a prized perception mirror. And the rusted daggers laying on the shelf next to him always landed where they intended.

"How did Gabrielle find you?" Andre asked, his eyes roving over a magic carpet as he followed the messenger to the back of the store.

And why has she never mentioned you to me? he wondered. It was his own fault, he supposed. Andre had found her leaving this store only days ago. He should've probed more then.

Jericho mounted the stairs, his breath coming in pants. "She followed bread crumbs."

Immortals and their puzzles; they loved nothing more than to make the worthy work for their messages. "What did she find?"

The messenger didn't speak until they'd stopped outside a door. "A means to her salvation."

"Don't give me hope, old man," Andre growled. He couldn't bear it. Gaining his mate only to lose her again.

The celestial pulled out a key, but made no move to open the door. His voice dropped. "But that is exactly what I am giving you. What I'm about to entrust to you must remain the most heavily guarded secret you've ever kept. Not even the devil has eyes into this place, and I've taken pains to hide from him what you're about to take. The seer's shroud still flows through your system, yes?"

"It does." The potion Hestia gave him would wear off

in several weeks. Until then, it hid him from the eyes of seers.

"That is fortuitous for it will hide you from the devil's sight as well. The seer's shroud no longer protects Gabrielle, as you might've guessed from the earlier ambush. She is the least safe from the devil and his spies, and that is why I am putting what rightfully belongs to her into your safekeeping. If the devil suspects anything, he will now come for me. So, I ask you again, can you guard what I'm about to give you with your life and keep it a secret?"

Andre gave a sharp nod, growing more curious about this object by the moment.

When Jericho opened the door, Andre leaned into the blast of magic that hit him. The old man shuffled over to a shelf, grabbing an object cloaked with canvas. He set it on the table and removed the material.

Dios mio.

Andre hadn't paid much attention to this particular detail in Gabrielle's note. The item that could save her. But the proof stared back at him.

Irrefutable.

"It's real?" Andre studied the iridescent feather trapped in the glass case.

"I plucked it myself," Jericho said.

A celestial quill. Salvation indeed.

Andre hadn't even known one to exist anymore. Truth be told, he'd thought such things were myths. Even his soulmate's letter couldn't convince him otherwise. Hope, after all, was a dangerous thing.

"This is Gabrielle's?"

Jericho inclined his head. "Nona and her mother paid a great price to procure this for her some time ago. It's been hers ever since."

"Tell me how a quill like this works," Andre said.

"Simple. All it takes is ink, a piece of paper, and a heart's desire. It's not how the quill works that's at issue. It's keeping the existence of it a secret that will be difficult. Creatures of both heaven and hell would rebel if they knew she owned such an object."

Andre rubbed his lower lip. "Why is that?"

"The queen of the damned requesting a favor of God?" Jericho gave a husky laugh. "The possibilities could be catastrophic for either side, depending on the request."

"But you're not worried," Andre stated, watching the messenger carefully.

"It is not my place to cast worry," he said. "But She isn't, and that's good enough for me."

"Why can't God just hear Gabrielle's complaint without use of the quill?" This method of requesting God's favor seemed uncomfortably close to buying indulgences, those papers that granted absolution.

Jericho began packing the feather and its glass case into a duffle bag. "God works in mysterious ways."

"That is not an answer, old man."

"It was a kind reminder that you are out of place to question Her motivations," he said as he worked.

"You cannot scare me into complacency. Why?"

Jericho stopped packing to meet Andre's gaze. The two stared at each other for a long minute. Then the withered edges of Jericho's face crinkled into a smile and a wheezy chuckle. "God wants all Her loyal followers to respect the decision. Angels and other celestial beings will not question the validity of a plea made with this quill."

Men of peace and their regulations. Andre felt an odd sense of camaraderie with hell. They handled things by right of might.

"And God will listen?" Andre asked.

"She is already doing so."

Andre folded his arms. "Then why are angels attacking my mate?"

"Because it takes masterful trickery to outmaneuver the devil, and God is well aware of this."

That could mean that angels were in on heaven's plans, but more likely, it meant that God was going rogue on this one, and only a select few, like Jericho and now Andre, were aware of it. Either way, they'd continue to attack Gabrielle.

This conversation was not helping Andre's black mood.

Jericho zipped up the packed duffle and handed it to Andre. Before the messenger let it go, he said, "A word of advice: Gabrielle should not use this until the time is right, and you should not make it known to her that you have possession of it. Otherwise, she'll be the devil's. Forever."

CHAPTER 16

Andre

Sunrise was less than an hour away when Andre returned to Bishopcourt and hid the celestial quill. Once he'd done so, he strode down the hall, ignoring the vampires that approached him.

He headed to the guestroom where Leanne was staying and flipped on the room's dim lights. He stalked inside.

"Mine *eyes*," Oliver said, blinking past the glare. The seer groaned next to him.

Sharing one room, one bed, when they'd been given two. Was this how modern men and women interacted?

"You better be looking for some late night nookie," Oliver said, "or else—"

Andre interrupted the fairy. "One does not command me in my own home."

"Andre?" Leanne's head popped out of the comforter.

She, too, fell silent as she took him in. Gabrielle's blood still stained his clothing and he was sure a bit of madness twinkled at the back of his eyes. Now was not a time to piss him off.

"What's up?" She gathered the comforter to her chest.

"If you want my continued protection," Andre said, "you will take me with you tomorrow when you retrieve, Gabrielle."

Oliver eyed him up and down. "Much as I would enjoy that, she's an earlier riser than you."

"I don't *fucking* care. You either do this, or be at the mercy of the Politia."

Things were going to happen a little differently from now on.

Gabrielle

A FINGER TRACED my lips.

I blinked my eyes open. Pluto sat on the edge of the bed I laid on, watching me intensely. My pulse jackknifed at his nearness.

"Home early, I see," he said.

I sat up, my mind jogging back. I didn't remember the return trip, not like yesterday.

I let out a squeak when I realized all I wore was a see-through teddy and skimpy lingerie beneath it. "Who dressed me?"

"I did." There was no apology in the devil's voice.

"You saw me naked?"

A hungry look entered the devil's eyes. "I did."

Breathe, Gabrielle. "Did you ... ?"

"Touch you while I was at it?" Pluto finished for me. "That does happen when you remove clothes. Did I violate you? No. When you become mine, I want you aware and enthusiastic."

My body reacted in vastly inappropriate ways to his words, and our connection jolted. Even the siren stirred. Having my head and heart and body all at war with each other totally sucked.

Hades sensed my reaction. He leaned over me, drawing closer and closer.

He's going to kiss me.

I couldn't do it. Not so soon after I'd left Andre's arms. I swear I still felt his fingers on my skin and his taste on my lips.

"What happened to me?" I asked.

His mouth was a hair's breadth away from mine, and I could see him weighing the benefits of ignoring my question.

"Asiri."

His eyes shuttered and he pulled away. "A mortal slit your throat."

I reached for my neck, but the skin there felt smooth.

"It wouldn't stop bleeding," I murmured, remembering.

"The blade was cursed to prevent you from healing. Otherwise, you would've survived it."

My hand fell to my side. "Am I dead?"

"You are immortal. So no, you are not dead."

I met Pluto's eyes. An inferno flickered at the back of them. Something about the devil was ... off. An agitation lurked beneath the smooth façade.

"What is it?"

Anger welled along our connection. "Don't presume to understand me," he snapped.

Tou-chy.

I began to get up. He pushed me back down, his face inscrutable. "I'm not done with you."

"Done with me?" My heart began to pound.

I'd pushed him too far, using his old name like that. And now here we were on a bed with me wearing no more than strategically placed lace, and crap, I might have bigger things to worry about than a kiss.

Pluto took several deep breaths, his chest rising and falling. "You tried to meet with the enemy. That ... *enrages* me."

Now I watched him closely, not daring to move. I'd recognized something about him was off, but I'd vastly underestimated just how dangerous he was right now.

"But what happened to you after that ... I am used to anger. I relish it. I cannot fathom why I feel it on your behalf. Especially after you continue to betray me." He picked up my hand and threaded his fingers between mine. Even this gesture was full of agitation, like he hated that he couldn't help himself.

His hand was in mine, and I hadn't once flinched at his touch.

I should've.

I'm changing ... and so is he. I'd seen the devil possessive, but not protective. I couldn't trust this.

"Perhaps I see my own nature reflected back in you. But I fear … " He shook his head, and whatever he planned on saying died on his lips.

"I've ordered the demons to strike angels and anyone fighting for them on sight. Our enemies are to endure the most painful deaths possible. Short of that, they are to be eliminated."

I shook my head. "I won't stand by and watch your demons attack innocent people." Even if most of those innocent people wanted me dead.

He squeezed my hand *hard*. "*Our* demons, consort, or have you forgotten who you are and who you're with? You are my queen and we will have a united front in this war."

War. There it was again, the reminder that no one could play nice.

"Are we agreed?"

I kept my mind carefully blank as I nodded.

His hold relaxed. "Good. Then we can move onto other topics."

He rubbed his thumb over my knuckles. "To care about someone, it is strange, yes?"

My brows knitted together but I nodded.

"I've had no one to care about until you," he admitted. "And now, with our connection, your death—temporary though it was—did crazy things to me."

My heart lurched. Fate had given him the wrong soulmate. Another woman might have been able to change him, another woman might've come to love him. There wasn't a happy ending for us.

Reluctantly, I placed my hand over his. "I'm fine."

He cast me an irritated look. "I don't care how you are."

Liar.

Hearing his words and the vitriol in them, I would've expected him to get up and stalk out of here. But if anything, I sensed that the devil wanted to be closer to me. I didn't know how I felt about that, and that indecision troubled me.

His eyes dropped to my lips, and oh God, oh God, oh God, he was leaning in, and there was nowhere for me to back up, and his lips looked far too inviting. The cord between us sang. This was so, so wrong, so—

Pluto's lips brushed mine, and before I could help it, I kissed him back. And, horror of horrors, I enjoyed it. The cord between us quieted. Through it, I could feel Pluto's vast, vast hunger. For me, for kingdoms, for anything and everything he wished.

Once the kiss ended, I opened my eyes. What I saw in his frightened me. I'd seen the look on Andre. I hadn't planned on seeing Pluto wear it.

"I'm not ready for this," I said, and then pushed back the covers, brushed by him, and spirited out of there.

He didn't try to stop me. But I could feel his eyes like a brand on my back as I left the room. I was sure he could read every single thought of mine right now—all those confused emotions and unwanted feelings surging through me. Maybe he took comfort in the fact that we both had no clue what to make of this.

Whatever he thought, he didn't share it.

I HAD TO go back.

I'd run, and that was all great and dandy, but chances were at some point I'd encounter another demon, and I wanted to be wearing more than just a teddy when that happened.

With no little amount of dread, I returned to our bedroom. I shouldn't have worried. The room was empty, the bed already remade. Wasting no time, I grabbed the first dress I saw—this one with a neckline that plunged past my navel.

C'mon. Leave a little to the imagination.

Okay, so I wasted a bit of time returning that one to the rack, only to pull out a spider silk crop top and skirt that joined together in the front. It still revealed a good deal of skin, but at least these sections were slightly less suggestive.

I donned the outfit and slipped back out, my mind consumed with disturbing thoughts.

I was at war with myself in almost every way possible. I wanted to do good, but I had a growing urge to commit wicked deeds. That didn't help my already complicated situation with Andre and the devil. My mind and heart knew whom I loved, but my body and soul pulled me towards Pluto.

Three days here, and my will was failing me completely. I needed to get to that quill before it crumbled completely.

Guilt led me out into the fields of flame. The fire didn't burn me, the heat didn't sear me. My senses should've been exploited by this place, but they weren't. The souls around me writhed and screamed and my heart wrenched at the sight. Such unending pain.

It only heightened my own guilt. Who was I to deserve to walk the earth when my soul rotted from the inside out? Who was I to deserve love when I could only tarnish it? And who was I to live forever as a queen while all these souls suffered?

Before I was conscious of what I was doing, I began to hum. All those poisonous insecurities of mine began to dissipate as I focused on the melody I created.

Perhaps I imagined the wails dying down just a bit.

The hum formed into notes and distinct words. I barely noticed the glow of my skin as the song poured out of me.

Now it wasn't my imagination. As I sang, the wails quieted. My heart knew the words to this song, and they fell from my lips. I sang about pain and suffering, and I sang about peace and redemption. I soothed these souls with my voice.

"What are you doing?"

I rotated to find the devil at my back. He looked spitting mad.

I kept singing, but now I reached out to him because I was batshit crazy. His gaze flicked to my hand. Reluctantly he stepped forward and grasped it, though the anger in his eyes didn't abate. Giving my hand a tug, he pulled me to him, wrapping his other arm around my waist.

The fire around us melted away, replaced by the cold bedroom of the palace. My voice wavered, but I didn't stop singing. Not until the devil captured my face in his hands and kissed me.

My music cut off.

Fuck. I was right back where I started with the devil.

For a sheer instant, hell was quiet. Then the wails rose up again, even louder than before as they lamented the return of their pain.

Pluto broke off the kiss. "You made them forget."

I blinked. I could apologize. He would want an apology. But I wasn't sorry.

Instead, I nodded. "For a time."

"You made them forget their pain," the devil said, squeezing my arms. I couldn't read the expression in his eyes. "It is my job to make them suffer, and you eased them of it."

I was waiting for his anger to beat down upon me, but seconds ticked by and it didn't come. His eyes searched mine. Then roughly he let me go and stalked towards the door.

"Asiri."

His entire body reacted to that name. Twice I'd used it today, and both times it affected him.

"I researched that name."

He didn't turn.

"You were once loved by people," I said.

"That was a long time ago." His voice sounded shaken.

"But it happened?" I asked.

Now the devil rotated to face me. "Why are you bringing this up, consort?"

My eyes roved over him. "Can you be that man again?"

Slowly he prowled back to me, his movements deliberate. It took all of my willpower not to back up.

"You said it yourself once—I am no man."

"You're Asiri."

He closed his eyes. I was uncovering a bit more of him every time I used that name, and the god that was revealing himself to me was markedly different from the one I was used to.

"I didn't give you that name to badger me with," he said.

"No," I agreed, "but you gave it to me for a specific reason." Tentatively I touched the side of his face. He grabbed my wrist, but rather than pulling my hand away, he anchored it in place as he leaned in.

"Can you be that man again?"

Why was I asking him this? What was the point? I didn't want to like him more. I wanted to hate him. And usually I did. But right now, all I desired was to give him some small amount of peace, just like the rest of the lost souls here.

His eyes opened. "For you, consort, I could try."

CHAPTER 17

Gabrielle

"I HAVE SOMETHING to show you," he admitted. He still hadn't released my wrist, and now he twined his fingers through mine and tugged me out of our bedroom.

My dress slithered across the onyx floors as we crossed the palace. Pluto could've instantly transported us to whatever it was he wanted to show me, but he chose to walk with me instead.

We didn't speak for much of the trip, which I was coming to find was decidedly not a good thing. It made me focus on the way his thumb drew circles on the back of my hand and the electricity that jumped between the two of us. But most of all, it made me realize that since our connection formed, I never felt more like myself than when I was with him.

Once we began to climb up a winding staircase, I had a good idea where we were going. But it was only when I saw the familiar doors to the library that I could be sure that was our destination.

I glanced over at him in time to see one corner of his mouth lift.

When we entered, I gasped. Floor-to-ceiling shelves now lined the room, each filled to the brim with books. Books that didn't appear to be bound in human skin.

Score!

I spun in place, taking it all in.

"Do you like it?"

I swiveled around at the sound of Hades' voice.

"You did this?" I asked.

His gaze passed over the shelves of books. "You've been bored, and you don't wish to come with me to the fields."

I suppressed a cringe at the word fields. He wasn't harvesting vegetables beyond the palace walls.

"You've been spending time in here. You needed a library fitting for a queen." He slid his hands in his pockets, wandering farther into the room, his gaze still glued to the books. "We will make it bigger. This is only temporary."

Bigger?

I still hadn't gotten over the fact that this was a gift. That someone could just give me a library. I didn't want to be moved by this or overcome with the vastness of this present. It wasn't something that I could repay in kind.

Suddenly, I was nervous. What *did* Pluto want in return?

Our gazes caught, and I swear he heard my thoughts.

For once I wished I could read his. In the depths of those unfathomable eyes was a world of unspoken things. They sat right at the tip of his tongue, but he voiced none of them.

Instead he bowed his head. "I will leave you here."

His words hit me in the gut, and I already felt the ache of his absence. I didn't want him to leave. Not when he was like this.

"Where are you going?" I asked. I crossed the room to where he stood.

The look in his eyes deepened as I came to him. "Back to work. I have a realm to run."

I touched the base of my throat. He hadn't tried anything. It was almost ... disappointing. I pushed that thought away as guilt rose up in me. I loved Andre, damnit. I needed to be with Andre. Fantasizing about the devil was not okay.

His jaw tightened. "Let him go, consort. He is not yours anymore. *I* am. This is not wrong; fighting it is."

The air changed, and Asiri, this strange god I'd caught glimpses of, retreated. "I will dine with you later. Until then, occupy yourself." With that, his form dissipated.

I rubbed my arms, thrown by his constantly shifting moods. No, not moods. Personas. He wore them like coats. Shedding one only to don another. It made me trust him less, not more.

After he left, I made myself comfortable. I discovered that Pluto had stocked the shelves with novels in a vast array of genres.

I felt like Belle, and the devil, my beast.

A heartless, scary-as-hell beast, but you know, a beast nonetheless.

Hours ticked by in that library. I read the final page in the first book I'd picked up. Closing it, I drummed my fingers along the cover. I wasn't ready to read another novel, which left me to my thoughts. I brought my fingers to my lips and absently rubbed them.

Earlier, the devil and I discussed some things, but it was what we didn't discuss that troubled me. He didn't mention me killing his demon. He didn't mention my meeting with Andre, and he hadn't done more than touch upon my attempt to find Jericho.

What was he keeping from me?

My thoughts turned to Andre. I held our earlier conversation close to my heart, hoping that he was having an easier time believing in us than I was.

A war between realms, a malleable god, violent angels, and me at the epicenter of it all. My free hand rubbed my locket absently. *The future is yours to claim.*

It didn't feel like it at the moment. If anything, it felt like the future was claiming me.

A BLOODY BODY was stretched out on hell's dining room table.

I shrieked when I caught sight of it, my hand going to my mouth.

"I can see you're acclimating well," the devil said. His feet were propped up on the table, crossed at the ankles. He sipped wine from an opulent chalice and somehow he managed to not look completely ridiculous while doing so.

Five minutes ago he'd telepathically rung me to come to dinner. Idiot that I was, I'd actually been eager to see him again. Whomever I thought he was earlier, I was wrong.

The body on the table moaned.

That man was ... alive?

He was laid out on his stomach, a pole running through the length of him. His hands and ankles were tied behind him, and someone had gone through and added what looked like cranberries and leafy greens around his body. He appeared uncannily like a spitted pig. Worst of all was his singed skin; someone had roasted him over an open flame.

"Why is there a bloody man on the table?"

"Archdemon," the devil corrected, swirling his glass of wine. Gone was the caring Asiri I'd spent time with. His eyes now challenged mine. "He disobeyed me. Now he's to be eaten alive."

I almost gagged. Nope, nope, nope. I'd go hungry. Whatever I walked into I was walking out of. Immediately. I swiveled on my heel and headed for the door.

The devil appeared in front of me, blocking my exit. "Where do you think you're going?"

"I'm not eating a freaking demon." I gestured to the charred thing.

The devil gave me an indulgent smile. "You misunderstand." He clasped my upper arms, and my skin crawled at his touch. "You won't be eating him. I'd never allow you to partake in something so barbaric. No, the lesser demons will be."

Now this was the devil I remembered. I needed to commit this to memory.

In spite of myself, I smiled. "You slipped up." I was embarrassed that tears pricked my eyes. I'd been so easily had.

The devil's eyes flickered and his face contorted in anger. "You want me meek? Loving?" He pointed behind him. "That's what happens when I soften. Demons rebel. Take a good look, my queen. The more kindness you ask of me, the more you will see this."

I SAT ON my room's balcony, my back to the wall. The flames that surrounded the castle crackled, the shrieks of the damned blending in with them. I hummed below my breath, not ready to call the devil's attention to me, but also unable to ignore all these souls' pain.

I cradled my head in my hands, waiting out the last of my time here for the evening. The devil had finally let me go, but not before he had me swear to join him the next time he hosted such a dinner. I wasn't banking on being here the next time such a dinner occurred.

The entire castle shook. I lifted my head from my hands. What in the world?

The tremors increased, getting more pronounced by the second. A minute later, the doors to our room slammed open. Dinner must be over.

Then the click of heels. The devil could move places instantaneously, yet he chose this entrance.

The balcony doors flew open. A shadow fell upon me.

"Are you trying to scare me again?" I asked.

"I have enough fear to prey upon. I want something else entirely from you."

I wrapped my arms around my knees. "I just want to be alone."

"And I want to be near you," he said.

Much to my dismay, he sat down next to me. "I scared you earlier?"

I looked over at him. "I don't understand you. At all."

He smiled, staring off at the fields of fire beyond the balcony. "That is because I am a god. We aren't meant to be easily understood. But one day you will." He turned to me. "I await that day."

My throat worked. "Why do you have to be like this? Just let me hate you."

"Little bird, I know you won't believe me, but I am all bad, and once I was all good, and I can be everything in between all at the same time."

"That makes no sense."

"In time you will understand this too. It is the logic of the gods, and you have only just come into your power. It will take eons to grasp this."

I watched his lips move, fascinated by them. On a whim, I reached out and traced them. My heart pounded faster and faster. He nipped at my finger, then took my hand in his.

"I enjoy your tender heart. It must survive much to live here. This will not be the last terrible thing you behold. And I will admit a part of me craves your terror, because

194

it is yours." He leaned his head back and sighed. "Everything about you excites me."

CHAPTER 18

Gabrielle

THIS TIME, WHEN I crossed over to earth, I felt water. As my body was forced upwards, the soil had gotten softer and softer. I'd cracked through the hard shell of the earth and was shoved into ... this.

Water.

After I released enough air to tell which way was up, I kicked my way to the surface. I gasped in a lungful of air, my hair plastered to my neck. I wrinkled my nose at the smell of sulfur.

Partially submerged columns surrounded me, and intricately carved, vaulted ceilings rose high overhead.

Irony of ironies, I'd found myself in the middle of a church, one that had been lost to time by the looks of it. The entire floor was underwater. I toed the ground, and tiny bits of ceramic brushed against my bare feet.

Whoops. In addition to all the really bad laws I'd broken in the past few days, apparently I got to add desecrating a sacred space to the list.

Only, I wasn't burning up like I'd assumed an unholy thing would. The disrepair of the place probably had a lot to do with it.

A growl had my gaze darting up. Gargoyles lined the bannisters and the exposed bars bracing the columns of this place, and their beady, red eyes tracked me.

Hold up. Beady red eyes?

Not gargoyles. *Demons.*

I spun in a circle; they'd fully surrounded me. And they eyed me like I was their next tasty meal.

Aww, hell.

A splash broke the silence. "Aaaaeeeei!" a familiar voice squealed. "Bloody fucking hell, Leanne. You couldn't have at least warned me we were landing in a moat?"

Not twenty feet away from me, Leanne, Oliver, and Andre appeared in the same pool of water I stood in.

My heart spasmed. Today Andre looked worse than he had yesterday, his skin tighter and paler than it usually was. Our broken connection was taking a toll on him.

He caught sight of me, and I could read the relief plain on his face. I wondered what he saw on mine.

"You need to shut up. Now," Leanne hissed, looking blindly around her. Neither she nor Oliver would be able to see much.

I began edging towards them, my dress plastered to my skin. My eyes darted up to the demons whose attention now moved between all of us with interest. Andre followed my gaze up to the rafters, and his entire body tensed.

The devil had been concerned about my safety here on earth. Perhaps he'd ordered these demons to watch me. Perhaps not. Either way, my friends were still fair game to them.

"When's Gabrielle getting here, Leanne?" Oliver asked, completely oblivious. "Because I can tell you right now, I can only take about ten minutes of this before I'm tapping out—*eww*, Leanne did you fart?" He scrunched his nose. "It smells rank in here."

Low growls echoed throughout the church.

Perhaps it was a bit optimistic to assume the demons were here to protect me.

Water splashed and shifted, and then strong arms wrapped around my waist. Even over the scent of sulfur, I could smell Andre's pheromones. He brushed a kiss along my temple and dragged me back to my friends.

One of the demons screeched, and it sounded an awful lot like a battle cry.

"Oliver," he said, placing my hand against the fairy's arm, "we need to leave, now."

All around us demons jumped from their perches, their leathery wings snapping as they stretched open. Dozens of them descended on us, the beat of their wings blowing gusts of air against my face.

"But Gabrielle—"

"Is right next to you," Andre said. "Now, Oliver!"

The last thing I saw was the bared teeth of several of them as their claws reached for us, so close that I smelled their acrid breath.

The basilica dissolved away. In its place were stone monuments and sand. My hands and knees hit the dry soil, and I stared up at giant columns and a wall of incised hieroglyphs.

That was all the time I had to appreciate the scenery. Someone yanked me back, and my surroundings were brutally ripped from me. If traversing ley lines with Oliver felt effortless, this felt savage, like I was torn through the fabric of space.

The Braaid appeared around me, and a cluster of men and women in uniform stood outside the circle watching. A knee dug into my back and magic flooded my senses.

Under attack.

My power built in response, but before I had a chance to release it, a spell slammed into me and the world went dark.

WHEN I WOKE, my hands were bound with spelled cuffs. My head leaned against a window and my body rocked gently.

In a car. On the road.

"It's just as Lila told us." The voice sounded far away. "She comes back every night. She can walk both realms."

I blinked as the last of the spell dissolved. My blurry surroundings came into focus. I sat in the back of a patrol car. I recognized the feminine voice that spoke. Maggie Comfry, my former boss.

I'd been ambushed. The Politia must've foreseen this.

Even with Leanne strategizing our next moves, she hadn't been able to catch everything. No seer's abilities were fool-proof.

I yanked on my cuffs, the jangling sound catching the officers' attention.

"Shit, she's already awake," Maggie said.

The familiar smell of shapeshifter coming from the driver's seat triggered my memory from last night. Byron Jennings grabbing my hair and slitting my throat. He'd found me again.

My anger rose like a whip, and with it, my power. He and the rest the Politia thought they could control me, hurt me, tame me.

I'd never felt wrath like this, and I no longer had the willpower to curb it.

It was a testament to how powerful I'd gotten that even with the containment spell wound into the cuffs, I retained enough power to out-muscle the enchantment. I pushed my energy out, disintegrating the spell. The full force my power flooded me, thickening the air in the car. Another push of magic and the cuffs snapped open, falling away from my wrists.

"What was that?" Maggie said, sensing a shift in the air. I saw the moment she realized the cuffs no longer contained me, her spine stiffening, her shoulders tensing. Slowly, she swiveled in her seat until our eyes met.

I smiled, and power pulsed out of me.

The windows and doors blew out. The sound of shattering glass and crunching metal echoed in the night. Wind whipped through my hair. I laughed as a howling gust of lost souls joined it.

Byron slammed on the brakes and the wheels locked. We spun.

My skin lit up at the chaos, and right in the middle of it, I leaned over the driver's seat and whispered into his ear, "You're going to regret what you did last night."

"Knock her out!" he yelled. "Knock her—"

The butt of a baton slammed into my temple, and the world went dark once more.

I woke briefly.

"Should we just kill her?" Maggie's voice.

"You want her coming back for you?" Byron's.

I blinked open my eyes only to see a black baton coming down on me once more. Pain slammed into my temple, and I lost consciousness again.

Eventually, the blackness bled away. A shiver wracked my body. I was too hot and too cold at the same time. My head pounded. It shouldn't pound.

I reached up to touch it and felt a lump.

Where I'd repeatedly been hit.

I rubbed my temples, trying to massage the pain away. Another shiver raced through me.

"Feels terrible, doesn't it?"

My body tightened at the voice.

I looked up. Iron bars separated me from Caleb. He sat outside my cell, his legs folded and his hands steepled against his lips. He watched me with tired, tormented eyes.

"This feels familiar," I said. Only this time I was the prisoner. "Are we in Castle Rushen?"

Caleb nodded.

Unlike the cuffs, the enchantments of this cell pounded away at my skin and sucked me dry of energy. Perhaps if I had been awake when they brought me here, I would've retained enough power to break free of the cell. But as I'd slept, the neutralization spell had drained me.

I rubbed my temple again.

"Yesterday, they meant to kill you," Caleb said. "Maggie was then supposed to get a read off of your body."

As a psychometric, Maggie had the ability to pull information off of whatever she touched, living or dead, animate or inanimate.

"Andre scared them off, then your body disappeared—or so they say."

I lolled my head back against the cement wall, letting him talk. This weak, I couldn't do much more than listen.

"That's why they captured you tonight. To understand you better."

So they could better understand how to defeat me.

"Why are you here telling me this?" I asked.

"You could've killed me, but you didn't," he said. "And last night, when you faced us off, you spared the officers then as well."

I just stared at him.

"I keep expecting death, not mercy from you," he said.

I didn't really care what he made of me. I wasn't doing this to prove anything to him.

He fell quiet, and for a long time we sat there together, me in agony, him in deep reflection.

"Remember our first date?" he finally said, shattering the silence.

My jaw clenched. I nodded.

"You asked me why I was interested in you, and I told you that you were mysterious. I hadn't known ... I hadn't known the half of it.

"And then Samhain came around." He swallowed. "That night I began to realize that you were really as doomed as you warned me you were." He blinked several times. "You were marked by the devil, but I believed I could save you. I truly thought that's what I was doing when I pulled the trigger four nights ago."

So this was Caleb's apology, part two, and I had to sit here and listen to it.

Lucky me.

"I still want to save you."

"There's no coming back from what you did," I said. "It doesn't matter how you defend yourself. You tried to murder me. We will never be friends again."

He held my gaze. "I know, Gabrielle. I've figured that out."

"Then why are you here?" God, I felt like shit. I was sure the enchantments of this cell were turning my organs to mush.

"Seers have been looking into the future," he said. "It's not good. But some have said ..." His eyes captured mine, "some have said that there's at least one future where you save us."

Bullets pinged in the distance, interrupting story time.

Caleb stood, his attention going to the end of the hall.

The gunfire stopped abruptly.

Both of us waited with baited breath.

A chorus of shots broke the silence, and after the ringing in my ears died down, I heard a dozen different screams.

Caleb cursed. "I have to go." He backed up and pointed to me. "We'll finish this later."

"Wait—"

"Later, I promise."

Caleb turned on his heel and took off.

"Thanks for letting me out of here," I muttered. Not that I should expect anything else. I'd done exactly the same thing only a couple days ago.

I pushed myself to my feet and wrapped my hands around the iron bars of my cell. I listened to the sounds of people dying. Whatever was out there was bound to find me eventually. I had no doubt this had to do with me. So I wasn't surprised when I heard the slow footfalls headed towards my prison.

I *was* surprised when I saw my sassy friend saunter up to the bars that separated us. He stared into my cell, a little moue of disappointment on his lips. "Fate's really sucker-punched you in the tits this time, Jailbait."

I raised my eyebrows. "Hello to you too."

Oliver held up a key, jingling it. "Lookie what I got. Just say it, I'm the best."

I exhaled, a smile curving my lips. "You are without a doubt the best."

In under a minute he had the cell opened, and I stepped out. As soon as I crossed the threshold, my power roared back to me. I sighed as my headache vanished and my injuries healed themselves.

I rolled my shoulders back.

Oliver gave me a gentle push. "C'mon, Corpse Bride, there's so much to do and so little time."

"What's going on?" I asked, following him.

He laughed, and it sounded so nefarious. "You're not the only one who can wreak havoc on the Politia. Your honey bee is de-*stroying* Castle Rushen and everyone inside. We need to move it. Dude has a track record of ruining castles."

His words were punctuated by a tremor that passed under us. The lights flickered out.

"Well shit. Can you see, Corpse Bride?"

"You really need to stop calling me that," I muttered, grabbing his hand and leading him out of the prison block, the walls shuddering around us.

Déjà vu hit me as we made our way down the back halls of the Politia's headquarters. I'd done this only nights ago, and only nights ago it had been Bedlam here as well. When we hit the crossroads, I looked down the halls. To the right was my exit out of here. Straight ahead took me to the training rooms, and to the left … that would eventually lead back to the main entrance of the castle.

I desperately wanted to go left.

Plaster began to fall from the ceiling.

"Son of a demon," Oliver cursed.

Son of a demon indeed. I had to get Oliver out before this place imploded … just as he said it would.

Andre really did have a bad habit of destroying buildings.

CHAPTER 19

Gabrielle

As soon as we burst out of the castle, I turned to Oliver. "Stay here."

"What? But that's no fun—"

I left him mid-sentence, darting around the castle and back to the front. Officers had surrounded the building, their weapons trained on the main entrance.

That awkward moment when someone's inside your headquarters and you're guarding against them coming *out*. Bet the Politia was forcing down a significant serving of humble pie right now.

When the officers saw me, they began shouting, and some of them turned their weapons on me. I lifted a hand, and with a flick of my wrist, wrenched their guns from their grips. Another flick of my wrist and the guns crumpled in on themselves.

Oh, I really liked doing that.

I felt the now familiar rage searing my veins.

Kill them all.

Kill. Them. All.

No. *No.* I fisted my hands and pinched my eyes shut.

Chill, Gabrielle. You are not a psycho. Correction: you are not a violent *psycho.*

I slowed to a saunter, then deliberately gave the officers my back as I headed inside, where the screams were coming from.

It was just as bad as I'd assumed it would be. Somehow, nearly every officer that wasn't outside was in that main room. Including Caleb.

The halls that branched to either side of the entrance had been barricaded with tables and chairs, preventing the officers from escaping.

And in the midst of all of this was Andre, his hair rippling. The air crackled with power. Two gigantic sheathed swords crisscrossed his back. He hadn't used them—yet. Still, that hadn't stopped him from wreaking havoc on the place.

Some officers lay sprawled in front of him, moaning. The smell of blood was ripe in the air, and each of these officers laid in a growing pool of it. The sight and smell excited the predator in me.

A closer look told me that all their injuries were non-lethal. A bullet to the arm, another with a hole through her calf. All gunshot wounds.

The remaining officers—including Caleb—clustered at

the back of the room, facing my soulmate down. I was surprised to find that I cared Caleb was unhurt. Not that he wouldn't be, and soon.

Guns pointed at their owners. And right when I walked in, they all cocked themselves.

"Come any closer and I will shoot them," Andre threatened.

"Andre," I said, stepping farther into the room, "do you not recognize my scent?"

At the sound of my voice, his shoulders tensed. He turned slowly, the static-y energy of the room ratcheting up.

"Soulmate," he breathed.

The weapons stayed trained on their targets, but he kept his back to the officers as he strode towards me. When he reached me he cradled the back of my neck and tilted my head up. His hair still rippled, and his eyes were largely unseeing. He leaned his head against mine, drawing in my scent.

"They took you."

I touched his cheek. "And you came for me. Thank you." A week ago I might've said this as a way of placating him. Now I meant it sincerely.

His eyes closed, his body relaxing. "I haven't breathed since they captured you."

He opened his eyes and kissed my lips, then my forehead. "I will eliminate these people, and then we will go home."

Blood roared between my ears.

Yes!

Andre began to pull away, and I stopped him, gripping his arms. I was missing something. I searched and searched before I remembered.

Ah.

"Let them live to see another day," I said. Even as I spoke, I rallied against my own words. I wanted them all to pay for what they'd put me and Andre through.

His nostrils flared. "They want you dead. I will not let your enemies live."

I clasped his cheeks with my hands, and forced his unfocused gaze on me. "I cannot be killed. They know this."

His unseeing eyes finally sharpened on me, and I thought I'd made a breakthrough.

Over a dozen weapons fired at the same time.

Mother fucker. He shot them.

"What've you done?" I gasped as more screams lit up the night. I felt those screams soak into my skin, along with their pain. Power burned through my veins.

Andre wrapped an arm around the back of my knees and lifted me up, his jaw hard. "Righted many wrongs."

My gaze moved around the room. The smell of fresh blood flooded it. My fangs, which had already descended, throbbed, and I swallowed down my unnatural thirst and all the dark thoughts that accompanied it.

My gaze connected with Caleb's. He clutched his bloody arm and gritted his teeth. He nodded at me, his way of telling me to go.

Not that I had much choice, trapped as I was in a power-crazed Andre's arms.

"You promised me no more mass executions," I said as

he began to walk.

The sound of groaning metal pulled my eyes back to the weapons behind Andre. Gun barrels bent themselves in unnatural angles. Then, as I watched, they clattered to the ground.

His lips brushed my forehead. "They are flesh wounds, soulmate. They won't kill them." Andre said, carrying me out the entrance. Even though his eyes had focused, his hair still undulated.

What was scarier than a blindly raging Andre? An aware and raging Andre. There was cruel determination in the set of his jaw.

Andre's grip tightened on me as he stepped outside. Since I'd been inside, several officers had acquired new weapons, which they trained on us.

I lifted my hand and whisked these away from them, crushing the metal with my magic, before Andre had a chance to react.

Behind the line of Politia vehicles and officers, Oliver leaned out of a black town car and was signaling to us.

I pressed my power outwards, forcing cars and people back and creating a walkway that ended at our ride. Andre squeezed me, but otherwise gave no reaction to my power.

He took his time reaching the car, glowering at every officer that watched. He was amped up and practically begging for an excuse to unleash more of his violent power. But no one lifted a finger. They watched the somber procession.

It was a strange, uncomfortable standoff, and I was thankful when Oliver opened the door of the town car and we slid inside. Once we were in, our vehicle burned rubber and we fled the scene.

I wiggled in Andre's arms. "You can let me go."

Instead of doing just that, he nuzzled my neck, breathing in deeply. His hold tightened. "Let me—calm—down." He forced the words out, pulling me close and inhaling me in.

Tentatively, I threaded my hands into his hair and tugged him closer. "It's alright, my life," I said, using an endearment he typically murmured to me, "I'm safe. You got me out."

"Ho *please. He* got you out?" Oliver said from my other side. "He was crushing skulls like a barbarian while I broke you out of that cell."

I threw my friend a look as Andre's hair stirred again. Now was not exactly the time for an argument. Not when Andre was ready to go on another rampage.

"Pssh, fine, whatever," Oliver said noticing my look. "He got you out. Happy now?"

My vampire's hand clasped my jaw and turned my head back to face him. "'My life'? I am still yours?"

I smiled. "Always."

As soon as we exited the car in front of Bishopcourt, Andre finally released me. At least, it was his version of releasing me. His hand still lingered on the back of my neck, his thumb absently circling my jugular. It was oddly erotic, and I had to shrug off the rush of heat that swamped my body.

"Men!" he shouted, gesturing to a cluster of individuals waiting for us. "I want four of you guarding my soulmate at all times."

I swiveled to give Andre a look. "You can't be serious." I was essentially a goddess. Of the Underworld. My powers were unparalleled, and, more importantly, I couldn't die. His soldiers could.

"I will not watch you bleed out again, you hear me?" he said, turning those intense eyes on me. The air blew his hair and his coat about him, and my God, he was the most staggering man I'd ever seen. "It will not happen while I have power to stop it. That means I will have you protected, no matter how ridiculous you think that is."

I could tell by the set of his jaw that on this subject, he wasn't going to budge. I gave him a sharp nod, my mood worsening as my attention moved to my new babysitters.

"I need to debrief my men, but I will find you once I'm done. And when I do, I will show you just how much I missed you." He gave me a final heated look, then left me.

"Well that was exciting," Oliver said when we headed into his and Leanne's room. The door clicked shut behind us, leaving my four guards out in the hallway.

Leanne was stretched out on the floor, her deck of tarot cards spread out before her. "So glad the last twenty-four hours are behind us," she said. She glanced up at me. "Hi again."

Apparently this was what Leanne had been up to while Andre and Oliver had broken me out of jail.

"No wonder you gave me the pep talk," I said. Oliver and I plopped down on the bed, and wrapping my arms around a pillow, I peered over the edge at Leanne and her cards. "Thanks, by the way, for all the visions."

"That's awfully appreciative for the anti-Christ," she said, her lips twisting in a wry smile.

I grinned back at her, though even now I struggled with my increasingly trigger-happy temper. "I'm trying to channel my inner Positive Polly. I've heard that no one likes ho-bag Holly."

"*I* do," Oliver chimed in.

Of course he did.

"Hey, where's the love for your rescuer here? I was in fact the one that got you out of that death trap holding cell. I don't care what that goblin of yours says."

"Thank you, Oliver," I said.

"Hmph."

I threw my pillow at him because sometimes, when it came to fairies, you needed to keep it real.

"Ow," he said as it whacked him. I bit my lip to keep from laughing.

I couldn't even begin to describe how good it felt to do and say normal teenage things.

He picked the pillow up and cocked his arm back.

"Dude," I said, rolling onto my back and putting my hands up defensively, "I'm a wrathful goddess now. You can't hit wrathful goddesses. Those bitches will go crazy on you."

I was only half-joking.

Oliver's arm wilted as his eyes narrowed. "Well played, Corpse Bride, well played."

I sighed at the name.

"I spoke with Nona." Leanne's words stopped me in my tracks.

"What?" I said.

Nona—or Cecilia, as I was fond of calling my former nanny—was dead as far as I knew. At least this incarnation of her was.

I didn't know how long it took other immortals to regenerate. Perhaps they returned just as quickly as I did.

"Where is she?" I asked, scrambling to sit up.

Leanne shook her head. "Not like that. I spoke with her in a dream."

That was no less spectacular, but I deflated a bit anyway. I missed her; there was no helping it.

"What did she have to say?"

Leanne gathered up her tarot cards. "Things," she replied cryptically. "Are you in the mood to sneak out?" she asked, setting her deck aside.

"Do you really even need to ask that question?" Oliver said for me.

In response, a devious smile spread across Leanne's face. "That's what I thought."

CHAPTER 20

Gabrielle

WE HUDDLED IN close, keeping our voices down just in case someone with supernatural hearing passed by the room.

"What's the plan?" Oliver asked.

"Gabrielle needs to speak with the messenger before she can use the celestial request quill."

I did? Well, that was news. Hopefully that would go a little bit better tonight than it had last night.

"The who?" Oliver asked. Loudly.

"Ssh," Leanne hissed. "The messenger. Jericho."

"Jericho ... ?"

"Aquinas," Leanne said. "Jericho Aquinas."

"That rings zero bells," he said.

"It doesn't need to ring any bells," she said. "He's waiting for us along the ley lines."

"Not at his shop?" I asked.

Leanne shook her head. "Oliver, we need you to take us to him. You should be able to sense him from his divinity."

The fairy huffed. "I'm nothing but a glorified cabbie."

"You're the best, and you're the only one who can do this," Leanne said.

"Buttering me up won't get you anywhere, Leanne. Anyway, Corpse Bride needs to shake her shadows," Oliver said, glancing meaningfully at the door in question.

"Let's grab something to eat, then think more on this," I suggested, a plan already taking root.

Leanne bit back a smile, and I suppressed mine. She already knew exactly how this was going down.

"I want chocolate and a piña colada," Oliver announced.

"What do think this is, a resort?" I asked as we headed out of the room, the four guards at our heels.

"Hell yeah it is," he replied. "Have you seen Andre's bar? For a guy with a limited appetite, he comes well stocked."

"*Very* well stocked," I agreed. The innuendo just sort of slipped out. So sue me, I was damned. Hell had rubbed off on me.

"You little hussy!" Oliver squealed giving me a push. "I *knew* it! Hung like a horse!"

Okay, this was quickly getting out of hand.

"You can have chocolate," I said. "We'll see about the fruity drink." Giving Oliver sugar was bad enough. Throwing alcohol into the mix was just asking for trouble.

I led my friends beyond the kitchen to Bishopcourt's

large pantry, the guards still trailing us. My skin brightened as I swiveled to face them. I noticed Leanne discreetly plug her ears. Oh, the perks of having a seer for a best
friend. Oliver didn't have to do anything; he could with-
stand my glamour since he was not of this world.

"Make yourselves discreet for the next several hours," I
commanded my guards. "If anyone asks where Leanne, Oliver and I are, tell them that Leanne's giving Oliver a private reading, and I decided to take a shower." It wouldn't
keep Andre away—not for long anyway—but it might allow
our absence to go unnoticed.

Once I finished giving orders, my guards retreated
through the kitchen. I closed the door after them, trapping us inside the pantry. I headed to the square door set
into the floor.

"Illegal glamouring is awesome and all that jazz," Oliver
said as I set to work opening the hatch, "but what exactly
are you doing?"

"Getting us out of here." My skin dimmed as I spoke.

Once I'd opened the door, the three of us entered Andre's cellar. Since I'd last been down here, someone had
installed new shelves and restocked the wines. I made my
way to the rack that hid the persecution tunnel. When I
got to it, I—carefully—pushed it aside, revealing the dark
passage beyond.

Praise Jesus for these shady passageways.

It took us about fifteen minutes to sneak off the property to the taxi waiting for us just outside the edge of Andre's property, courtesy of Leanne's earlier planning. It
took us another fifteen minutes to make it to the nearest

ley line entrance, and then an instant for us to find our-selves in an entirely new land.

I stared out at the ruins. Arid plants grew between stone slabs and craggy rocks. A chilly wind blew over us, carrying with it the distant smell of the sea.

"Where are we?" I asked Oliver.

"Ancient Troy," a soft voice responded. I turned in time to see Jericho making his way to us, his aged body curved inwards.

As soon as I caught a whiff of his divinity, the need for violence assaulted me. I fisted my hands and fought the urge off.

"Why here?" I asked as he approached me.

"Ah, I see you assumed I called for this meeting."

I furrowed my brows. "You mean you didn't?"

"No, I did in fact arrange this."

I tilted my head, thoroughly confused.

His eyes met Leanne's, and he nodded to her. Without a word, she melted away from us, dragging a reticent Oli-ver along with her.

Jericho took my hand and patted it. "Assumptions, my dear, are dangerous, as you well know."

He could say that again. The good guys wanted me dead, the bad guys wanted me safe, and the devil wasn't nearly as ferocious as I'd always imagined him.

We began to walk, the shrubs thrusting themselves as far away from me as they could. Small plants withered beneath my feet. I locked my hands together and squeezed them to tightly leash in the urge to attack him.

"You'll have to excuse me," Jericho said. When I

glanced over at him, he appeared chagrinned. "Now is not the time for lessons in perspective. This mind is, at times, a maze I wander through. Often I lead myself down wrong avenues."

A shiver raced up my spine at his words. Not his mind, *this* mind. The form he'd taken.

"Do you have the quill with you?" I asked.

"I don't," he admitted.

"Then we have to get back to your store."

"It's not there, either, I'm afraid."

It took me a second to process his words, and even once I did, they didn't compute. Not really. "Then where is it?" I asked.

"Gone."

"Gone?" I raise my eyebrows, disbelieving. I squeezed my hands harder. "Where did it go?"

He shrugged, and I didn't know it was possible to be this angry at a divine thing.

"Jericho, I need that quill." I was desperate, so, so desperate. I was going to lose the last of myself soon. I could feel it in my bones. Already it took most of my energy to just appear normal when a maelstrom of negative emotions swept through me.

"Another whom you trust holds it for you, but I will not tell you who."

My wrath was rising. "Why not?"

"Your very being betrays you. The devil can see into your mind, and the world watches your every move. Too many people are looking in. Once you find that quill, you will have minutes to use it before the powers that be will try to converge on you."

I rubbed my forehead at his cryptic words, some of my anger ebbing. I still wasn't over the fact that he'd moved the quill behind my back. "Couldn't all those people figure out that I'm looking for the quill from this conversation?" If people were watching me and my future, then they'd see this.

At least I assumed so, until Jericho spoke.

"I'd imagine not," he said. "The seer's shroud still runs through your friends' veins, and as for me ... I can block prying eyes from foreseeing my future when I want. No one save for perhaps the devil will know of this conversation."

So Jericho had taken precautions I hadn't even considered.

"You'll have one chance." Jericho lifted his head to the sky. The wind was picking up, and I could faintly hear the violent crash of the surf in the distance.

"Your presence affects not just the people, but the very nature of this realm," Jericho said. "The skies and sea rebel. Fires blaze, the earth quakes. If you don't take it when the time comes, then this all ends.

"Heaven and hell are moving in. Beings that have no business traversing this plane are now entering it." He picked up my wrist. "Some through your blood rites, some through the celestial gates.

"You are the cause hell fights for. The cause heaven fights against. But—" Jericho's eyes got devious, "the quill will allow you to right these wrongs and return the world to the way it once was."

220

I narrowed my eyes at him. What was so damned special about this pen? "Can't I just tell a few angels that I'm on their side?"

"And why would they believe you? You are the devil's wife—the Deceiver's wife—and the queen of the damned. *No one* will believe you."

"Do you?"

"It is not in my place to judge."

"And a glorified pen is?"

"It can only scribe true intentions. You use the quill, you bind your entire essence with it."

Alright, it was a pen with a built-in lie detector.

"You only get a single chance to use this quill," he said. "One. So whatever you write, you must think long and hard about it." His eyes went to the sky again. "And you must wait until the time is right before you use it."

Apprehension tightened my stomach. "What's that supposed to mean?"

"Last time we talked, I told you that you wouldn't be able to use it until you died. Now I am telling you that you will not be able to use it until you feel compelled to."

Was he serious? I spent half of my day in hell. "But I already feel compelled to use it."

"No, you don't. At some point, you will though. And that, my dear, is when you must scribe your plea."

"*But I don't know where it is.*"

"That too will be apparent in time." He closed his eyes and breathed in the air. "Hell rises, heaven falls, and earth rebels. I must go."

Jericho stepped away from me. "Remember my words,

Gabrielle. A war emerges that will rip worlds apart, and only you can stop it."

CHAPTER 21

Gabrielle

"NO PRESSURE OR anything," Oliver said, sauntering back with Leanne's hand tucked in the crook of his arm.

"You heard that?" I picked my way around the ancient stone structures. The moment Jericho left, the violence riding me receded. I could finally relax my muscles now that I didn't fear I'd jump someone in a fit of rage.

"I'm a fairy. What did you expect?"

Good point.

Next to him, Leanne stared out, her eyes unfocused. She murmured under her breath. The words that I caught—such as *bloodbath*, *death*, and *damnation*—I chose to ignore.

"How long has she been like that?" I jerked my chin towards her.

"The real question, sweets, is when is she not like this?"

Another decent point.

My poor friend. It was largely my fault that she had one foot in the present and one in the future.

I rubbed my forehead absently. "I don't even know where the quill is. And here I thought my biggest problem would be figuring out how to word my request."

"Pssh," Oliver said. "That one's easy. Just write, 'Yo God, hook a bitch up.'"

I gave him a look.

"*What?*"

The beat of wings interrupted us.

Oliver and I glanced to the heavens. Thick, ominous clouds hid the source of the noise.

"What're the odds that those are just birds?" Oliver asked.

"Zero," Leanne replied, her eyes still unfocused.

"And what are the odds that whatever's up there means us no harm?" he asked.

"Zero," she said again.

Figures emerged from the clouds, and iridescent feathers glittered above us.

"Fuck," I swore as my rage welled up once more.

"You can say that again," Oliver stated.

I glanced over at him, but he wasn't watching me. And he wasn't watching the angels. I followed his gaze.

"Double fuck." A swarm of demons cut across the sky, dipping lower as they got nearer. They were heading straight for us.

We were surrounded, the demons from one side and the angels from another. Just when our luck seemed to have run dry, the two groups caught sight of each other. A demon let out a sharp screech, and the swarm changed its trajectory, aiming instead for its winged enemies. The angels drew their swords.

"Okay, my best bitches," Oliver said, "thumbs out of our asses. It's time to go." He extended his arm, and Leanne and I latched onto him.

The demons had begun to shriek, and the angels bellowed out their battle cries. The last thing I saw was the clash of claws and steel and the last thing I heard was the wet sound of ripping flesh. Then, thankfully, we disappeared.

A VERY TALL, very pissed off vampire glared down at me, his arms folded. "Where have you been?"

He'd been waiting for us in the kitchen. Fury rolled off of him. His fangs were clearly visible, and he didn't bother retracting them.

I got his meaning loud and clear—he was seriously debating eating us all. Okay, maybe not me, but I'd also bet that my unholy blood would give him indigestion.

Andre's eyes moved over my friends. "I give you shelter, and this is how you repay me?"

I stepped in front of them, recapturing Andre's attention. "They're helping me, as they always have."

"Why was I not informed?" he demanded, his eyes moving from me to my friends, then back.

I reached out and touched the side of Andre's face, half expecting him to swat my hand away. I should've known better. Almost unconsciously, he leaned into the touch. "You're busy dealing with the Politia and your coven. And you didn't need to be there."

Beneath my hand, a muscle in his cheek jumped. Ho, he was pissed. "When it concerns you, I always need to be there."

That was sort of sweet, in a super overbearing kind of way.

"And I *will* be there from now on." He turned his glare towards Leanne and Oliver. "Your continued stay here depends on it."

Righteous indignation bubbled up. He did not just threaten my friends. "Don't you—"

"And *you*, soulmate, are not to glamour my men."

I turned his face so that my lips brushed the shell of his ear. "I could've done a lot worse and you know it."

His jaw tightened.

"I wanted to do so much worse. Keep talking, and I might."

"Oooooooh," Oliver said from behind me.

Andre swiveled his head to narrow his eyes at me. I pushed past him, not nearly ready to deal with Andre's sour mood when I was still struggling with my own dark impulses.

He caught my wrist as I passed.

I yanked it from his hold and stalked away.

The air stirred behind me, and then he swept me off my feet, holding me in his arms for the second time that night. He hauled me out of the kitchen, where he'd cornered us, and pretty soon it was clear where, exactly, we were heading.

"I've led armies, ruled a coven for centuries, and kept every important supernatural player in my debt. Yet I cannot seem to manage one itsy bitsy siren."

"I'm not *itsy bitsy*."

His nostrils flared. Our heads were so close together.

"You drive me insane," he said. "You know that, right?" The edge had left his tone. The thing about Andre was that it really was easier to ask for forgiveness rather than permission. And when his bad mood melted away, as it was doing now, his hot, schmexy side made an appearance. He pulled me in closer and bumped his nose against mine.

"What were you thinking, leaving like that?" he whispered. "I was ... scared. I don't do well with fear."

I tightened my hold around his neck. "For the record, Andre, I wasn't trying to get myself killed or running away from you."

"I know, soulmate, and I expect you to fill me in on exactly what it was you were doing." His warm breath brushed against my cheek as his mouth crept closer. "But for now ..."

He stopped talking so that he could press his lips to mine. Unlike some of our other kisses, this one wasn't frantic or hungry. It was romantic and reverent. I wrapped an arm around his neck, pulling him closer, when we heard it.

"*Regina*," a voice glided in from outside.

Andre stiffened, his mouth breaking away from mine. We both looked to the end of the hallway. The voice had come from beyond the back balcony.

He set me down, and we followed the voice to the rear of Bishopcourt.

When we reached the French doors that led out to the balcony, Andre stopped me. "You are not to exit this building until I okay it."

And this was why I always asked for forgiveness rather than permission. His commands practically begged me to break them.

"*If* I okay it," he amended.

Begged me.

I nodded absently, having no intention of following his orders.

He flashed me a stern look, like he didn't trust me—smart vampire—and he stepped up to the doors.

"*Regina Inferna.*"

The hair of my arms stood on end at the sound of that voice. A slip of a woman walked out from the garden beyond the balcony, and the blood drained from my face.

"She can't be real," I whipered.

She really couldn't. After all, I'd already killed the woman in front of me.

CHAPTER 22

Gabrielle

I PRESSED A hand to the glass. "Lila." I breathed the name. The cambion had tried to kill me back in Romania. I'd beat her to it.

Or so I thought.

"Regina." Her voice carried along the wind.

A pulse of energy lashed out of Andre. Never a good sign.

"Stay here," he warned me. He opened the door to the balcony and strode to its edge.

Lila watched Andre exit, and I watched her. Her smirk, her calculating eyes, the sexuality that dripped from every one of her features.

She was a phantom. She couldn't be real.

Andre stopped at the balcony. "You know how this

ends," he said. "Leave."

"As soon as you hand my queen over, I'll be gone."

I couldn't see Andre's face, but I didn't need to. A wave of power rippled through me. It was a magical warning shot of sorts.

"You test what little patience I have, sneaking onto my property and demanding my soulmate."

"She is not yours, Andre."

"She has always been and will always be mine." His hands slammed down on the balcony, his power fissuring out. Bishopcourt shook violently as the blast tore through it. I braced myself against shockwave, even as it knocked Lila to the ground.

I was moving before the cambion pushed herself up.

"Get back inside," Andre said, not turning around. Bits of the balcony crumbled beneath his hands as he dug his fingers into the railing and fought to maintain control of his power.

"Not without you," I said.

Andre swiveled to face me, annoyance and love flashing in his gaze.

Peering through her curtain of hair, Lila's eyes darted to the roofline, and she smiled. I followed her line of sight, and my breath caught.

Perched along the roof were dozens upon dozens of demons.

Well, damn.

They dove.

"Andre!" I shouted.

Hearing the urgency in my voice, he shoved me to the

ground. My fear forced a burst of power out. It wasn't very strong, and my aim was sloppy, but Andre grunted as it passed through him, the demons screeched as it hit them, and I heard a muttered "motherfucker" from Lila.

"Inside!" Andre roared, grabbing my upper arm and yanking me up.

Too late. Several demons latched onto his skin, their claws and talons slicing through it. More descended on me. I threw my power out, this time directing it towards our attackers.

I'd been ambushed for the second time this evening, and I was having none of it.

Several sets of footsteps pounded towards us. A moment later, Andre's men and some of his coven joined the fighting. Already my soulmate was a blur of movement. He pulled out a dagger he'd been carrying on him and began mowing through his opponents.

I had no such weapon.

The creatures kept coming at me and I blasted them off with bursts of energy, but it only stunned them. I needed a strategy. I knew that other beings that wielded magic could shape the power itself into a weapon.

Once I blew the latest round of demons away from me, I imagined honing my power into a long, thin blade. When the next creature came at me, my power slashed out, and I envisioned it slicing my opponent through the chest.

He stumbled back as my magic hit him, and a tiny scratch appeared across his pectorals.

Epic fail.

While I was distracted, several demons swooped low

and plucked me from the balcony. I twisted in their arms as we rose rapidly into the air.

"No!" Andre shouted. His power grew, and I could feel the electricity of it charging the air.

The flap of demon wings was a drumbeat, each one taking me farther and farther from Bishopcourt. Andre's mansion was beginning to look like a toy.

My skin brightened as my own power built, fear and anger driving it onwards. Energy flooded my system, more by far than I knew what to do with. Thunder roared overhead as magic blasted out of me, ripping me from the demons' grips. I began to fall from the sky, the ground rising to meet me.

I heard Andre's shout, saw his form blur as he raced towards me. Several more demons swooped in and caught me before he could.

I kept shooting my power out, trying to shake them, but the demons had swarmed. They packed in tightly around me until I could see nothing but red eyes and leathery skin. Nowhere for me to go. They growled as I struggled. A meaty fist smashed into my temple, and the world went black.

WHEN I WOKE, it was to a nightmare. A dozen grotesque faces peered down at me, and twice as many hands held me down. I struggled against them, but for the second time that night, I felt exhausted.

I cast my senses out. Wherever we were, it was dark and cool. I could barely smell the earth over the iron tang of blood.

Pain flared down my forearm, and I realized that was what woke me. I let out a moan as warm liquid trickled down my arm.

Blood.

That fucking hurt, and held inert like this, I couldn't see what was happening. Just the excited, hungry looks of the demons as they stared at my limbs.

Another sharp pain sliced down my arm. I hissed in a breath, even as my fangs throbbed.

What's happening to me?

I tried to move again. A set of claws clamped my head in place, but even with the tight grip, I managed to tilt it enough to catch a glimpse of my body.

My blood was everywhere. On my arms, dripping onto the altar I laid upon, collected in goblets and removed from sight.

As I watched, a demon slashed its claws down my pale flesh, reopening the wound that had only just stitched itself together. I screamed, more from shock than from pain. Another chalice appeared, and the demons used it to collect the liquid seeping out of me. I tried to catch my breath and control my panting, but you couldn't put a leash on fear.

Lila's face joined the others, her dark eyes glittering. "Regina Inferna, finally a goddess in the flesh."

Even in the dim light I could see she was real. Alive.

"How?" I croaked, my throat parched. I watched her die after I'd delivered the deathblow. I saw her last breath leave her lips and heard the final beat of her heart.

Her lips curved into a satisfied smile. "Resurrection."

Resurrection? That was actually a thing? Why had no one told me that—

I screamed as they began cutting into me again.

Lila reached out and dragged a finger down my cheek. "I know it hurts. I remember how it felt." Her eyes grew distant, and her finger dug into my flesh.

My skin blossomed as the siren joined me. "Let me go," I commanded, my voice much weaker than it ought to be.

Nothing happened. I hadn't been expecting the siren to affect Lila or the demons, but I had hoped they'd listen to me because I was their queen. Especially the demons. In the past they'd listened to my commands. Sometimes. But when they didn't, it was because ...

Because someone of higher rank had ordered them otherwise. There was only one person who outranked me in hell.

The devil.

Andre

"WHERE IS SHE?" Andre demanded, stalking through his house. He threw his dagger to the side. Best not have it with him when he confronted the girl. Not when he was like this.

His shirt was in bloody tatters. God, he wanted to run something through with a sword. Those beasts had grabbed Lila shortly after they'd seized his mate, whisking away the one person he'd really enjoy gutting.

"Where is my soulmate?" he bellowed. "Leanne!"

How had she not seen this? Why had she not warned him?

He stormed into the room she shared with Oliver. He found the two snuggled in bed, ear buds in their ears, a laptop between them. Both of their eyes were closed, and their heads leaned together.

"Leanne!"

She blinked her eyes, groggy. "Hmm?" She squinted through the darkness.

Andre came over to the side of her bed, grabbed her upper arms, and shook her. "Gabrielle. Where is she?"

That roused her. "With you?"

"Guess again," he said, his hold tightening.

"Ow, okay, okay, give me a minute," she said.

"We don't have a minute."

"Why do you people think I'm all knowing? Not even Nona knew everything."

Next to her Oliver stretched, and a yawn shook his entire body. He perked up further at the sight of Andre. "What's going on?"

A muscle in Andre's cheek feathered. "Gabrielle's been taken."

"Again?" Oliver said. "This is obviously becoming a thing."

When the girl's eyes unfocused, he released her. She gazed at nothing for a long time. Long enough for the fairy to get dressed. She sucked in a sharp breath, and a shudder racked her body.

Dread flooded Andre's system; it was becoming a familiar bedfellow.

Leanne closed her eyes.

"What've you seen?"

She shook her head. "It doesn't matter. You'll see it for yourself soon enough." Her eyes fluttered open, and it heartened Andre to see resolve in them. "We are going to rescue Gabrielle," she said. "And we might be too late."

Gabrielle

THE DEVIL ORDERED this. *He ordered this.*

The betrayal hurt worse than I thought it would. I shouldn't have been surprised, but damn me, I was. I'd expected different because *he* was different.

At least I thought he was.

I was a stupid, stupid girl, and I got played worse than the rest of those fools that made deals with the devil.

"... We need your blood," Lila was saying. I honed in on her as the demons continued to slice through my skin. "It has the power to build armies."

The second awful insight of the evening hit me like a freight train.

They were using my blood to make more demons. Enough, perhaps, to take over the world.

My struggles renewed. "Let me go!"

The demons' grips tightened.

I thrashed, screaming at them. When that didn't work my voice dropped low, menacing. "I swear, if you don't let me go, I will hunt each one of you down and kill you."

Okay, it was an empty threat, but—

I cried out as one of them cut behind my knee. I felt the

236

press of cold metal and the drip of blood as they collected it in another container.

"Stop, please," I begged, my eyes finding Lila's. A shameful tear snaked out of my eye.

She petted my hair back. "You look so pretty when you cry. It's going to be alright."

More pain followed her words as the demons continued to bleed me. I reached for my power again, but it was so weak. The demons didn't even pause when it battered against them.

Lila clucked her tongue. "That'll only make this take longer."

I was going to die, and the very things I unwittingly created were going to be responsible for it. They'd make it slow, too.

I had to remember who was really responsible for this. The devil promised that he'd never hurt me. He'd lied, as usual, and I was the sucker that believed him.

Black dots danced in front of my eyes. My breathing became labored. What was the point? I felt my muscles relax and my mind began to slip, slip away.

"Get her some blood!" someone shouted—Lila, I think.

Off in the distance, I heard a shriek. It cut off abruptly, followed by a gurgle. A chorus of screams rose in response. The smell of foreign blood grew stronger, and I forced my eyes open. I hadn't realized I'd closed them.

A demon holding a cup pushed through the group and came to stand next to my head. I could smell the metallic scent of blood and the fear that had been taken with it. The creature extended the glass, pressing it to my lips.

Those earlier screams ... they'd butchered and bled someone, and now they were feeding me that person's blood. Bile rose up again. I tried to turn away from the cup, but the other demons had me pinioned. I pressed my lips tightly together.

Another creature grabbed my jaw and squeezed, placing more and more pressure on it. Still I kept my jaw clamped shut. I wouldn't do it. They couldn't get me to drink it.

But they could.

Claws tore into the skin of my cheeks; my jaw felt as though it was about to break. My lips reluctantly parted, and the demon began to pour the blood down. I began to cry in earnest as I unwillingly drank it. The siren wept with me. Lila watched the entire time, a creepy little smile on her face.

The blood kept coming, and when I'd finished the glass they'd poured down my throat, they replaced it with another, forcing the liquid down until I no longer fought them.

The demons hadn't cut me for a while, and I thought, rather optimistically, that perhaps they were done. As soon as they removed the chalice from my lips, I felt the first prick of pain. I thought wrong.

They began to cut into me again and again, collecting my blood and carting it off. I had to deal with the very real possibility that from now on, my nights would be like this—sliced and bled to create an unholy horde of them. And then they'd wipe out the earth.

I wanted to scream and rally against that. I wanted to strike down each and every one of them. But even after the blood, I was still weak, and with each cut I grew weaker.

My eyes drooped again, and again I heard more screams. A minute later they forced more blood down my throat. My strength returned, awful consciousness returned. My fear and my horror returned. Then the cutting began once more.

Over and over again it went, each round more brutal than the last, and I recovered less and less. How long had it been? Minutes? Hours?

Darkness rimmed the edges of my vision. It crept closer and closer. I couldn't push it away, not even a little. And then it embraced me completely.

CHAPTER 23

Andre

THEY WERE TOO late.

The intricately carved rooms that made up the Mogao Caves Oliver led them to were already abandoned, the smell of burnt blood thick in the air. It mixed with the stench of the newly dead. On either side of him, time-faded paint clung to the earthen walls, depicting Buddhist imagery. Now bright speckles of blood partially obscured them.

A year ago Andre wouldn't have recognized the emotion that had his chest rising and falling faster and faster. Now he was familiar with the tight grip of fear.

Screams floated in from beyond the ancient walls. It was the sound of dying dreams, dying lives. Had the situation been different, Andre might've tried to help, but right now he had to find his soulmate. That ran on loop in his head.

The farther in they walked, the stronger the smell of flesh and blood.

"Oliver, Leanne, don't leave my side. And ... prepare yourselves."

Andre followed the smell, his strides purposeful. They passed through beautiful rooms cut from rock. Sacred rooms. But not Christian ones that could keep demons—and Andre—out. If they could, he would be a pile of ash resting at the threshold of this place.

The next room they walked into halted Andre in his tracks. He'd been expecting the carnage, his nose had prepared him. But there were some things the eyes were never ready for.

The room was full of butchered innocents. Slashed throats, glassy eyes, mouths open in silent screams. Blood and gore covered them and the ground they lay upon. It was a shock every time evil showed its true face.

A small noise slipped out of Leanne's lips.

Andre's fear only deepened as he studied the wounds of the dead. They'd been torn apart, no one death exactly like the other, but each always had one consistent wound. A cut along an artery.

If they did this to innocents, what did they do to his mate?

His mouth tightened as he passed through the room. None of the bodies were Gabrielle's. Her body would no longer exist on this realm if that were the case.

The smell of so much blood had distracted him from

Gabrielle's scent. Now he caught a whiff of it, and it overwhelmed his senses.

He was moving before he was even cognizant of it.

Her blood.

Her blood.

Her blood.

Too much of it outside of her body. Far too much to survive. And that excluded all the blood that had hit the ground and vaporized.

Andre almost fell to his knees then. Leanne had warned him they'd probably be too late. He'd braced himself for it, but just like seeing great evil, there was no preparing for the reality of losing the love of your life.

No matter how many times it happened.

Masochist that he was, Andre pressed on. When he entered the chapel, he saw her.

Dios mio.

He stopped at the threshold, his feet taking him no farther.

Gabrielle lay on a stone altar, her arms folded across her chest, her face serene. She wore a crimson gown, the color saturated with her blood and the blood of the dead. The fabric stuck to her skin, and he could see rivulets of the viscous liquid dripping down her arms and snaking through her hair. Even her bare feet were mostly coated with it.

Drip, drip, drip.

Blood snaked down the sides of the altar, drenching most of what had probably once been a holy surface. Only her face was untouched, and she looked ... serene.

So long as Andre lived, he would remember the sight of her so at peace amongst this bloodshed.

Behind him he heard the pattering of Oliver and Leanne's footsteps.

When they got to his side, the fairy gasped. "Is that—? Did she kill—?"

"*No.*" Andre couldn't believe Gabrielle was responsible for the carnage in the other room. He wouldn't.

"What happened?" Oliver asked.

They stared at the one person who might know, but she was as still as death.

Tha-thump.

She lives.

The sound of her heartbeat jolted him into action. Andre moved as fast as his legs could take him, crossing the room, his boots splashing through puddles of blood. Whatever had happened to her, she'd at least survived it. Finally, finally, some of Andre's fear dissipated. The desperate need to protect her grew in its place, borne from the possibility that she really was losing herself to the devil.

He dragged her off the altar and into his arms. With one hand, Andre cradled her head and shoulders against his chest, uncaring that the blood of so many men and women now seeped into his clothing. His soulmate, his beautiful, tormented soulmate.

He'd been here before, done this before. And now he'd do it again.

Andre brought his wrist to his lips. His fangs dropped, and he used them to slice open his skin. Blood welled and he pressed the wound to Gabrielle's lips.

She wasn't responding.

His wound sealed up, and he had to reopen it, again and again. On the seventh try, he felt her mouth latch onto his wrist. His body relaxed as she drank from his vein, and he pulled her closer.

"I will never give up on you, my sun," he whispered to her in Romanian. "I will pull you from the dark, just as you have me."

Leanne and Oliver watched from the doorway, not daring to come any closer.

Andre pushed the blood-matted hair away from his mate's forehead. Her skin brightened, either from the blood or the close contact, and after another minute or so, her eyes fluttered open.

"Soulmate," he said.

Her mouth left his wrist and her throat worked. She stared at him as he pulled her more fully into his arms, a strange look on her face. Her throat still worked and her nostrils flared. She began to shake in his arms. And then, all at once, she came apart.

She let out a shuddering sob. Her eyes grew faraway as the trembling increased. He'd seen this before, usually from men freshly removed from battlefields. Trauma.

She drew in a long breath and closed her eyes. When they opened again, she was back with him.

"My blood. They took it. The demons. They held me down and took it. Then they forced me to drink blood of the people they killed, so they could take more of mine."

Christo. The horror of it all weakened his knees; if he

hadn't already been kneeling, that would've brought him to the ground. They did this to the most powerful woman he knew. They did this to the person that released them. They did this to his soulmate.

The power he kept locked away rose, as it usually did when Gabrielle's life was threatened. Oliver and Leanne, who had crept closer at the sound of their friend's voice, were now pushed back by the force of it.

Something built at the back of his throat—a roar, a wail, *something*. The bulk of his power gathered around it, building, building—

A cry cut through his awareness.

"Oh my God. *Oh my God. Get it off of me.*"

He glanced down at his soulmate to see her clawing at the bloody robe she wore, horror plastered across her face.

His power dissipated as he focused on her. Now wasn't exactly the time or place to change. Demons were still wreaking havoc outside these walls—if the screams were anything to go by—and they could be back soon. Not to mention that on any other occasion, Gabrielle would be terrified to expose herself in such a place, especially when she didn't have clothes to change into.

But he couldn't bear to see her traumatized, and she couldn't bear to wear the clothes her tormentors must've given her.

"Oliver, Leanne, turn around."

"Don't need to ask me twice," Oliver muttered. "Boobs hold no sway over me."

Andre turned his attention back to his soulmate as her friends faced away from them. Gabrielle was already ripping the fabric, uncaring that she was exposing herself as she did so.

Andre shrugged off his jacket and wrapped it around her shoulders. He grabbed her bloodstained hands and clasped them in his own. She yanked against his hold, but he wouldn't let them go.

"Andre—" she sobbed out.

"Look at me," he commanded. "*Look at me.*"

Reluctantly she did so.

"Let me do this, love."

She frowned, her lower lip trembling—her entire body trembling. And damn if the sight didn't break something in him. He would tear out her enemies' hearts and dance upon their ashes for this.

She released a long breath and nodded.

Andre ripped the dress down the middle, scowling with each yank. The devil did this. He'd been given this covetous bond, this radiant woman, and he was destroying her piece by piece. Andre's resolve hardened into place. They would trump the devil at whatever game he was playing, and they would do it *soon*.

Once he'd ripped the dress off, he removed his shirt and used it to wipe off the blood that stained her skin. He couldn't get it all off, but he did the best he could, even toweling off her hair. His soulmate pulled his jacket closer around her.

"Thank you," she whispered.

He paused, then grabbed her chin. "Never thank me for something like this."

Before she could respond, he kissed her. She latched

onto him, falling into the kiss like it was the only thing tethering her to the earth. He clutched her close, breaking off the kiss to whisper. "I will always come for you. I will always follow you, and I will always, always try to save you."

Gabrielle

I LAY CRADLED in Andre's arms as he, Leanne, and Oliver led me back to Bishopcourt. As far as coping went, on a scale of one to ten, I was at a two. Physically, I might be in the arms of my soulmate, but mentally, I was still pinned to that altar, being sliced open over and over again.

Lila and those demons disrobed me at some point. I'd been unconscious and they'd changed me. And they were minions of hell.

Don't think about that.

I must've let out a sob because Andre tightened his hold. "You're safe, soulmate."

He whispered to me in Romanian, pressing me close to his chest. He'd finally gotten the damsel in distress that he always wanted. I was pretty sure he now regretted ever wanting her.

The demons took so much blood. They had to have brought hundreds—if not thousands—more to life. That many could destroy entire cities within a day. The world was in serious trouble.

It was a sobering thought that I really was the anti-Christ even against my will. I didn't want to bring the blight to earth, but I had. The time for denial was over.

"I have to see him." I whispered more to myself than anyone else.

The devil, the man who forced me to hell and ordered me to be cut and bled, would be waiting for me on the other side of dawn.

Andre didn't respond to my words, so I continued to speak. "He did this, and now I have to see him."

Andre gathered me closer to him. "I swear I will spend every last breath hunting him down."

Bloody tears slipped out of my eyes. There was no armor strong enough to protect me from the devil.

I drew deep on my own need for retribution and vengeance.

"*I* will be the one to stop him." My voice came out colder and stronger than I'd planned. "I will be the one to end this once and for all."

CHAPTER 24

Gabrielle

THE BRUSH OF lips against my wrist roused me. My eyes snapped open, taking in the vaulted onyx ceilings and the agonized faces that seemed to be carved into the stone itself.

I jerked my hand away from the *thing* that kissed it, my chest rising and falling faster and faster as I became more aware of my surroundings. I pushed myself into a sitting position, noticing absently that I'd woken up in the bed I'd dreaded so much only days ago. Now betrayal overrode fear.

The devil watched me, his face passive. He'd been bent on his knee next to the bed when I woke up. He stood.

"You said you'd never hurt me." My voice broke as I spoke.

He winced, and the sight of it infuriated me.

"Don't pretend you feel something," I snapped.

I needed off this bed. I needed to pace.

"Oh, but I do," he said, those strange eyes of his taking me in. "For the first time in a long time, I do feel."

"Your demons held me down and cut me over and over again." My voice broke. "I know you were the one that ordered it."

"I did what I had to do for us both."

There. He admitted it—and savaged my heart while he was at it.

"You did it to *punish* me," I clarified. I knew enough about him to know that he'd punish me for betraying him like I had over the last few days.

"No," he said obstinately.

I would've been surprised had I actually believed him.

He grabbed my shoulders. "I am telling the truth."

I pushed his hands away, turning my face from him. I couldn't stand to look into those eyes.

He grasped my face and rotated it so that I was forced to gaze at him. "I did it for us, and I would do it a *thousand* times over." Wrath clouded his features.

A thousand times over.

I barely survived it once.

I needed to get away from this monster. I scrambled off the far side of the bed. He stood as I rounded it, seeking to cut me off. The doorway out was on the other side of him.

I ignored his presence as I made a beeline for the exit. My body was too small to contain all the anger, all the pain, all the terror that coursed beneath my skin.

The devil didn't like me ignoring him. He caught my arm and spun me around.

"Let me go." I pushed at his hands.

"*Listen* to me."

"Let me go!" Now I struggled in earnest.

"You will not be mad at me."

"Fuck you. I'm not mad at you—I *hate* you."

Our connection throbbed, weeped. We were wrapped up in each other, our destructive natures circling one another.

"No," he said, grabbing my upper arms and squeezing them.

I pushed against him. "Yes," I hissed. "I hate you so much it's hard to breathe."

His face was the epitome of anger. His eyes traveled over my features, his upper lip curling. Then he reeled me in and he pressed a kiss against my lips.

I pushed against him, fought as his mouth pried mine open. And then I tasted him, the brimstone and ash and blood. The taste of endless death and pain. My power flared, and I slammed it into him. He stumbled back, but once he regained his footing, he moved into my space again.

"How dare—"

I slapped him, putting the full brunt of my strength behind it. His head whipped to the side, and he froze in that position.

My breaths came in angry heaves, and I didn't care. I was done being used, done bending to an unbending man. Done with this.

He touched his cheek. "You hit me." His face twitched like it couldn't decide what expression to wear.

I did, and I wasn't ashamed to admit that it felt good. I'd be high-fiving angels right now if I could.

Suddenly, the devil whirled on me. He grabbed my neck and swiped my legs out from under me. I hit the ground hard, and the devil came down with me. All I could sense from him was his barely contained nature. All that evil pressing down, peering at me through humanoid eyes.

I so did not sign up for this shit.

His face hovered right over mine, and the fingers around my throat dug in.

"Do it," I wheezed. "Hurt me worse than your demons did. Give me another reason to hate you." It was so much easier to ignore our terrible connection this way.

He released my neck and slammed his fist into the floor. "Bloody fucking *hell! I'm sorry*," he said, his eyes flashing.

My breath caught in my throat. He'd never apologized before.

"You think I'm happy about this? That the key to my power lies in another? That I must be made vulnerable to her—to you? I've guarded myself against this for so very long, but the enemy still found a way in, and I welcomed Him with open arms."

"What are you talking about?"

"Our connection."

"What does that have to do with anything?" I asked.

"What *doesn't* it have to do?" He stroked my cheek as though he couldn't help himself.

"I've been planning my war and my great escape for millennia. I knew there'd be costs—I'd expected pain, sacrifice. I thought it would be physical. I hadn't expected you. I hadn't planned on watching you take my pain and making those sacrifices for me.

"More than anything else, I hadn't planned on my pain and sacrifice being emotional. I hadn't expected it to hurt here," he touched his chest, "where I can't so easily heal myself."

I didn't breathe.

The Deceiver had been deceived. He hadn't planned on using me to build his army on earth; he'd just improvised. He also hadn't planned to care about me, but through our connection he'd been forced to.

What had he said? He'd let the enemy in?

I stared up at him as realization set in.

Of course. *Of course.*

Soulmates were bonded pairs. Love, among other things, passed through that connection. And from all that I gathered, God and love were synonymous.

The devil *had* let his enemy in.

"Yes," he said, reading me, "you finally understand the chink in my armor."

"Why did you take me if you knew this?" I asked.

He pushed himself to his feet and extended a hand to me. I hesitated.

"Little bird, for once this really isn't a trap. I have answers for you. Take my hand."

Though I was loathe to touch him, I did so, grasping his hand. He hauled me up.

We left our room. "The reason I took you, despite the risks, is really quite simple: you give me access to Earth."

"Once upon a time, there were three fates." The devil and I walked through the castle gardens. I hadn't spent much time here, so close to where all those screaming souls were. The sound of so much agony chaffed against my spirit—and it was already so downtrodden.

The devil called this place the glass garden, and I understood why. Trees, bushes, and flowers were hewn from obsidian. They seemed to grow straight out of the lava rock beneath us, so lifelike I could see minuscule veins on the leaves, and rough bark on tree trunks.

I touched the petal of a flower we passed. It felt ... *alive*. This was a strange, disturbingly beautiful place.

I withdrew my trembling hand. I was putting myself back together piece-by-piece after last night, but I was still shaken by all that had happened.

"These three fates sought to appease the old gods," the devil continued. "So they formed husbands and wives for them. One of those gods was me."

He snapped off a nearby rose. "You were to be my gift."

Ah, the good ol' days when women could be given like presents.

"Some of the other gods had received husbands and wives, and some had married each other. Each union diluted the power of the gods—one pie, too many pieces. They fell, and the remaining gods claimed their power. I saw what these marriages did, and I knew I did not want

254

you."

The feeling was mutual.

Even as I thought that, my connection tugged me closer to the devil.

"Initially," he clarified, picking off the rose's obsidian thorns one by one and tossing them to the side. "Don't misunderstand—I very much liked the idea of my own woman—someone made specifically for me who would spend eternity at my side—but I was ambitious, and I wanted to share my power with no one.

"But the fates promised me that my wife would make me powerful, that she wouldn't lead to my destruction like the wives of so many other gods had. And this place ..." The devil surveyed our surroundings. I followed his gaze. Beyond the obsidian hedge that bordered the lush garden I could see the tips of flames reach high into the sky. Its brightness reached far, but it couldn't drive away a darkness above it. "This place can make even a god go mad, if left alone for long enough."

Methinks that was exactly what happened.

He led me to a dark stone bench, and we sat down, his body angled towards mine. "They gave me a glimpse of you." He reached out to touch my hair. "And I was gone. You'd taken me completely. They made me a mate who could unearth who I once was, before time and power and loneliness warped me into this."

"This is not just about you," I said.

Sure, somewhere in that twisted form of him, there was a kernel of love, and I had the ability to lure it out of him. My heart ached with the need. But what if he broke me first?

There was no use rehashing what happened to me last night. He knew about it, and he had to realize how close he'd already come to cracking my mind.

"I would never break you," he said.

"Stop reading my thoughts."

"I cannot. You were made for me. That is how much a part of me you are."

He rolled the stem of the glass rose in his hand. "I've always believed thorns rather than flowers incentivized people." He took my hand and pressed the rose into it, curling my fingers around it. "Thorns haven't worked with you. I'm trying flowers."

I stood, holding the strange flower in my hand. "I don't want this." I stared down at the obsidian rose in my hand, then looked up at him. "I don't want you."

I felt full with emotion. Hate and fear and pain filled me, but underneath it all was love. Through our connection, God did in fact penetrate this place. I swallowed down my rising sickness. My one last link to God lay in this connection. This connection to the devil.

This was so wrong.

He stood, and he caught me before I could leave. Cupping me cheeks, he said, "*Asiri.*"

I furrowed my brows.

"Say it," he said.

"Why? What's the point?"

"Say it."

I sighed. "Asiri."

He closed his eyes. When he opened them, more than

just an infinite swirling abyss stared back at me.

"Let me go," I said, latching onto his wrists. I'd pry them off of me if I had to.

"Don't you see it? We are *more*, Gabrielle. You know this. We hate more, but we can also love more.

"Let me in, consort. Let me into the heart of yours. I swear I won't betray it."

First an apology and now a request.

"You're already in my heart." Thanks to the connection I could feel him with every beat of that organ.

"By design I am, yes. But not by choice. Let me in."

"I wouldn't even know how."

"You need to give in. Give in."

"To what?"

"Your heart."

It was already taken, and the man that held it lived in a different realm.

I closed my eyes.

"Look at me."

I shook my head.

"Teach me how to be better. Open your eyes and show me how to live. How to love." His voice was so gentle, so soothing. I desperately wanted to believe that he wasn't an evil being.

A tear trickled out of my eye, and I felt his thumb brush it away.

"Please," he said.

All at once, it broke.

I broke.

The damn that held back my rising pull to him and all

the emotions that went along with it poured out.

My eyes snapped open and I drew in a shuddering breath. "*Asiri.*"

"Consort, I feel you. I finally, truly feel you." He smiled, and angels should weep at the sight. It was almost too much, and I was falling, falling, falling. Down into those eyes of his, down into our connection. There was nothing separating us except two sets of skin and the space between us.

He pulled me to him, and kissed me.

I could feel him. *Him.* This ageless, timeless thing. His soul was full of whitenoise, of shrieking souls and pain.

I wasn't sure where I was. My lips were on his, and I could taste him and feel him, but that was distant, background noise to the feel of him. I'd reached inside him, and he'd let me in. Of all the beings out there, Asiri seemed like the most closed off, and he let me in. Only his soul, or whatever this was, battered against mine. I was surrounded by a terrible howling noise, and I could feel the discontent that festered inside of him.

So I began to hum, softly at first. I pulled on the siren, brought her through the connection, and together she and I began to sing. The storm inside Asiri settled, the howling quieted, and it calmed the raging madness inside of him.

The air shifted, and we were back in his bedroom—our bedroom. He moved us to the bed I dreaded so much.

And then I was running my fingers over his wing scars. And then I was kissing them.

"No more pain," I whispered against his skin. He laid

me on the bed before joining me. For the first time ever, I saw an expression on his face that was free of the violent tendencies he was so well known for.

Only one thing lay in his eyes now.

Hope.

CHAPTER 25

Gabrielle

WHAT AM I doing?

I felt like I was surfacing from a dream. One where monsters and gods played with mortals, and I'd tamed the worst of them.

My thighs rested over sculpted shoulders. A mouth pressed against my core, giving me the most intimate kiss. Not a shred of fabric covered me. Without thinking, I fisted my hands—hands that gripped already mussed up hair.

The color was wrong.

Not Andre's.

What in the bloody hell am I doing?

Every fiber of my being focused on the naked man kneeling between my legs. He paused in his ministrations to kiss my inner thigh, and I saw his face.

My heart almost died of fright.

The devil was going down on me.

OhGodohGodohGod.

This was my own personal nightmare.

I shook off what felt like the aftereffects of a drug.

"Gabrielle." His lips moved against my skin.

I yelped and tried to disentangle myself from him. I'd willingly let the devil into my heart, and I'd lost myself in the process. I could still feel him there, making himself comfortable. He was in me and I was in him.

His hands captured my thighs and held them in place. "No sense being shy now, little bird," he said, his hungry gaze moving over me. "You are going to finally, completely be mine."

Cue internal screaming.

No, no, no, no, no.

I squirmed against his hold. "That can't happen."

His eyes narrowed, and I felt the shift in his mood as though it were my own.

"You say this to me now, even exposed to me as you are?" He glanced meaningfully at the juncture between my thighs—which was, to my utter mortification—spread before him.

"I love someone else."

He glared down at me. "You gave me your heart, and I gave you mine."

I don't want your charred husk of a heart, and I want whatever I gave you back.

I'd made a grave, grave mistake, and I might lose the only man that had ever mattered to me because of it. Kisses were one thing, but this? Relationships died every day for less. The devil and I might not have done the deed, but we were naked in his bed, and I'd been participating in some heavy petting. Andre would have every reason to leave me.

Contemplating that hurt too much. I pressed the heel of my hands against my eyes. I might've already lost him, and I knew it. I knew it.

I was a goddamn fool.

Whatever I'd soothed inside the devil now fell back to chaos. He slid out of bed, naked from head to toe, and all I wanted to do was call him back to me. I *hated* that. Our connection had betrayed me. I had divided loyalties, and I really, really shouldn't. Not after all the pain the devil had put me and countless others through.

He paced. I could see the scars trailing down his back where his wings had been ripped from him. "It's the vampire, isn't it? Even after everything, it's still him you want?"

"It will always be him," I whispered.

The devil turned from me and leaned a hand against the wall as though catching his breath. He let out a roar and slammed his fist into the stone surface. Flakes of obsidian chipped away beneath his fist and the entire building shook from the power of the blow.

"*No*, Gabrielle." He swiveled to face me. "You are mine, and I vow to you, those words of yours *will* change. You've just made this a whole lot easier for me."

Goosebumps broke out along my skin at his ominous vow.

"It really doesn't matter at this point," I said. "I lose

something, no matter what."

The devil drew in a long breath and collected himself. "The longer we live, the more we lose. Innocence, virginity, friends, time, and if you live long enough—and you will—memories.

"Few things survive. Andre won't survive you, but I will." His calm demeanor was all the more frightening now that I could see right inside him. I could feel the torment of his emotions battering against mine. "You've already opened your heart to me. Your mind and body will follow soon enough."

He grabbed his clothes and began pulling them on. I gathered the bed sheets to me, covering myself. Once he was dressed, he headed to my armoire and threw an outfit onto the bed. "Get dressed. The time for secrets is over. I will show you your legacy."

COMING HERE WAS a mistake.

Not that the devil had left me much choice. As soon as I'd donned another gown, he'd roughly grabbed me and transported us out of the bedroom.

We stood amidst the burning souls, the flames fueling the devil's inhuman anger. Every so often I sensed another emotion flicker beneath that rage of his. Hurt was the most common, followed by frustration. Love wasn't something you could compel another to feel. He understood this, but he didn't have much patience or practice waiting for me to love him. From what I gleaned from our connection, he felt entitled to it.

263

But ever since his final words back in the bedroom, he'd acted calm, as though he weren't a ticking time bomb set to go off at any minute.

He raised his hands to the fire, which roared and crackled. "This, consort, is power." Souls screamed around us, clawing at themselves like they might be able to tear the pain off of themselves.

"So you can make souls feel pain. How big of you."

The devil was not right in the head. Maybe I'd broken him before he had the chance to break me.

"Their pain is what gives me power."

Like I said, not right in the head.

The devil narrowed his eyes. "You misunderstand. I'm not talking about *enjoying* their pain; I'm talking about using it. An engine needs fuel to run and a person needs food and drink to live. I am no different. As the fire burns these souls, it creates usable energy, energy that feeds my power, and now yours."

Mine?

I set that horrifying thought aside. Otherwise, it would distract me from the fact that the devil was giving up his trade secrets, one of which was that essentially, hell was nothing more than a glorified steam engine.

And the devil was the terrible machine it propelled.

"My power gets its source from pain—both emotional and physical. The more souls I have, the more power I collect.

"And now you create chaos and mayhem, fear and anger and pain topside," he continued. "I could never feed on the emotions of the living before you became my queen."

Alarm raced through me. "And now you can?"

He inclined his head. "And now I can."

I almost stopped breathing. "How?" I whispered.

"Through our bond."

I stumbled back. The roar of the flames the screams of the damned became background noise to the pound of my heart.

It was so much worse, so much worse than I'd imagined.

"You think you are the only one held here against her will? My eyes see no real sunlight, my lips taste no real food. I smell only brimstone and rot. I live off of corrupted souls."

He held his arms up and gestured around him. When he faced me again, something incredibly tragic entered his features. "This has been my prison for as long as I can remember.

"But now that you're here, that all will change."

He harvested the dead and I harvested the living.

I placed my fingers to my temples and rubbed. This entire time I hadn't realized ... All that power. I thought it came for free. I should've known better. Everyone pays a tithe. Especially me.

I dropped my hands. A long time ago Andre told me that the devil did all that he did for one sole purpose.

Power.

My gaze slowly lifted to his. "What will you do with all that power?"

He cocked his head. "Isn't it obvious? We take over other realms, one by one. Earth first," he said, sauntering to me, "because that one's the most powerful and the most corrupt. And now it's accessible.

"Limbo will fall shortly after that. Then the Other-world—I've already begun to claim it, but this will be the proverbial nail in its coffin. The fae are delightfully nasty things; it will be nearly effortless to bring their world into the fold. And eventually ... the Celestial Plane. Heaven."

Horror, true earth-shattering horror, dawned on me.

He meant to take over every world in existence, and I was the key to them all.

CHAPTER 26

Gabrielle

I WAS BACK.

The earth spit me out into snow, and I dug my hands in it. The devil wanted this place, and he would use me to get it.

World domination. Excuse me, *worlds* domination. *That* was his end game.

A shudder worked its way through my body. Now that I was here, an increasingly large part of me wanted to see his plans actualized. It was the same part of me that fed off of suffering.

However, knowing how my power worked allowed me to better control it, and through it, my tumultuous emotions.

The devil had shared his secrets, but I hadn't shared

mine. I didn't dare think about them. My mind was no longer a safe place for even me to linger.

But I was finally ready to act on those secrets.

Well, as soon as I made it back to civilization, I thought as I took in my surroundings. Snowcapped mountains jutted up around me. I saw no houses, no streets, no signs of life—other than frost covered grass. And that looked pretty dead to me too.

I was dusting snow and dirt off myself when I heard the hiss of breath. A moment ago, where there'd been empty space, my friends and Andre now stood. And Andre ... Andre's heart was breaking, I could see it on his face.

He must've smelled the devil on me or seen my sins in my expression.

He stepped forward, then fell to a knee, like his legs could no longer support him. The weaponry strapped to his body clinked as he did so. "What did he do to you?"

I wasn't going to get a chance to see that smile of his before I confessed. I stumbled over to him, kneeling in the snow in front of him. We were close, but we weren't touching.

Andre was having none of that. He scooped me up around the waist and pulled me close to him.

Somehow this was even worse. To be held in his arms while I confessed.

His nostrils flared at the smell of my guilt and—hopefully—my remorse.

I glanced at my friends. They were now going to witness this conversation. Oliver looked like he wanted a bag of popcorn.

I exhaled a shaky breath. "The devil and I ... did things."

"What things." Andre's voice was flat, but I could see the world breaking in his eyes.

How to explain the sensation of letting the devil in. It hadn't felt like it did with Andre, this warm presence that was a part of me. The devil staged an aggressive takeover. He'd seized my heart and decided to occupy it. I'd lost myself in the process, by the time I surfaced I'd found myself in an intimate situation with him.

Andre squeezed me tightly and shook his head. "Forget it. It doesn't matter."

"Of course it matters," I whispered.

"No, it doesn't. What matters is how you felt about it, and how you feel about me."

At his words, bloody tears dripped down my face. "I can't fight him off, Andre. He ordered me to be held down and bled and not twenty-four hours later, I allowed him to get close to me." Admitting that hurt something fierce. "How do I feel about it? Disgusted. Horrible. Evil."

"*Enough.*" Andre's voice cut through the night.

My mouth snapped shut.

"Do you love me?" he asked.

I swallowed thickly and looked away.

"Do you love me?" he repeated, turning my head to face him.

"With everything that is good in me, *yes*," I said.

Most of the pain in his eyes seeped away at that. "That is all I need, Gabrielle. Through thick or thin, I am yours."

I searched his face. My heart was thawing, my mind was disbelieving. "You're serious," I said.

"You think I don't understand?" he said. "I have lived for seven hundred years, soulmate. I may have lost much in that time, but I have also gained some wisdom. I knew going into this what you faced. I hate that you shared something physical with that abomination, but not as much as I hate that he shares a bond with you." He tilted my chin up. "But most of all, I hate that this has fallen on your shoulders." He held me close. "When it comes to you, nothing is beyond my forgiveness. I am yours, soulmate. Are you still mine?"

Our bond had withered away, but even without it, and even after seeing into the devil's soul and being with him, I still chose Andre. I would always choose Andre.

I nodded.

He smiled, and I'd been wrong earlier when I thought the devil was the most attractive creature to ever exist. Because that title belonged to the man that held me in his arms. I felt small and unworthy and tainted, yet Andre stared at me like the sun rose and set on me.

He gave me a squeeze. "Say it."

"Andre, so long as I live, I am yours."

SHORTLY AFTER OUR conversation—and shortly after some meaningful looks from Oliver that demanded I fill him in once we were alone—the fairy tapped into the ley line and took us back to the Isle of Man.

Or at least he was supposed to.

I knew something was wrong immediately. I couldn't experience ley line traveling the same way fairies could, but I'd gotten used to Oliver's techniques. And these weren't it.

A second later, I understood why.

I hissed at the feel of natural light on my skin. It didn't burn like it would've a week ago, but whatever creature I now was, I preferred darkness to light.

As my eyes adjusted, I took in my surroundings. I wasn't back on the Isle of Man, nor was I amongst the snowcapped mountains I'd arrived at.

A huge stepped pyramid towered in front of me, and surrounding it were waves and waves of people and demons. More winged beasts crowded the sky. Every single one of them had their eyes trained on me.

Holy crap. This was going to be the devil's revenge, part two.

Gray claw tips dug into my skin, and I realized this demon must've snatched me on the ley line. He now dragged me forward. I tripped over my bare feet, my spider-silk dress slithering behind me. Last time I'd been in this situation, I hadn't acted fast enough.

I wouldn't make the same mistake twice.

Power built inside me. I was going to blast this dude to Aruba. I'd already pulled my arm back to release the energy when I realized that it wouldn't matter.

Too many of them.

I was laughably outnumbered, and if I tried anything, at the very least another demon would replace the one I obliterated. And that was being optimistic. Knowing my luck, I'd get the mob descending upon me.

The wind kicked up as we reached the base of the stone

structure, and off in the distance I caught sight of rolling storm clouds. They were heading this way, and fast.

I got a close look at the pyramid the demon now dragged me up.

Chichen Itza.

I was a little rusty when it came to world history, but I was pretty sure this was one of the places where the Aztecs ripped out the beating hearts of their victims.

Considering that I hadn't treated the devil's too kindly, I could only imagine what lay in store for me here.

The devil's revenge, part two, indeed.

I was so screwed.

Andre

MOTHERFUCKER!" OLIVER CURSED.

Andre glanced around and his heart dropped. "Where is Gabrielle?" They stood in front of Nona's ruined cabin and his soulmate was decidedly absent.

"Um," Oliver said.

"*What happened to her, fairy?*" Rage rising.

"A demon was waiting for me. He snatched her as soon as I tapped into the ley line."

Andre's fangs descended. "A demon was waiting for her," he repeated.

This was the second time in two days that she'd been captured along a ley line. First it was some goon working for the Politia. Now this. He could feel the storm brewing beneath his skin. God, he needed to hurt someone.

Oliver squeaked. "They ambushed me. It's not like I

gave her to them."

Yet the fairy was here and she wasn't. Again.

He grabbed the fairy's shirt and leaned in. "Take me to her."

Andre would be damned if they had a repeat of last night. And if there were demons waiting for them—all the better. He owed them for what they did to his mate.

Leanne, whose eyes were hazy, spoke up. "No, Andre. You'll have to sit this one out."

Andre turned his glare on the seer; the look was lost on her sightless eyes. "Why."

"Because where she's being held, the sun still shines."

Gabrielle

I MIGHT NOT have blasted the demon to smitherines, but I was definitely dragging ass when it came to following him up the pyramid. He growled and yanked on my arm. I glared up at him as I tripped up another two stairs.

"You have *got* to be kidding me."

I whipped around at the sound of Oliver's voice, a smile blooming along my face. He and Leanne stood at the base of the pyramid, right in the middle of the crowd of demons and not-so-nice-looking people.

"Shi-it, Corpsie," Oliver said, assessing the crowd, "you really did a number to yourself this time." When he caught the eye of a human next to him, he said, "What? Never seen a fairy before? Yeah, that's right, back off."

The demon jerked me nearly off my feet, and I stumbled up more steps.

273

"Freaking-A." That was it. I hadn't used my power up until now because I had no means of escaping this place. But now that my friends were so close, I was done with the man-handling.

My skin glowed, and I heard gasps ripple through the crowd at the sight, reminding me that I had a huge audience. I wasn't going to think about why they'd gathered. I *wasn't.*

Energy formed in my palm, and I threw it out at my captor. The demon flew back. I didn't wait for him to hit the stone.

Demonic howls rang through the skies above me as I ran down the staircase. I noticed ominously that no one else dared to step onto the pyramid.

With each step I took, the stairs shook and the sky rumbled. The already howling wind picked up and that storm I'd seen on the horizon was now directly overhead. Flashes lit up the clouds and the entire clearing.

Lightning struck the top of the step pyramid. I covered my eyes. Once the brightness dimmed, I lowered my arm—and froze.

All that is holy.

Standing at the top of the ancient structure was the devil.

CHAPTER 27

Gabrielle

THE DEVIL LIFTED his hands in the air, and the crowd bellowed. The excitement here was full of lust—for battle, for chaos and bloodshed. Rows upon rows of demons and humans watched him.

I kept backing up until I bumped into my friends. The crowd closed in on us from all sides.

"How did he get here?" Oliver asked.

I stared up at the devil as he surveyed the land. "I have no idea."

"Think he'll go away?"

"No," Leanne said. "He came to claim earth, and he came for Gabrielle."

"Me?" I squeaked. He already got me in hell.

He *shouldn't* be here. Traveling to earth was my power.

But somehow he'd managed it.

The devil began descending the steps. Cameras and phones were aimed at him, and dread pooled in my stomach. Clips of this would hit the Internet. Word would get out of his existence on earth. There was power in fear, power that the devil knew how to harness.

Another world to feed upon.

"Whelp, coming here was a bad idea," Oliver commented.

The devil's eyes searched the crowd. After a moment, they found mine. He extended an arm towards me. And then he smiled. "Come forward, my queen."

I froze at his voice, as did the audience. The crowd parted, and an aisle was created that led directed from the stepped pyramid right to yours truly.

Shit, shit, shit.

A thousand different faces turned to me, some of this world, some not.

Members of the crowd had pulled Leanne and Oliver away from me—the latter of whom was giving his captor the stink eye.

"Bow to your queen," the devil continued. "My consort."

And now a thousand different beings bent at the waist. My eyes darted from them back to the devil. Our connection pulsed and then I felt a pull from his end. The bastard was siphoning off my energy.

You aren't using it.

I narrowed my eyes at him.

He smiled at me, stepping down stair after stair. "She is

mother to the demons here, our lady of chaos."

Thunder rumbled overhead, flashes of light brightening the dark clouds.

"What's going to happen when he gets to me?" I threw the question over my shoulder to Leanne. Those that held her frowned at me, like I was supposed to be in-the-know when it came to the devil. Ha!

"I already told you, Gabrielle. He's going to claim you."

My eyes bulged. "Like in the Biblical sense?"

"I don't know. Maybe. Definitely a kiss at the very least."

I was still stuck on *maybe*. My attention flittered back to the devil, who stalked down the pyramid steps and towards me with purpose.

Fuck maybe.

My power surged and I blasted it forward, making sure to avoid hitting Oliver or Leanne. Humans and demons flew into the air, knocking others over like bowling pins.

Lighting struck the ground with a thunderous boom a hundred yards from the pyramid. A chorus of screams punctuated the blast.

I strode forward. First I grabbed Leanne's hand and then, after blasting another round of beings off of Oliver, I grabbed his too.

Another bolt of lightning speared a tree at the edge of the clearing. It caught fire, the branches going up in flame.

Run, little bird, and hide yourself good, because when I find you, you'll regret crossing me.

I stared up at him. Fifty yards and hundreds of people lay between us, but when our gazes locked, I could feel him in me and me in him. We were back in his castle, his soul laid bare. Anger and hurt so deep it was bottomless rose up to greet me, and even now I reached out and began to hum. We were the point and counterpoint in the universe. He was a wound and I was the needle and thread that would sew him up.

I fell into those eyes and under that spell once more. I sucked in a bite of air, and when I released it, our surroundings disappeared.

THE CHANGE OF scenery was so sudden, and the devastation in front of me so extreme, I staggered back.

"Whoops," Oliver said. "Wrong exit. Hold on."

"*Wait*," I said.

San Francisco sat across the bay, the tightly packed buildings dotting the landscape. Only, much had changed since the last time I'd seen it.

The Bay Bridge canted sideways, part of the roadway dipping towards the water. Beyond it, I could see the partially exposed skeletons of several skyscrapers, like some great beast had taken a claw to them.

"What happened to this place?" I asked, my voice desolate.

"Demons," Leanne said.

I swiveled to her. Her eyes, which had been going in and out of focus, were sharp once more.

"This is the work of demons?" I asked.

"Mainly. Some of it was just collateral damage from human and angel counterattacks. They're fighting back."

The world blurred as I blinked back tears. Indirectly I'd

caused all of this.

"Oliver, can you show me more?"

"You know I hate to be the voice of reason," Oliver said, "but we shouldn't linger on ley lines more than necessary. Especially not when that possessive vampire of yours is waiting for you back on the Isle of Man. I don't know if you've noticed, but patience isn't his strong suit."

"Please," I said. "I want to see what I've done."

"She'll be fine," Leanne said. "Show her two more cities."

Athens was smoldering, the Parthenon all but wiped away. Rio de Janeiro had been all but leveled, and the city's Christ the Redeemer statue was nothing more than a pile of rubble.

I gasped when we returned to the Isle of Man. We ended up next to Nona's cottage.

An instant later, Andre was clasping me to him. He pressed a kiss to the crown of my head before pulling away. "Soulmate, are you okay?"

"I'm fine."

He searched my face. "What has put the darkness in your eyes?"

"The devil has arisen to conquer the world," Leanne said, back to focusing on nothing. "He uses borrowed power to live and breathe, and he has come here to destroy."

Dread settled beneath my skin. While I'd been fighting for my life, the devil had been taking over the world. I felt him pulling from my connection even now.

"The devil is here?" Andre said, releasing me.

"*Yes*," Leanne hissed. "And he comes for you and your mate. Beware of Bishopcourt. The battle between worlds has begun, and the heart of it will play out inside its walls. To go there is to face certain death, but you must if you wish to save the world."

All at once her eyes rolled back and she pitched forward. I caught her as she fell.

Dazedly, she blinked up at me. Her gaze sharpened. "You know what you must do."

My jaw set in grim determination. The time for running was over. "I need to end this."

"You need the quill," Andre added.

I turned to him, forgetting for a moment that I'd told him about the celestial quill in the letter I'd left him several days ago. "I do."

Andre whipped out his phone, and called one of his men.

Quill? The devil's voice flowed like water through my mind.

I released Leanne to massage my temples, trying to not think about anything.

"Soulmate?"

What are you hiding from me?

"Stop it," I gritted out.

"Who's she talking to?" Oliver said.

"The devil," Leanne answered.

Andre closed the phone. "Bishopcourt is already surrounded," he said, taking my hand and rubbing his thumb over my knuckles. "Many beings are expecting our return."

Consort, I'm coming for you.

I made a noise at the back of my throat. "He knows something's off."

That was all the warning Andre needed. He scooped me into his arms. "It's alright, soulmate. We're ending this now. The fairy is right, you need that quill. I know where it is, and I'm going to get it for you."

The vampire has put the nail in his own coffin.

"Oh God," I moaned, "the devil's listening. He wants you dead, Andre."

"What's new?" he said. He rotated to my friends. "Oliver, Leanne, a taxi is coming for you. It'll drop you off at a nondescript apartment in the city." He looked down at me. "From here, soulmate, we go it alone."

The countdown had begun. Now it was a race to save the world.

WE'D LEFT OLIVER and Leanne back at the ley line, and began sprinting towards Bishopcourt, the place Leanne had foreseen us dying.

Both Andre and I chose to not touch on that topic.

"You know where the quill is?" I said as we ran. It made sense now, why Jericho was so cryptic and so unworried. He left the quill with the one person I was closest to.

"Yes."

I didn't bother asking how or where it was. That would only serve to feed the devil more information. Andre would show me, hopefully before it was too late.

It is already too late for him, the devil hissed.

He hadn't left my mind alone. I could feel him lurking at the back of my eyes, watching, waiting.

We sprinted across the countryside, using our inhuman strength to carry us over fields. By the time we could see Bishopcourt, I could tell we had some big problems on our hands. Angels and demons blanketed the skies. The Politia and dozens upon dozens of other individuals crowded Bishopcourt's lawn.

"*Christo*," Andre swore.

"Was it like this when you left?" I asked.

Andre shook his head. "Many supernaturals had come to our gates, but my men and my coven had held them off."

Something had obviously changed within a short period of time.

I could see vampires tearing out the throats of humans and demons alike. Demons lashed out at anyone they could, even their own when they got in the way. Angels seemed to focus their attention on the demons, but as I watched, I saw one bring down a vampire. Andre choked back a cry as several other individuals who'd been fighting turned to ash.

We wouldn't be the only victims the battle claimed tonight.

Stop thinking like that, I chided myself. *The future can change. End this quickly enough and no one else has to die.*

"The quill's inside?" I asked. I bit my lip as soon as the words were out. The less I knew, the better.

"We're going to use a passage you've never taken before," Andre said instead. "Follow me, keep quiet, and try not to attract any attention."

A.k.a., don't light up like a Christmas tree.

We ran toward a squat stone fence. Bishopcourt was still a ways away, and from what I could tell, no one had noticed us.

I've noticed, consort.

"The devil is still watching," I said.

Andre began shoving stones away from the wall. "Doesn't matter."

Beneath the stones was an old iron door. I could sense the cloaking spells that had long ago been cast, as well as several hexes and a few curses meant for unwelcome intruders.

Andre ripped the door open, the metal screeching as it was forced from its resting spot. I glanced to the battle to see if anyone had noticed, but there were too many beings to account for.

Andre reached for my hand and helped me down into a subterranean passageway. My feet hit the stone floor, and a moment later, Andre's did as well. He closed the metal hatch as best as he could, and then we were off, my bare feet splashing into puddles.

For Andre's benefit, I let the siren peek out enough to illuminate where we were going. One of the powers I'd acquired as queen of hell was the ability to see even in absolute dark. Andre, however, even with his night vision, couldn't see when there were no light sources.

Eventually, we came to the end of the passage. To my dismay, it ended with a wall of brick. If there'd ever been a door here, now it was long gone.

Andre whispered something in what sounded like Romanian, and I felt the release of a spell. He took my hand and pulled me *through* the wall.

For the merest of moments, I felt like I was trapped under the ground again. But then we stepped out, onto the other side.

I glanced around, my mouth parting in surprise as I took in Andre's secret library. I studied the wall we'd just come from. It was one of the few areas of the room that was bare of bookshelves or furniture, and now that I could sense magic, I could feel the spell woven into it.

Turning back to the rest of the room, my eyes honed in on the glass case sitting on Andre's coffee table. In it rested my salvation.

No! The devil's roar echoed inside me.

I clutched my head. No place to hide from him.

"Soulmate," Andre said, capturing my hands and lowering them, "if you are ready, use it now."

I nodded as the last remnants of the devil's voice died away.

I'd only taken a single step towards the quill when a clap of thunder shook the walls of Bishopcourt.

Andre and I looked at each other.

The devil was here.

CHAPTER 28

Gabrielle

ANDRE DASHED ACROSS the room.

"*Where are you going?*" Desperation laced my words.

Andre turned to me. He was already at the foot of the stairs that led to his bedroom. "I'm buying you time."

"Please don't go." If he went out there and tried to stop the devil, he could die. The king of the damned was no longer a phantasm; he was a god made into flesh.

In five long strides Andre was across the room, clasping me tight in his arms. He pressed a kiss to my lips.

"I love you. I'll be all right, soulmate. Use the quill and finish this."

Andre was being brave. I could be brave too.

I nodded.

Before I had a chance to do anything else, he released

me, and in a flash he was gone.

My body went weak with fear.

He'll be all right. He'll be all right.

The sooner I ended this, the safer we'd all be.

I dropped to my knees in front of the coffee table and lifted the glass that caged the quill. The sight of it took my breath away. I reached for it, only to hear a growl tear through the hidden tunnel that had led me here.

A moment later, the wall shuddered as something large rammed into it.

I swiveled just in time to see the wall explode inward, brick and plaster clattering to the ground. A plume of dust rose into the air. As it dissipated, a demon stepped through.

First I saw a large clawed foot. My eyes rose, taking in gray, muscular legs and then wide, wide shoulders. The demon's face was more beast than man, its huge teeth too big for its jaw, its nose nothing more than two slits, and the pupils of its red eyes horizontal.

It—or rather, *he* (I was studiously ignoring *that* part of his anatomy)—growled low in his throat.

Today would not be like yesterday. This creature would not hold me down and bleed me. He'd been sent to deliver me back to hell.

We stared at each other for a second, and then the moment popped like a bubble. I lifted my hand as he dove for me, fangs bared.

I threw my power out at him, sending him careening back out the opening he came through.

My gaze darted about the library. I needed a weapon.

286

Andre had to store some here. This room was, after all, a final defense against enemies. If someone else managed to break in, Andre would have a stash of weapons to defend himself with.

I scanned the walls and shelves, but saw nothing that came close to a lethal instrument.

The demon roared as he got to his feet.

Aw, crap.

I flicked my wrist at a nearby row of books, and using my power, flung them at the demon. He growled and lifted an arm as they smacked into him. With another twist of the wrist I emptied an entire shelf of books, silently apologizing to Andre as some of them exploded into an array of pages.

All I managed to do was piss off a demon and discern that no weapons were hidden behind the books.

I hoped Andre was having better luck than I was.

Andre

ANDRE RESTED A hand on his chair back and waited for the devil in his study. If it was time to end his long life, then he'd do it for Gabrielle. Gladly.

But not without a fight.

Even from here he heard the howling wind rip the front doors open. There were no screams to punctuate the devil's entrance. Bishopcourt had already emptied itself of its occupants. They'd either fled, or they were now outside, battling for their lives.

Heels clicked against the entryway floor, moving away

from where Andre waited until he could barely hear the footfalls. A minute later they returned, making their way towards him. They paused outside the study.

The door crashed open, and the devil stepped inside. The two men stared each other down.

"You can't have her," Andre said.

"She's already mine."

The devil had a sword sheathed at his waist. He'd come prepared like a mortal might.

The devil clasped his arms behind his back. "Who would've known all those centuries ago that it would come to this?" He surveyed the room before his eyes returned to Andre "You've made a good life for yourself. Pity it all has to end."

Andre reached over his shoulders and pulled his swords out. He rolled his wrists, loosening up his arms.

The devil raised an eyebrow but made no move to draw his own weapon. "I granted you not just mercy, Andre; I gave you *immortality*, a gift other men have died for. Had you lived your mortal life, you would've been no one. Your bones would've rotted to ashes by now. You wouldn't have been alive to steal my bond and my mate."

Andre flared his nostrils. "You stole my father's soul and damned me with this curse."

"I didn't see you regretting my goodwill when you took my queen to bed." The devil said the words aloofly enough, but an inferno scorched at the back of his eyes. "You are the only reason she rebels, the only reason she fights my will." The devil's eyes narrowed. "Can you even fathom how much this angers me? I am Rex Inferna, the king of hell. Legions fall to my feet. Billions fear me; billions more worship me. I am *no one's* second choice."

At that, Ande's mouth curved into an unpleasant smile. "You are most human's second choice. That is all you will ever be."

Now the devil didn't bother masking the fire blazing in his eyes. He pulled his sword from its scabbard. "The world tilts and changes and yet it comes back to where it all started: you, me, and Old Man Death."

Gabrielle

THE DEMON GRABBED me by the throat and tossed me across the room. I smashed into the coffee table, my body landing on top of the quill's glass case. It shattered beneath me, and dozens of different shards dug into my back.

I rolled away just as a meaty fist came crashing down, splintering the coffee table where I'd laid not a moment before. I stumbled to my feet, my eyes frantically searching for a weapon. Blood dripped from the nicks on my back. I heard a hiss as at least one drop hit the ground.

Seriously? Can't a girl catch a break? I thought as another demon began to take shape. This was like fighting a freaking hydra.

Spotting a walking stick in the corner of the room, I called it to me. And then I went Gandalf the Grey on the monster's ass. I smashed the cane across the demon's face, whacking him again and again until the staff broke and he collapsed to the ground.

A growl came from behind him as the other demon finished forming. Dropping the remnants of the cane, I ran down an aisle of shelves. I needed a better weapon than a walking stick. Feet pounded at my heels as the demon bore down on me. A hard body slammed into my back, tackling me to the floor.

I fell to all fours, pinned in place by a hulking piece of demonic flesh. If I died now, the world was—pardon my French—so fucked.

Ahead of me, my eyes caught sight of a chest tucked away in a forgotten corner.

Lifting a hand, I levitated it off the ground and catapulted it at the demon holding me down, the one who was giving an evil little laugh now that he had me where he wanted me. The chest beaned him, wood and metal exploding against his flesh. He slumped to the side, half on, half off me.

Praise Jesus and all the baby angels in heaven, a dozen different weapons scattered out of the remains.

Sliding out from under the demon's deadweight, I lunged for the sword closest to me. In one smooth movement I'd unsheathed it, and in the next I brought it down upon the demon's neck. His head didn't have time to roll before he turned to smoke and ash.

I was stalking towards demon number two when I heard the clash of swords in the distance.

And they were getting closer.

Andre

"Doesn't this feel familiar?" the devil said. He and Andre

began circling each other. "Only then you had a pitch-fork."

The devil disappeared. In the next instant Andre felt a boot at his back. It had been a long time since anyone had caught him off-guard. The devil shoved him forward.

Andre didn't fall, but as he caught himself, the devil twisted his wrist and snatched one of the swords right out from under him.

"Like taking candy from a baby," the devil said, testing the weapon out in his hand. "And I'd heard so many tales of your skill with a sword." He backed towards the door, sheathing the sword he'd come with now that he had Andre's.

Andre followed him, chafing at how easily the devil divested him of one of his weapons. "Wrong sword, Lucifer," Andre said. "Ask Gabrielle. She can tell you all about my skill with my sword."

The devil gave a wordless shout, swinging Andre's stolen weapon at him. Andre smiled as he parried the blow. He'd wanted to get under the devil's skin, and he'd succeeded.

They fought their way out of Andre's study. Steel clinked and sparked as their weapons collided with unnatural force. They were blurs, moving down the hall as they traded blows. There was no mistaking where the devil was leading him. Andre's room got closer and closer, until they were passing through the door. His heart skittered as he caught a whiff of sulfur and the remnants of his soulmate's blood.

The distraction nearly cost him.

The devil's stolen sword arced over Andre's head, ready to split him right down the middle. At the last second he blocked the blow.

Their swords locked. "What a disappointment you would've been to your father," the devil said, "whoring and killing your way through the centuries. Tell me, do you think he would've traded his soul for your life if he'd known what you'd do with it?"

Andre slid the devil's blade away and kicked him in the chest, sending the dark god sliding to the entrance of Andre's secret library. "You're going to have to do better than that, Lucifer," Andre said.

"Andre?"

His blood froze as he heard his soulmate's call. The devil was between them. Andre wasn't fool enough to think that she'd already used the quill. If she had, it would be unlikely that he and the devil would still be fighting. And positioned as they all were, Satan could kill her now and their one chance at salvation would evanesce.

The devil seemed to realize this. He smiled at Andre and disappeared.

Andre ran for the doorway, his body doused in fear. It had all been one elaborate trap. The devil wanted Andre to watch his soulmate die, along with the last of his hope and that of the world's.

Andre stood at the top of the stairs when the devil appeared in front of him, dropping the sword he stole to wrap a hand around the back of Andre's neck. And then the devil's other sword was in his hand.

With a hard thrust, he shoved it into Andre's chest.

The blade parted skin and pierced Andre's heart, exiting through his back.

Andre's mouth opened, but no words came out. He touched the wooden blade that impaled him and knew he'd indeed been tricked. Only, it wasn't Gabrielle who would die, and it wasn't him that would be forced to watch.

The devil clutched him close. "Feel that, vampire? That is death." He pulled the sword out, the blade making a wet, slick sound. "It won't be fast, but it will give you enough time to think about what exactly waits for you on the other side."

Gabrielle

I DROPPED MY sword after the second demon dissipated into smoke and ash. My breaths came in great heaves. The clash of swords grew louder, until it was right above me.

I scrambled through the debris, searching for the quill. Before I came upon it, I heard a familiar voice.

"... *to do better than that.*"

"Andre?" I called.

Another sinisterly familiar presence tugged at my heart. The devil had already consumed so much of it that I hadn't noticed that throb of his closeness. He was right up there with Andre.

I couldn't think about that.

I began turning over the ruins of the coffee table and tossing aside scattered books, my heart pattering like rain on a rooftop.

There.

It shimmered amongst the debris, not a single vane of the feather out of place. It had survived the fight.

Just as my fingers closed in on it, my back arched and pain seized my heart. I clasped the skin over it, gasping for breath. My first thought was that it was my body's reaction to touching a holy object. Then I heard the devil's voice and the slick slide of a blade leaving flesh.

My pulse pounded in my ears.

I smelled the blood before I saw it.

Borrowed blood.

Oh God, *no.*

A moment later a body tumbled down the spiral staircase that led into the library. My knees weakened. "*Andre.*" I ran, stumbling over my own feet in my haste to get to him.

"Soulmate," he said. I'd heard that voice say many things in anger, in love, in sadness, in agony. Never had I heard it so weak.

I wound an arm underneath his shoulders. He clutched his chest as I dragged him to the couch. Blood sluggishly seeped between his fingers.

"Why isn't it healing?" I asked, my voice rising with panic. I had his torso propped on my lap.

"Love." The endearment was little more than a whisper. In that one word was an explanation, one I didn't want to hear.

Nononononononono–no.

"*Why,* Andre?"

His head lulled against my breast. "Staked. The sword

... was wood."

"*No*." There were only a few ways you could kill a vampire; a wooden stake through the heart was one of them.

I didn't realize I was crying until my tears hit his cheek.

"Don't cry, my life," he breathed.

"Andre, don't leave me. *Please*."

He gave a slight shake of his head. "Never." His hand groped for mine. I helped him, slipping my hand into his. His skin had never been this cold.

I couldn't breathe. Heaven above, this was what loss felt like.

Only one way left to save him. I still clutched the quill. My grip tightened.

This ends now.

Desperation fueled me. My eyes frantically searched the room. A leather-bound book rested below the coffee table. I grabbed it and ripped out the first page.

I wrapped Andre's hand around the quill. "We're doing this together."

"No—please, soulmate. It's yours."

I ignored his plea, bringing our joined hands to the paper. Belatedly I realized that I didn't have any ink for it.

Fuck.

My eyes searched the room. I could fumble through all the odds and ends in Andre's private library, but he could be dead by then.

You know this can't possibly save him anyway. I pushed the thought away. I would save him. That was what soulmates did; they saved each other. And fate be damned, he was my soulmate.

Only, it was looking like there was no ink to transcribe this.

And then a horrible, macabre idea entered my mind when my gaze returned to Andre.

Blood. I could use his blood.

A sob slipped out. I pinched my eyes shut as I dipped the quill into a pool of Andre's spilled blood.

What mischief is my little queen up to now?

The devil was suddenly, staggeringly present. I could feel him like a swift wind brushing past me. The question he asked was irrelevant. He knew what I was doing, what I had. I realized then that he'd been watching from the shadows, waiting for me to come this far only to snatch victory from my grasp.

I had seconds—if that—to finish this.

The devil began to coalesce in the room.

"Leave, soulmate," Andre pleaded with me.

"Never," I said, throwing his words back at him.

I began writing, dragging Andre's hand along with mine, glancing up at the shadows as I did so.

S-A-V-E

The letters were a mess. Blood was poor ink, and my normal difficulties with quills were only exacerbated by the unwilling vampire who kept trying to pull his hand away.

U-S

Smoke wrapped around me, souls screaming.

A-L—

The quill was ripped from my hand before I'd been able to write the final "l" in my message. I hadn't even managed to write a full three words.

The devil snatch the sheet from me.

"*No—!*"

I reached for the paper only to watch it go up in flame in the devil's hand.

I counted my breaths, in and out, in and out. I waited for divine judgment to strike me and Andre. For us to be whisked away from the room.

Nothing happened.

I failed.

I *failed.*

The world as we knew it would end. Andre would die, and I would rot away in hell for an eternity. It was almost too much to comprehend.

The devil turned his wrathful gaze on me.

"*Consort.*"

Never had I heard so much anger packed into a single word. Betrayal gleamed in the back of his eyes. I hadn't expected that. Not from the Deceiver.

I stared at him, a stubborn part of me still holding out for some sort of divine intervention. But the seconds ticked by and deliverance never came.

It really didn't work.

It was a good thing I was already sitting, because if I wasn't, my legs would have given out.

"Even in my native tongue, there are not words for what you've done," the devil said, speaking to me in Demonic.

I swallowed back bile. If Andre and I weren't going to be saved, then things were about to get very, very bad. I would not face them sitting down.

Andre groaned as I lifted him enough to slip out from under him.

The devil seethed, the shadows around him expanding

"This is not your native tongue, Asiri," I responded, moving away from Andre so he'd avoid the devil's attention.

"*How* dare *you use that name with me now of all times!*" The walls of the room shook under the force of his words, and my hair whipped around me.

Having the devil's love was bad. Slighting the devil that loved you was far, far worse.

He disappeared only to reappear directly in front of me. He grabbed me by the neck and dragged me across the room, slamming my body up against the wall. The entire time he stared me in the eyes. I could see pain in those inhuman irises, pain that stemmed from love.

I choked as he lifted my body up, my feet leaving the ground. "I banish you to the deepest, darkest region of hell, consort. May you rot until you've paid your penance, then rot some more."

The words were barely out of his mouth when I felt the devil draw on my power. I gasped as I felt my life force sucked from me. I could hear wood begin to splinter far below us. I knew what was coming.

"*No.*" This came from Andre, who was trying to stand.

The devil spared him a glance, his lips curling with his anger. He swept his free hand out, and a wave of energy hit Andre square in the chest.

The devil's hold on my neck cut off my scream. Andre fell back, and this time he didn't move. The world turned red as tears leaked from my eyes.

"You cry for him? *Him?*" The devil grew bigger and more powerful as his pain fueled him. So much hurt lay in those eyes. Right now, the all-powerful devil was a wounded thing. I couldn't have created a more dangerous creature.

The room filled with static electricity.

Even with him feeding off his own pain, more and more of my energy drained from me. I heard stone crack and wood splinter as the floor lurched and shifted.

"Asiri," I said.

He squeezed my throat until he crushed my windpipe completely. As black dots spread across my vision, the vines snaked around me, and then they dragged me down to hell.

CHAPTER 29

Gabrielle

THE DEEPEST, DARKEST region of hell was exactly how the devil described it. Deep and dark. I could feel the weight of the very earth itself press against me.

I blinked my eyes, but I saw only blackness. Oblivion. One could go crazy down here. I reached around me, but felt nothing. Perhaps this all just went on and on. Nothingness, forever.

Andre was down here somewhere—or he would be very soon—burning in the flames, damned to unbearable agony. My blood chilled at the possibility. Fear triggered the siren in me, and my skin began to glow.

Wherever this place was, it was no longer the darkest region of hell. On a whim, I reached for the locket around my neck and yanked it. I heard the dainty clasp snap, and

I tossed it away from me.

No more doubt, no more uncertainty, no more straddling two men. I knew whom my heart belonged to. I'd spend every last second of my undying life trying to free Andre from this place, regardless of the punishment the devil doled out. It didn't matter what the fates had decided; he was my destiny and I was his.

But first I needed to escape this place.

I began walking in ever increasing circles, reaching out in search of walls. When I'd done this for several minutes and came across none, I stopped. This place could be endless.

I reached above me. My arms met only cold air. The only surface I'd come in contact with was the earth beneath me. So I knelt against the floor, pressing my hands to it. My blood thrummed as I did so, and power raced down my arms and into the ground. It poured from me until instinct commanded that I reclaim the magic I'd only just released. So I called the power back to me, drawing it up from the ground.

I didn't know exactly what I was doing until a wisp of golden light curled up from the earth, thickening and coalescing as I watched. My power was making it corporeal. My brows furrowed as the golden wisp became a silhouette and the silhouette became a man.

Not a man, a *soul*. A damned soul that had been trapped beneath the floor of the darkest, deepest region of hell.

Souls couldn't die. Not even damned ones that had been spent of their energy. They just became a part of the matrix that made up this place.

Once I'd pulled the soul from the ground, the urge to repeat the process rode me.

I continued to pour my power out of me, only to pull it back from the earth. Each time I did so, more souls took shape around me.

I couldn't say how fast time passed down here, or how long it took for those wisps to fill out into the semblance of people. But even after they'd filled out, they stayed by my side. Each gave off a slight glow, and the deepest, darkest region of hell brightened.

As I worked, I wondered about the devil. I hadn't heard him in my head when I should've. It took effort to yank one of my hands from the earth and put it to my heart, the power that gripped me reluctant to let me go. I could still feel the devil inside me, but I sensed a cocoon of magic swathing our connection. Thousands of intricate threads of magic had woven themselves around it.

I had no finesse when it came to magic. Spells were a witch's forte, not mine, and while I could now sense magic and understand it at a rudimentary level, I knew in my bones I couldn't have made the enchantment that wrapped itself snug around our connection. I could, however, sense this spell's function. It blocked the devil from sensing what I was up to without closing him out completely. It was the magical equivalent of feeding security cameras benign footage to cover up a heist. The devil could feel me, but he couldn't sense what I was up to.

I knew enough about spells to know this one was powerful—strong enough to outwit the devil. The back of my neck prickled. Whatever instincts were conducting my movements had also led to the creation of that enchantment.

At that, the tingle in my hands became almost unbearable as power built up. The itchy feeling beneath my skin forced me to resume my efforts. The ground pulled my hands to it like a magnet, and I resumed my task.

What seemed like an eternity later, the earth released my hands with a pop, and my power ebbed back inside me. I leaned back on my haunches as the last spirit finished taking form. That was when I realized there were hundreds of them—maybe thousands. All hovering around me, casting that eerie light on this place. They waited, staring at me, and I stared back.

Alrighty.

This situation was ... weird. Weirder than normal. And my normal wasn't exactly all that normal.

The souls didn't speak, but they began to crowd me. I really didn't want to hug this out, but there was nowhere for me to go. I felt their bodies brush against mine. Instead of the usual agony that I'd come to expect when I brushed up against the souls of this place, I felt ... peace.

They began to touch me. My skin still glowed, so I assumed that even in death the siren appealed to them. Until, of course, those hands latched onto me and my feet left the floor.

I let out a yelp.

I yanked against their grips, putting my supernatural strength into it, but any hands I shook off were replaced by others. Glancing down, I noticed with dismay that spirits were now beneath me as well as around me. I tilted my head up. Dozens crowded the space above me. They surrounded me completely, sheltering my body with all their forms.

We rose up, moving as a unit. Each of their faces was turned skyward. Their features blurred then sharpened. I'd given them back their form, but they no longer had physical bodies to hold those forms in rigid place.

As I watched, some of the spirits disappeared above me. First their heads, then their torsos, and finally, their legs. I realized that was because we'd finally come across a ceiling. Only I wasn't a spirit. I'd smash up against that ceiling, and then I'd fall back down.

I renewed my struggles as more souls disappeared. Like before, I couldn't break their holds. And then the ceiling was above me, and there wasn't any more time to struggle.

I gritted my teeth and held my breath, preparing myself for impact. But instead of smashing against the stony ceiling, I moved through it much the same way I moved through the ground when I traveled between worlds. The spirits dragged me through it, and as they did so, my power flared. I could sense more spirits trapped in this section of hell. My power whipped out of me and then it retracted, pulling souls out from the earth as it did so.

Once I broke through the earth, the spirits released me, continuing to float upwards. I dusted myself off, noticing that I stood inside the palace, the black stone walls arching high above me.

Home sweet home.

I stood in the middle of the great entrance hall. Across from me, two large doors led out to the fields of fire.

The place was utterly abandoned. Not that this was unusual in and of itself. This time, however, I could feel it. All the heavy players had been released from hell.

A manic need took hold of me. It thrummed through my veins. I was a vessel. A vessel for this power that demanded I release more souls.

I lifted a hand and aimed it at the double doors. I blasted them open, and then I stalked outside, down the palace steps.

It was time to pull souls from the fire.

Andre

ANDRE BLINKED UNTIL his surroundings came into focus.

Devil stabbed me, banished Gabrielle to hell—

The scrape of steel on steel and the boom of thunder filtered in from somewhere far beyond the walls of his library.

And now the bastard is waging war outside.

He tried to sit up, but his limbs were weak. So, so weak.

I'm dying.

It was almost unbelievable. He'd been alive for so long, been the most powerful being around for so long, that he thought he might be impervious to death at this point.

But all it had taken was a wooden sword. A child's play thing. He recognized it earlier as one of several usually stashed in Bishopcourt's training room.

With much effort, Andre lifted a hand and probed the wound. He hissed as it screamed. The skin around his heart felt raw and ragged, and blood oozed out. Andre let his hand fall back to his side. Time to get on with the business of dying.

He laid there as his life slowly seeped out of him, his eyes fixed on the ceiling. His mind spun.

As soon as he died, Andre would drag the last of his coven to hell. A part of him wondered if they could sense his encroaching death. If their limbs moved slower, if their bodies weakened.

Then his mind moved to less pleasant places. He'd be bound in the fires of hell, burning for eternity, and he'd have to watch that monster with his soulmate. He couldn't decide what was worse—witnessing the devil's cruelty towards Gabrielle or his kindness. Likely Andre would have to see both. And he couldn't do a single thing about it.

The nearby grandfather clock ticked down the final minutes of his long existence. They said that when you died, your life flashed before his eyes. But it wasn't his life Andre was thinking about.

Gabrielle's smile. Gabrielle's laugh. Gabrielle's bad jokes. Gabrielle's clumsiness. The way Gabrielle looked at him when he moved inside her.

He couldn't give that up. Not yet.

Andre gripped the edge of the coffee table next to him. A cry tore out of him as he pushed himself up.

This was nothing. He'd seen men with arrows wedged between shoulder blades and sunk deep into guts. He'd seen their bodies sliced open and bludgeoned in, and still they fought. And fought for what? Their country? Their religion? If ever there were worthy causes to fight for, fighting for his soulmate and his world would be them.

While there is life left in you, live.

Gabrielle

I HEADED STRAIGHT for the hellfire, led by some unseen hand. As I passed through the flames, my instincts tugged me forward, toward a soul that needed saving.

I halted in front of a sexless gray wisp. This one had almost been swallowed whole by this place. I fed it power and a form took shape. Thick, rounded limbs and soft skin. A woman, I realized, as she filled out. Then color came. Long auburn hair, brown eyes. Each feature became more distinct until her image had fully filled out.

When I arrived here, in this damned land, I knew instinctively how to place a soul into the fire. Releasing one was a little different, a little trickier, and yet I knew the movements intuitively. I wrapped my power around the woman and tugged, like pulling a weed from the ground. Once she was free from the flames, I released her. She floated up, up, up. A bright light in the darkness. The screams quieted as they watched.

I moved through the fire once more, my power driving me towards another soul. This one, after he regained his contours, was a burly man. He smiled at me before he drifted upwards, joining a collection of souls gathered far above me.

I repeated the process again and again. Why I passed by certain souls and stopped at others, I couldn't say. Some other force guided my hand. I didn't know who these souls were or why they called out to me, but I did know

307

that I wasn't liberating all of hell's prisoners.

The devil said it wasn't possible to release a soul from the fire. What he meant was that it was impossible for *me* to release a prisoner. But that was before he'd thrown our connection wide open, thrown it open so that he could tap into my power.

He'd dipped into my power, and now I was dipping into his.

Time lapsed as I freed souls, and the more I touched, the more dissociated I became. I lost my identity somewhere in those flames, and thank God for it. I would've gone mad otherwise. The sheer number of souls I freed, the faces of those I bypassed, the power I wielded—it was all too much for even an immortal like me to bear.

Until, that was, I came up to my father.

My identity rushed back to me all at once. Unlike the other souls, this one was personal.

In front of me was the man who died to save me. The man I'd dreamed about intermittently for a decade. I couldn't stop the wetness that welled up in my eyes, both from the agony that contorted his features, and from the knowledge that I'd get to free him from that suffering.

That realization led to another: There was a method to this madness. The souls I released weren't picked at random. Each had arrived here unjustly.

My power gushed through me the moment I touched my father's soul. The terrible agony that consumed him fled.

I ran my hand reverently over his essence as his form brightened and filled out. It didn't take much energy to revive his soul completely.

A shimmering hand reached for me. I looked up, meeting my father's gaze. I felt the brush of his spirit as he ran his phantom fingers down my cheek, gazing at me with stark adoration.

I leaned into his touch, and I smiled at him. "I've missed you, Dad," I said, blinking back my tears. He moved his hand to his heart, then back to me.

I nodded, understanding what he couldn't say. "I love you too."

I released his soul from the fire, and stepped back to watch his ascent. My heart rejoiced as he floated up beyond the reach of the flames, where they could never get to him again. I stayed rooted in place until he joined the other souls gathered far above me.

When I resumed my work, I allowed my body to be directed by the power once more. I kept vigilant, however. My father's release had reminded me that Andre was down here somewhere. With the same senses I used to locate souls, I searched the vast fields of flame for him.

I couldn't feel him. Where was he? Could he still be ... alive?

Hope flooded me, only to get squashed a moment later. He'd told me himself; he'd been mortally wounded. He might not die right away, but he was indeed dying. And that was a soul the devil *would* claim.

But as I continued to work, I didn't sense him, nor did I come across him. My steps began to slow as I realized, ominously, that my power was coming to a close and I still hadn't found my soulmate amidst the flames.

And then my feet dragged me forward one final time. I could feel it inside me—this soul would be the last I released.

I swallowed as I came to a stop in front of a reedy man with hollow cheeks and sparse white hair.

Not Andre.

I'd released thousands upon thousands of individuals. Among them I'd seen some vaguely familiar faces from Andre's coven—an alarming discovery since I believed many of these individuals to still be alive—but I hadn't come across my soulmate. Worse, I still couldn't sense him.

I stared out across the roaring inferno that spanned as far as the eye could see. Despair curled around my heart like a lover.

My soulmate was lost to me.

CHAPTER 30

Andre

ANDRE STUMBLED DOWN the persecution tunnel set into his library. He clutched a hand tightly to his chest, staving off the slow drip of blood through his wound. Now that he was moving, something beyond his own determination compelled him onwards. Fire burned through his blood. No longer could he feel the magic draining from him. No longer was the pain so horrible that it seized up his muscles.

Andre paused to lean against the wall and rub his eyes. His fingers came away with blood.

The celestial request quill hadn't worked. Gabrielle had one chance, and she wasted it trying to save him. He hadn't been strong enough to pull away, and now the quill was gone, along with the last of his hope.

The world would have to save itself. God wasn't listening.

Ahead of him the ground rose where the iron hatch fit into the ceiling. It took far longer than it should've to shove open the metal hatch. A dying Andre had little more strength than a mortal man.

He hissed as he pressed a forearm against the iron and pushed, the position causing his wound to tear further. His lips curled inwards at the searing pain, but he pressed on, the need to be outside now singing through his veins. With a deep groan, the door released, smacking into the ground with a heavy thump.

Andre braced himself for more agony as he hauled himself up by his arms. It was all he could do not to cry out like a babe.

Bloody heavens above, that hurt.

Once he dragged himself onto the grass, he rolled to his back, took a fortifying breath, then pushed to his feet. His free hand went to the hilt of his sword as he scanned the horizon.

The fields surrounding his home were overrun with supernatural creatures. Among them were the Fallen, the devil's most coveted demons because, like him, they were once angels. He caught sight of Lila, that hateful cambion, urging men on with her voice.

Distinctly fewer vampires were out here now. He had to press his lips together when he caught sight of the piles of clothes. They'd died defending him, knowing as they fought that if they fell, it would be to their doom. Had he ever doubted their loyalty, he did no longer.

Flashes of light arced across the sky as witches and sorcerers threw spells. Sparks flew as the swords of angels clashed against the claws of winged demons. The entire place looked like a swirling stew of light and shadow.

Chaos.

Andre could imagine it devolving further—each creature losing their form, creation unmaking itself until the world returned to the primordial place where it began.

He blinked and the sharpness of the landscape roared back to life around him. As soon as fighters caught sight of him, he'd become a target. And just about everyone out here wanted him dead.

He gritted his teeth as he pulled the sword from its sheath, the metal zinging as he did so. To die on the battlefield was a glorious death.

Right in the middle of the melee, the devil slashed through beings indiscriminately with Andre's sword, a maniacal smile on his face. He must've felt Andre's stare because he turned and his gaze locked on the vampire king.

The devil's eyes narrowed.

Straightening his stance, Andre stalked forward. The devil should've taken his head when he had the opportunity. Andre was going to make him regret it.

Only he never got the chance.

Gabrielle

I SEARCHED THE fire for my soulmate, used every sense I could to probe the vast reaches of hell.

Nothing.

Despair was giving way to panic.

"Andre!" I shouted. My voice got lost in the roar of the fire and screams of the doomed.

Above me, the souls I'd released were descending back towards the flames. Why were they returning? My power rushed over me, pushing my selfish thoughts back, urging me to lift my hands to these souls and embrace them.

No.

I dug my heels in and fought against the instinct to give in.

"Andre!" I shouted again, moving away from the souls.

They followed me, closing in from all sides. I tried to push past them only to feel their phantom hands latch onto me. I shrugged them off only to feel more grab me.

They'd done this before, but then I'd had no real reason *not* to follow them. Now I had plenty. I forced my way through them, noticing absently that the fire no longer had the ability to burn them.

I managed to slog several feet before too many had hold of me. I called on my power, seeking to magically force them off, only to feel it shy away from me.

Traitorous thing!

My feet left the ground as the souls lifted me up.

"Wait, stop!" I struggled against them.

The spirits wouldn't let me go, and together we rose high above the flames. The souls that remained tethered to the fire screamed louder, echoing my own thoughts. "Let me go!"

A familiar soul brushed against my cheek. I opened my

eyes, and my father stared back at me. He shook his head then tilted his face to the darkness above us, where thousands upon thousands of souls floated. He took my hand, and with a small smile, led me up.

His message was clear enough. We were all leaving this place.

"N-no," I sobbed out.

This should've been joyous. My father held my hand, and we were rising from the pits of hell. But the farther away we moved, the more certain I was that I would not be returning. I couldn't save Andre if I never came back.

Then and there I made myself a vow: I'd see this through. And despite whatever came to pass, I wouldn't rest until Andre was in my arms again. Only then did I stop fighting and allow these souls to sweep me away.

The darkness above us receded as thousands of glowing spirits illuminated our surroundings. So many surrounded me that I could barely see beyond them. I caught the barest glimpse of the Underworld's cavernous roof.

It struck me then just how finite this place actually was. The land of the damned really wasn't so big. It might stretch on for leagues and leagues, but it had a floor and it had a ceiling. No wonder the devil was so eager to leave this place.

Souls crowded around me, their faces upturned. All these people had been bound unfairly to hell, all so that the devil could gain a bit more strength. I'd righted his wrong and freed them. That counted for something. More than just something. That counted for a lot.

I reached the ceiling and, like before, the earth parted

to make way for me. I could still feel my father's hand in mine. Beyond all that peace that suffused his touch, I could feel his deep love. It was all going to be okay.

Unlike the other times I'd pushed through the earth, this time the ground didn't fight me. I flowed through it, gaining speed along with the specters. Together we rose higher and higher until I could sense vestiges of life.

All at once, we burst through the ground, and then we were on earth.

CHAPTER 31

THE GROUND SHOOK as angels, humans, demons, and everything in between fought. In the sky, underwater, on land. With swords and guns and claws and fangs and talons. Red blood and black blood and blood that seemed to be weaved of light all spilled. Beings that stared eternity in the eye fell alongside mortals.

The elements stirred themselves into a frenzy as good and evil fought for dominance. Waves crested hundreds of feet high, swallowing up ships and crashing into coastlines. Gale force winds tore at buildings and swept away homes. Fires blossomed in thick forested areas and spread like a disease, descending upon entire towns. As worlds fought, the earth rebelled, ripping apart like all the prophecies feared it would.

The ground trembled, so subtle at first that it couldn't

be told apart from the quakes that already shook it. It was just enough to scatter pebbles and further disturb the already agitated bodies of water.

A high pitched noise sounded in the distance. It rose in volume as the earth's tremors built on themselves. The noise grew louder and louder, until battle cries could no longer be heard over the sharp whine.

All at once, the sound cut out.

Fighters lowered their weapons in the silence.

And then, with a cataclysmic boom, the dead rose.

Gabrielle

I EMERGED FROM the earth alongside the souls I'd freed. They lifted into the sky, their forms taking a warm golden hue. Beyond them, I could make out Bishopcourt.

I'd surfaced in the middle of the battlefield. I only had a moment to take it in, soaked with blood and broken bodies. Those that hadn't fallen on the field watched me and the souls rising. My skin hadn't stopped glowing, and now it shone as bright as the angels that hovered in the sky.

My entire life had led me to this moment, and my one true purpose was to return these souls to their rightful home. I realized that now as they continued to ascend.

My father brushed a kiss against my cheek, just a whisper of contact, and then he let me go. I felt the loss deep within me; I would see him again, but not for a while yet. But he had his fate and I had mine.

He was the last one to leave me. I watched his form

grow smaller and smaller as the heavens finally claimed him.

"Consort!"

The devil's voice shattered the peace. He stalked forward, his face twisted in anger. That fury had no place here.

Even though the souls had released me, I kept rising, my toes skimming the grass only for a moment. The magic within me drew me off the ground and into the air. I could feel it crawling beneath the skin, burning, burning—

"Consort!" he yelled again.

Power was filling me up. Too much of it. The blinding light of it obscured my vision, but I made out the devil's form. He stalked towards me, deep shadows shrouding him.

The pain of so much power dug its claws in me. I could barely focus on him over it. And conscious thought ... that was going too.

Still a vessel ...

The devil stopped in front of me, his inhuman rage mingling with a yearning so deep it shone out of his eyes. I reached down for him as I rose, beckoning him to take my hand. I was still low enough to grab his if he gave it to me.

He stared at my outstretched hand. His yearning won, and he reached for me.

I realized what was going to happen an instant before it did. And in that instant, I hesitated—briefly.

Even after all the carnage and destruction he'd wrought, a part of me didn't want to see this being hurt. But I was just a vessel, and a far more generous being steadied my hand.

The devil grasped it, and his eyes locked on mine. For one earth-shattering second, everything else fell away.

I saw the future.

A lifetime of endless night. Years and decades of coaxing kindness from whatever this being had left of his heart and nurturing forgiveness from mine. Then centuries of affection given freely between us. Finally, an eternity spent creating something else out of his prison beneath the ground and the worlds he'd conquered, something that seemed closer to paradise than damnation, something closer to happiness than hate.

Amidst all those nights of change, I was there, in his arms, in his mind, in that slowly healing heart of his. All those nights he cradled me close, whispered words of wondrous praise. And I came to love him, and he came to love me. Together we vanquished the monster within him, and hell as we knew it became nothing more than a horrific nightmare of a time before forgiveness.

I almost screamed as the vision cut off. That future was the future the fates had plotted all those centuries ago, one that would change worlds and lives and afterlives. I'd held that future in my grasp. But now, now it slid through my hands like grains of sand.

Even no longer mortal, I couldn't handle life on the scale of gods, love on the scale of gods.

I was just a vessel. A vessel nearly used up.

The world came back into focus, and for one terrible moment, I saw Asiri staring back at me, the benevolent god of the dead. Hope brightened his eyes an instant before he realized the future we saw would never be his.

With a loud clap of thunder, my connection to the devil snapped. That strange, inhuman presence that had filled my heart was now shoved out.

Reflexively, I loosened my grip. The devil's hand slid from mine, and the earth opened beneath him. His lips parted, but no words or screams came out. We shared one last piercing gaze, and then he was falling, falling farther and farther down that chasm in the earth. The entire time he made no noise, but his eyes—his eyes said a million things.

The ground sealed up above him, and the devil, for the second time in his long existence, fell to the pits of hell.

Andre

ANDRE STAGGERED AT the sight of his soulmate. She'd always been unearthly, but rising from the ground, her skin shining brighter than he'd ever seen it, leading countless souls from the earth ... in that moment she truly was not of this world.

His broken heart sang at the sight of all those glowing souls. The devil had banished Gabrielle to hell, and instead of following orders, she'd coordinated some sort of widespread prison break. For once Gabrielle's rebellious streak was causing someone else grief. A smile wavered along his lips.

That's my girl.

The entire field watched raptly. Everyone, save the devil. His chest rose and fell, rose and fell.

"Consort!" he shouted. The shadows around his form

expanded, and energy poured off him. He wasn't masking his otherness like he always had. And an angry Lucifer wasn't good. It fed right back into his power. "Consort!"

Andre began striding forward, gripping his sword tighter.

Gabrielle reached for the devil, her body levitating off the ground.

The devil grasped his soulmate's hand. Something about the embrace made Andre halt his progress. He couldn't see the devil's face, but he could see Gabrielle's. For the first time in a long time, he couldn't read her. She was utterly devoid of expression. This woman of his, he finally caught a glimpse of what she might look like after the eons chipped away every last piece and parcel of her humanness. She would've been nothing like Andre. Time would've fashioned her into a distant but humane goddess. Someone far loftier than him.

Andre swallowed. This had always been above and beyond him. He could see that now. Gabrielle rode the power; the power didn't ride her. She was the sun, and the devil that held onto her was the deep blackness of the universe.

And then the electricity that filled the air, the magic that coated his tongue, something about it ... changed. A clap of thunder echoed in the dark sky. Below Gabrielle, the earth split open, and she released the devil's hand.

The dark god fell silently, and even from this distance, this angle, Andre could tell that the devil hadn't looked away from Gabrielle. The ground resealed, and Andre's soulmate had done away with Satan as though he were the mortal and she the goddess of old.

Demons, angels, and supernaturals all watched her in horror, in wonder. Andre's bleeding heart squeezed at the sight.

She tilted her head skyward once more. The power that drenched her now bled away the black attire she wore, replacing it with iridescent robes. They rippled around her body, moving as though the air was as viscous as water. Whatever magic this was, Andre was sure he'd never seen anything like it.

She had hovered in the air while she held the devil's hand, but now she rose until she levitated twenty feet above them. Angels shifted their sword arms, preparing themselves to fight her. But she wasn't attacking. She wasn't aware at all from what Andre could tell.

His soul cried because he couldn't see his Gabrielle in this woman.

Gabrielle

POWER ROARED THROUGH my veins, continuing to brighten my skin and tear me apart from the inside out. I'd thought it might settle now that the devil was gone. I hadn't thought it could hurt worse than it already had.

I was wrong on both counts.

My eyes didn't see, my ears didn't hear. I was pain, limitless pain. My power built on itself, boiling my blood as it did so. I blindly stared at the heavens as it drew out the damnation within me like one would a poison. But it also felt like it was killing me.

My back arched and I screamed, the sound like nothing of this earth as the siren rode my voice.

Oh God, the pain. Just a vessel, a vessel for darkness and light to battle, and either might win, but I would lose.

The power stole the rest of my thoughts. It stole everything.

For one brief second, the world came to a halt as I hovered in the air. And then the power burst through my skin, ripping me apart, and Gabrielle as I knew her was nothing more than smoke and memory.

Andre

SOMETHING WAS WRONG. Gabrielle's skin continued to brighten, and her face contorted.

Andre had frozen in place, just like everyone else out here.

He forced his feet into action. It felt like pulling himself from a bog, each step difficult. He sheathed his sword as he staggered towards her.

Gabrielle continued to brighten, her body arching. She opened her mouth and let out a scream. The noise brought Andre to his knees.

Beautiful anguish.

Then it all stilled. He felt the silence and the breath of magic against his skin.

Dear Lord, it was too late.

Andre roared as light consumed Gabrielle's body. And then that light, that blinding light, blasted from her. It was so bright it lit the night sky, so bright it drained their surroundings of color.

It swept over the field, and Andre saw the demons closest to Gabrielle combust, flames ripping through them, before the light swallowed that too. He heard Lila's shriek a moment before it consumed her.

The shockwave raced towards him, and he only had a split second to realize that the light would burn through him. He dropped his sword and opened his arms to embrace his death.

Andre didn't even have time to scream as it ripped through his body, incinerating muscle, bone, and seven hundred years of life.

And then the curse of vampirism was finished, once and for all.

CHAPTER 32

Gabrielle

MY SKIN THROBBED. Each cell felt like it had its own pounding pulse.

Bit by bit, the blinding, all-consuming light drew away from the edges of my vision and color seeped back. With it came sight.

The sky had lightened since I last gazed upon it, now a dusky dark blue. In the east, pinks and purples bled into it.

My body began to descend and I dimmed. My earlier power fled, draining me of the last of my energy.

Weak. So unbelievably weak. My feet gently touched the grass, then the backs of my thighs, then my shoulders and head. Laid down by some unseen being.

I barely had energy to move, but I managed to tilt my

head to the side. The grass beneath my cheek didn't wilt or flatten itself away from me.

Bishopcourt stood off in the distance, smoldering. Around me, a field of men and women lay, some dead, some stirring awake. No one had been left on their feet. Well, aside from the angels that hovered in the sky, but they hadn't been standing in the first place. The only beings wiped away completely were the demons. Not even their bodies remained.

Banished to hell along with the devil.

As the last of my power left me, my heart jolted, and I felt a familiar tug as my bond flared to life. I placed a hand over my chest and felt the pump of that organ.

I'm alive.

After all that I'd done, I was sure the energy would eat me up.

I heard a gasp in the distance, then, "*Soulmate.*"

A jolt flared through my body, and my connection throbbed.

It couldn't be.

I pushed myself to my forearms, the air stirring my hair. Across the field, Andre stared at me, his gaze intense. Shocked.

I thought he was dead. I thought I'd lost him. But there he stood, looking very much alive.

He glanced down at the torn and bloodstained material that covered his chest. His fingers rubbed over the skin. The wound that the devil delivered, the one that should've killed him and sent him to hell, had vanished, and his heart—

I closed my eyes, just to make sure I heard correctly.

Tha-thump. Tha-thump. Tha-thump.

It beat. His heart beat.

How was that possible?

I opened my eyes as wonder spread across Andre's features. He strode forward, his movements somewhat stilted. I got the impression that he might be just as weak as I was.

As he got closer, our connection got stronger.

Our connection.

A sob slipped out of my mouth. I forced myself to my feet and stumbled forward. I tripped over myself, but then he was there to catch me in his arms. One of his hands skimmed up my neck and tilted my jaw up.

Our connection—*our connection!*—throbbed. And then our lips met, and it went blissfully silent.

I couldn't imagine any mouth could feel this soft or anyone could taste this good. Andre's lips glided over mine, his arms tightening around me. I'd seen a future with the devil, a future that stretched on and on, and in it I was happy. But it didn't hold a flame to a single lifetime with this man.

Neither of us expected this, neither of us thought it was possible. We'd fought and fought, and I wasn't sure we ever truly believed we'd make it out alive. And now I was in Andre's arms, my hand pressed against his beating heart.

Eventually we had to come up for air. An hour ago, we wouldn't need to catch our breaths. Now we did.

Andre still held me tightly against him, his hand cupping the side of my jaw. His eyes searched mine, his chest rising and falling. "What is the meaning of this?"

I blinked back watery tears.

Watery tears. Not blood.

"I think it's over, Andre. It's finally over."

"*Dios mio*," Andre whispered.

He reeled me back into his body, trembling around me. A tear hit my cheek, sliding down into my mouth. I tasted salt and water, and as my nose buried into the crook of Andre's neck, I could smell him. Not his pheromones. *Him.*

We truly were no longer vampires, which meant we weren't damned. Only, I wasn't sure we were human, either. I still retained my ability to smell and hear things normal mortals couldn't.

Above us, the sky brightened. We gazed to the skies, our arms still locked around one another's.

The angels stared at me now, their brows pinched together, their mouths frowning. And as people roused themselves, they too studied me until they caught sight of what was happening above us.

Light backlit the dark clouds. They parted, and a beam of light stretched from beyond them to the field. Not light from the sun, which was rising in the east; light from on high.

The atmosphere inside the beam of light shimmered and coalesced into a man with iridescent wings and dark skin and eyes that seemed to contain the entire universe.

He had the same otherworldly beauty as all the angels, but I could feel the power of this man eclipsing theirs.

He wore golden gladiator sandals and a cloth made from the same fabric as my own attire that draped around his hips. And he wore little else.

"I, the messenger known on earth as Jericho Aquinas, come bearing an edict for heaven, earth, and hell," he said, his voice carrying over the field.

That was what Jericho really looked like? Holy heavens, the dude was a *babe*.

"In response to a plea made on a celestial request quill, God, our holy mother, has intervened." He held up a scroll that shimmered. "This is Her edict."

He unrolled the paper and began reading. The language he spoke wasn't meant for human ears.

Teoian, my mind whispered, *the language of the gods*.

The sound of it reverberated in my bones, too powerful and vast to be understood. I caught the sound of my name amongst the words.

He paused. When he resumed speaking again, it was in another foreign language, one that enveloped me in a peaceful embrace. I felt the brush of divinity in this language not because of its power but because of the holiness that washed over my skin.

The angels stared at the messenger in growing shock as he spoke.

Jericho paused once more, and this time when he spoke, it was in English. "In return for freeing those unjustly imprisoned in hell, God has granted amnesty to all who were tricked by the fallen one once known as Lucifer.

God has additionally granted amnesty to those both directly and indirectly involved in the release of these souls.

"The curse of vampirism has been lifted from those still living, along with their immortality. Whatever magic their body retains will be theirs to keep until the day of their death. Their sins up to the present day have been expunged.

"Lucifer, who sought to break this world to his will, has been stripped of those powers he so recklessly wielded and divested of a mate he sought to entrap. The bonds that he broke in the process have been mended.

"God's vessel, Gabrielle Fiori, is to be recognized for her involvement in stopping the devil, as is Andre de Leon, Leanne Summers, Oliver Borealis, and Nona, the weaver of life. Any wrongdoing on their part is absolved by this heavenly decree.

"With these words, heaven acts out its will. May these times not be forgotten, lest history dare repeat itself."

Jericho lowered the scroll and stared out across the field. His eyes briefly landed on me before continuing on. "Be good, humankind, for gods play with mortals and our reckoning is mighty and final."

With that, his form shimmered out of existence, and the ray of light dissolved away.

ANDRE'S HAND TIGHTENED on mine as he stared towards the lightening sky. The angels had left shortly after Jericho, and the remaining supernaturals scattered like dust in the wind. The only other beings that lingered were the last of Andre's coven. There weren't many, and I recognized even less.

We watched the horizon. The sun crested in the east, and for the first time in seven hundred years, Andre felt its rays on his skin.

He sucked in a ragged breath, and I saw a tear slip down his face. He closed his eyes as he drank the sensation in, and then he was laughing, his whole body shaking from it. I couldn't tear my gaze away from him. I'd thought he'd been beautiful before, but under the glow of the sun, he was magnificent.

He picked me up by the waist and twirled me around him. I cupped his face, drinking him in. The sun didn't incinerate his skin, no vines rose to claim me. Our hearts beat together.

"You did it soulmate—you saved us all," he said. "My God, we're finally free."

CHAPTER 33

Gabrielle

Two weeks later

IN THE END, I had led to the extermination of vampires, just like the prophecy said I would. The curse of vampiricism now lifted, there were no more vampires. Just a bunch of scary-ass mortals.

Unlike the devil, God gave words and intentions the benefit of the doubt. My plea to save us all hadn't even been fully written, and I hadn't clarified who, exactly, I'd been referring to. But God had divined my intentions nonetheless and she'd expanded it to include everyone throughout the ages who'd been duped by the devil. God hadn't just saved our souls, she'd saved our lives.

I set down the brush I'd been running through my hair

and stared at my reflection in Andre's bathroom mirror. My skin glowed softly from the song I hummed underneath my breath.

We might be mortal, but neither Andre nor I were human. I was still a siren, and I could definitely still beguile Andre with my voice—not that he fought it too much. Our bond had reestablished itself, a feature distinct to supernaturals. But most of all, we retained some of our power.

We'd kept the heightened senses that came with vampiricism—including night vision—and we still both had extraordinary strength and speed. Even more extraordinary was that both of us could still call on small amounts of magic, and I maintained the ability to sense it. It was a mere echo of what we once wielded, but it came with no strings attached.

There was no longer a name or classification for us. We now fell outside the categories given to supernaturals. It made me wonder if other beings had come into existence as solutions to past battles between good and evil. I guess I would find out once I had children of my own whether they'd inherit these same abilities.

My gaze moved to the packet of birth control pills sitting on the bathroom counter. Speaking of children, I had to have the vastly uncomfortable conversation with Andre about contraception, a conversation that he, unlike me, didn't find awkward in the least. He did, however, enjoy watching my face flush with embarrassment.

Behind my reflection, I caught sight of a broad, muscled chest just as a hand snaked around my waist. Andre leaned in from behind me, pressing a kiss to my cheek, then nipping my ear playfully. "What has my soulmate flustered?"

I swiveled around in his arms to face him. "Sneaking up on people is not nice."

He nuzzled my neck, breathing my scent in. "Mmmm, it's not, and you *are* flustered." The hand around my waist stroked my skin languidly. "Are you still thinking about last night, as I am?"

See? No qualms.

My face heated, and Andre flashed me a wicked smile. His eyes strayed briefly to the packet of pills, and the smile vanished.

And that was the other thing. Now that kids were back on the table for him, I was pretty sure Andre wanted them. Eep. No—please and thank you. I wouldn't be crossing that bridge for a *long* time.

A long, long, *long* time.

"Sooooooooooouuuuuuulmate!" Oliver screeched from the hallway.

Andre flared his nostrils. "Why is he calling you that?"

"Because you do, and he loves nothing more than irritating the wrong people."

We met the fairy out in the hall. On his heels was Leanne.

"Has anyone told you that your bed sucks?" he said by way of greeting. "I bet you've laid on stone slabs softer than that thing."

I narrowed my eyes at Oliver. He'd unofficially taken over my dorm room, much to his former roommate's delight and much to Leanne's horror. Andre'd balked at the idea of me returning to the dorm rooms now that I was enrolled at Peel Academy once more. A day after Jericho delivered his message, I found my packed belongings sitting at the foot of Andre's massive bed.

"Are we going to discuss this?" I'd asked him.

"I've left you with the enemy for far too long. I'm not making that mistake again."

I'd all but rolled my eyes at that, but I didn't fight him too doggedly on this issue. After moving heaven and hell for him, I wasn't all that eager to leave his side.

And, two weeks later, I found there were few things better than falling asleep and waking up in the arms of a former vampire king.

It might all come to an end in two days, however; that was when my mother was scheduled to arrive. We'd see how *that* would go over.

She'd learned along with the rest of the world that gods and devils existed—as did supernaturals of all shapes and sizes—and that her daughter was both the anti-Christ and the girl that saved the world from the devil.

My mother was obviously having some issues processing all of it.

"Oh, and I'll have you know that I put a hex on Doris to make her nose hairs grow to her chin," Oliver said, pulling me back to the present.

"Oliver!" I gasped.

"What? She was rude to Leanne and you, and she casts those judge-y eyes of hers at me. Anyway, that's not why I'm here." He grabbed my wrist. "We need to go to Castle Rushen. Now."

The *remains* of Castle Rushen, that was. They were still renovating the building after Andre demolished it, and they would be for some time.

"We're not going anywhere near that castle," said my still-so-over-protective-it-hurts soulmate.

Since the world almost ended, Andre and I had become something of a sensation. Both the supernatural world and the human one were captivated with our story. It was all nice and well, until you wanted to grab a cup of coffee and someone recognized you.

"*Oh my god, you're Gabrielle Fiori, aren't you?*"

"*Were you really fated to the devil? Did you actually have to marry him?*"

"*Can I have a picture with you?*"

"Told you," Leanne said, back in the present.

Oliver huffed, then glanced at me, raising his eyebrows. I gave him a look that said, *What do you want me to do?* I had to pick my battles with Andre, and this was not one of them.

"Fine, *fine*. We won't go, spoilsports. Do you have a television?"

By means of answer, Andre brushed past us and stalked down the hall.

Oliver leaned in. "Broody-as-hell. Gah, you lucky bitch," Oliver said, eyeing his backside.

The three of us and a couple of Andre's men entered his conference room and circled the television. Oliver picked up the remote resting on top of it and clicked to the appropriate channel.

A news station popped on the screen. In the background I could see Castle Rushen and a number of vehicles with flashing lights.

The caption that ran along the bottom of the screen read, *Cult and Corruption within the Politia.*

I sucked in a breath and glanced at Oliver. He wore a smug grin, and when he caught my eyes, he wiggled his eyebrows. Behind me, Andre leaned forward, splaying his hands on the conference table.

On the screen, Byron Jennings was carted away into one of the police cruisers. *Human* police cruisers.

The revelation that paranormals really existed was met with mixed reactions. But here on the Isle of Man, where supernaturals had been an open secret for centuries—if not millennia—the police force was happy to aid us.

Byron's eyes briefly met the screen, and I shuddered. Darkness dwelled there. I hadn't noticed it before, but having once felt its touch, I recognized it in others now.

I was surprised to see that Byron hadn't shifted and escaped his captors. Whatever cuffs held him bound, they must've been spelled to contain a shifter.

"He already confessed to three attempted murders," Oliver said, staring at the screen.

I glanced over at my friend, my eyebrows nudging up. Something cold and hard entered the fairy's features, and I realized that I'd only ever seen a happy Oliver. Well, okay, sometimes I'd seen him miffed, but never like this.

"Three attempted murders?" I repeated, confused.

Oliver sighed. "That moment when you realize your friend is such a badass she doesn't remember those times someone tried to kill her. One was outside of Jericho's

Emporium a couple weeks ago, and the other was at the beginning of the school year, at Andre's club Mystique."

I touched my throat, remembering the knife biting into my flesh. The other instance did require me to paused and think back. I flipped through my memories and—*yes*, I remembered. I was in Andre's VIP suite when a man attacked me. He tried to stab me in the heart. He'd been captured but he'd later disappeared without a trace ...

"Holy shit."

"Yeah, and the individuals responsible for capturing Leanne's doppelganger on the night of Samhain?" Oliver's chin jutted to the screen. "Officer Maggie Comfry and Byron Jennings—again. Bastard. That was murder attempt *numero tres*."

I swallowed down a lump as my eyes met Leanne's. I'd worked alongside both inspectors.

Andre spoke. "You did this?" he asked, his attention focused on Oliver.

My friend buffed his nails. "Mhm. I cleaned the Politia *out*. House of Keys knows everything, thanks to my sleuthing."

My eyes widened.

Oliver nudged me. "This is why it's always a good idea to be friends with a fairy. We are in the business of vendettas."

Note to self: never get on Oliver's bad side.

He hadn't so much as let on that he held any interest in the attempts on my life and Leanne's. But he had. It reminded me of all those other times he'd noticed things. He'd figured out the Samhain murders before I had, he'd been the one to point out the killer in Romania had been a cambion. Oliver noticed things and, despite his reputation for having loose lips, I was beginning to understand that he calculated a great many things.

"Byron and Maggie aren't the only officers involved, either," he said now.

"There are more?"

"Oh, honey, *lots* more. So you know how I'd been sleeping with the chief constable?"

I suppressed my shudder. Oliver, however, didn't bother suppressing his. "By the way, remind me never to date old men. They're all wrinkly, and saggy, and—"

Ew.

"Don't date old men," I rushed out.

He clucked his tongue. "You're not supposed to give me that advice right *now*, Corpsie. Anyway, I'll have you know I screwed that man for you."

I scrunched my face. "Please be lying."

"'S all in the line of duty. He made terrible grunts though. You know, when he—"

"Oli*ver!*" *Eeeeeewwww!*

"Relax. Wouldn't have pegged you for a prude." He opened his mouth to continue, eyed Andre, who watched the fairy with flinty eyes, and clicked his teeth shut. He cleared his throat. "As I was saying, men talk when they feel good, and Chief Constable Morgan had quite a lot to say about the Eleusinian Order. Do you remember them?"

I nodded. They were the cult that wanted to reunite me with the devil. They'd believed he was Hades and I was his Persephone.

340

"The wrinkly old constable admitted everything in a few moments of weakness. Apparently there are a number of Politia officers working with the order, and several more who are in it. Seems being a part of it is a pretty high honor. It's the kind of exclusive club that draws in fat men with little arms and big egos ... and hotshot Politia members. Byron's a part of it. So is Maggie, and—" Oliver paused and looked at me regretfully, "Caleb was being groomed to join."

That news didn't hurt nearly as much as it once would've. "How long was he aware of them?"

He shook his head. "I don't know that, sweets. But I don't think he ever officially joined."

On the T.V. Chief Constable Morgan was led through the crowd.

"How did you accomplish all this?" I asked.

Oliver cocked a hip, an irreverent grin pulling at his lips. "You mean besides boning an old man?"

I scrunched my face. "Besides that."

"Camera phone, recorder, a few favors—" he lifted a shoulder, "the usual."

I nodded, breathing deeply as some weepy emotion welled up in me. "Why did you do all this?"

Oliver took my hand. "No one fucks with my friends." He gave it a squeeze. "No one."

Damnit, I was going to cry.

"Also, I enjoyed the shit out of being sneaky."

I sniffled and laughed, then I yanked on his hand and reeled my friend in for an epic hug.

"Whoa," he said, as I squished him to me. "Hey there—

don't mess up the hair," he wheezed. "And maybe let up a bit. You're still strong."

"You're seriously the best." He'd gone out of his way to bring me and Leanne justice.

Andre stepped around me and clasped the fairy on the shoulder. "Oliver, I owe you for meting out my mate's revenge."

The fairy in question preened under Andre's words. "I like being owed. And I believe that's two favors I'll have to cash in at some point in the future."

I noticed Andre tense slightly under the reminder, and I bit back a snicker.

I was looking forward to this normality. Worrying about your boyfriend meeting your mom and your friends all getting along together. My life would never be typical, but finally it would be free of darkness.

I pulled Leanne aside a little while later. Andre had wandered off to catch up on his many business ventures, which he'd neglected while we were on the run. Oliver, meanwhile, was in the kitchen, dictating to the in-house chef what he wanted to eat.

Leanne and I reclined on one of the couches in Bishopcourt's sitting room.

"Should I be worried about the future?" I asked.

She shook her head. "It's all finally over, Gabrielle."

I released my breath. "Logically, I know it is, but sometimes I can't help but worry it's not." Over the last two weeks I'd suffered from nightmares. In them, I was still in hell, still bound to the devil, and Andre was down there with me. He'd rouse me from them and kiss my terror away, but the memory of them still lingered.

I stared down at my hands. "I'm not used to good things happening to me—I always expect something"—or some*one*, more precisely—"to take them away."

Leanne looked thoughtful. "The future is ever-changing. Nothing about it is certain. I can't promise you anything more than a possibility of what's to come, but what I do see is a life filled with lots of happiness and very little pain. And if that ever changes, I can tell you that I'll be there for you, through thick and thin. As will Oliver. And, most especially, as will Andre."

She scooched over on the couch and gave me a hug. "And like anything else, when it comes to the future, all I can really tell you is this: safe travels."

I squeezed her back. "Safe travels."

EPILOGUE

Gabrielle

5 years later

"I STILL CAN'T believe you didn't let me wear white." I stood in the bedroom of Andre's house in Cluj Napoca, trying not to let nerves get the better of me. Being someone's soulmate was one thing. Marrying him amongst an audience of hundreds of people was another.

Oliver fussed around me, arranging my wedding dress.

"Sweets, you're the queen of darkness, and the queen of darkness doesn't wear white to her wedding."

"The queen of darkness probably doesn't wear pink, either."

"Ombre," Oliver sniffed. "And I did give you a little white."

Technically he *had*, right around the bodice. It just wasn't much. At least the shear back didn't drop so low, like his original mockups. I had to fight him on that one.

"You can see my back dimples," I'd said, when he unveiled the first iteration.

"Yes, and they're *adorable*."

"I don't want people to see my back dimples," I'd protested.

"Listen, ho, this is already a prude wedding dress for a fairy."

"And I'm not a fairy."

"You're an honorary one in my book." There he went sweetening me up. "And way too bloodthirsty to be considered otherwise."

Back in the present, I let my "mate" of honor make last minute adjustments to the dress he'd designed.

"Leanne," he asked over my shoulder, "got any evening forecasts?"

"For the fifth time, Oliver, I'm not telling you whether or not you're going to get laid tonight."

He huffed. "What is the point of having a seer friend if she's not going to even tell you these things?"

Before Leanne had a chance to reply, my mother entered the room, holding my bouquet.

The first time she met Andre, like any reasonable mother, she might've freaked a little. The guy had bad news written all over him. But Andre had won her over fairly quickly, like he tended to do when it came to women. It helped that he was my soulmate ... and that the other man I'd been fated to had been the devil. That kind of put things into perspective.

"Sweet daughter of mine," she said, her eyes tearing up as she took me in, "you look radiant."

"Thank you, Mom." I had to breathe through my nose. Gah, I was going to cry too.

Pull it together, Gabrielle.

She handed me my bouquet, then leaned in and gave me a kiss on the cheek. "The car's here. Are you ready, honey?"

I blew out a breath and nodded as a nervous smile pulled at the corners of my mouth. "Yeah, I am."

In the holy stillness of St. Michael's church in Cluj-Napoca, beneath the stained-glass eyes of angels and saints, I married Andre de Leon, my soulmate and the former king of vampires.

The moment I'd caught sight of Andre standing at the altar, his hair brushed back from his tanned face, I'd lost myself in those dark eyes of his.

Jericho read the marriage rites, wrapping our hands with a silken cord. The symbolism wasn't lost on me. The fates had woven our threads together. But we hadn't simply been given this love. We'd fought and earned it.

Andre's jaw worked as he stared down at our joined hands, fighting back some strong emotion. He smiled at me when he realized I'd noticed. Even if I hadn't, the electric connection between us would've given him away.

"You have declared your consent before the Church," Jericho said. "May the Lord in Her goodness strengthen

346

your consent and fill you both with Her blessings. What God has joined, men must not divide. Amen."

Andre's lips pressed to mine. The kiss was gentle, reverent. A promise to cherish our mortal life together as well as our immortal afterlife—one free of damnation, devils and eternal pain. Our stained souls had been cleansed.

BACK AT ANDRE'S home in Cluj, the wedding reception was in full swing. After greeting a barrage of people and taking way too many wedding photos, I'd gotten a brief respite with him and Leanne.

My smile felt like it was about to fall off.

"So," Oliver said, swirling his glass of wine and giving an eligible bachelor a predatory look. The man stumbled into an older woman, spilling her wine all over them.

Oliver tore his gaze away. "Are you going to go all *Twilight* on us and push out a vampire baby within the next year?"

I rolled my eyes, bringing my own glass to my lips. "Andre and I are no longer vampires."

"Hmph." Oliver pursed his lips. "Well, if Andre knocks you up and the baby pops out of you Alien-style, I'm shooting it."

"Oliver, shut the hell up," Leanne said, snatching an hors-d'oeuvre from a passing waiter.

"I'm just saying."

"Why is anyone talking about babies?" I asked. Geez, I got married mere hours ago.

"Seriously, sweets?" Oliver lifted his fingers and began

ticking off reasons. "One, this is a wedding. It's everyone's excuse to rush your life the hell up and make you feel as uncomfortable as possible. And two," Oliver gave my groom, who was chatting with some of my relatives across the room, a once-over, "that man is a stallion. He can just look at you, and boom, you're pregnant. If it weren't for your birth control, the dude would probably have to wear two condoms when you did the nasty, just to be safe."

"I'm so not comfortable with this discussion," Leanne said, making a face as she ate her appetizer.

Andre glanced over then. Even from across the room his heated gaze burned into me.

Oliver leaned in. "Boom. Pregnant."

I gave him the side-eye. "Say that again and I'll make you my unborn child's future nanny."

"Ew, a nanny to a little monster? That would be ... acceptable. He'd be the cutest little shit ever, and I could be his fairy godmother ... oh, I dig."

"'He'?"

"Sorry to inform you Gabrielle, but that man," he nodded to Andre, "shoots straight Y's." The man in question had returned to his conversation. I noticed his lips twitch, however. The punk was totally listening in.

My mother came over then, wrapping her arms around Leanne and me, and gave us a squeeze. She rubbed my arm affectionately. "What are the Three Stooges up to now?"

"The Three *Musketeers*," I clarified.

She snorted. "That will be the day."

Did I ever mention that my mother was snarkier than

me?

Oliver jumped in. "I was just telling Queen of the Damned here to lie back and think of England tonight."

"Ugh," I said, wincing, "that is *so* not appropriate."

My mother, however, didn't seem to mind nearly as much as I did. She peered over at Andre, then turned back into our huddle. "England?" She shook her head. "That would be a waste of some perfectly dirty thoughts."

Oliver squealed. "You did not *just*!"

She gave him a wink and pulled away. "I'm parched and the wine here is good." From the nice pink tinge to my mother's cheeks, I was thinking that she'd already had plenty to drink. "Try not to get up to too much trouble—I'm looking at you, Oliver."

Oliver placed a hand to his chest. "*Moi?*"

"Mhm."

"*Never,*" he said.

Leanne and I exchanged a look, and then broke out into laughter. Oliver swiveled back to us and raised his glass. "To best bitches, forever and ever."

We joined our glasses with his and clinked them together. "To best bitches, forever and ever."

THE RECEPTION WAS winding down when Andre took my hand and led me back to our room, flashing me a secretive smile that had my heart racing.

Early on in our relationship I'd assumed that even soulmates' passions cooled as the newness of their bond wore off. But, if anything, time had deepened the sweet ache I felt for Andre.

He glanced back as he led me through the halls of his—*our*—house, and his nostrils flared at the scent of my desire. Once we were out of sight of any prying eyes, he scooped me up in his arms.

When I wove my arms behind his neck and pressed a kiss to his cheek, he raised an eyebrow. "No objections to being carried?"

I shrugged a shoulder. "I'm willing to go with tradition just this once."

His lips quirked. "I'll make sure to savor it then."

He placed me down only once we were inside our bedroom. I took in the hundreds of flickering candles that lit the room up. The sight of them had my skin brightening.

The door to our bedroom clicked shut, and I swiveled around. Andre leaned against it for a moment as he drank me in. His look was all predator. He'd kept himself away from me for over half the day entertaining guests, and before that, preparing himself for the wedding.

He was done waiting.

In two swift strides, he caught me. An arm snaked around my waist, the other cradled the side of my face as our lips met. The current between us amplified at our closeness.

Andre pulled away. "Gabrielle de Leon," he rolled the name on his tongue, "my *wife*."

A smile split across my face. "Andre de Leon, my husband."

He flashed me a blinding smile of his own. "We did it, soulmate," he said. "We survived the devil, a near-apocalypse, and—most insidious of all—a wedding."

A surprised laugh slipped out at that.

Andre's eyes fixated on my mouth, and then he leaned in, capturing my laughter between his lips. With a moan, I fell into the kiss, pulling his head closer to me. By the time our mouths parted, we were both breathing heavy.

"Soulmate, I am the most blessed man to walk the earth," he said, his voice husky with desire.

His gaze turned heated again, and the time for talking was over. We tugged at each other's clothes, making our way to the bed. Our movements only relaxed once skin met skin and Andre settled over me.

I gasped as he slid himself inside. Using both his hands, he brushed away the hair that framed my face.

He moved against me, and I broke eye contact for a moment to close my lids and enjoy the sensation of being joined with him.

When I opened my eyes, it was to find him staring at me like I invented happiness. "I love you soulmate," he said. "Forever and always, I love you."

Letter to My Readers

Thank you for walking this journey with me. It's been over two years since *The Unearthly* first hit shelves, and six years since Gabrielle's story first began to haunt me.

For me, this is a bittersweet moment as Gabrielle, Andre and the gang were the first fictional characters I wrote, and this is the first series I've had to end. These books have become very dear to me, as I hope they have you.

I will continue to write plenty of paranormal novels in this world. Even another–*gasp*–siren's story. Despite what the supernatural world thinks, another siren's out there, and her story will be told in *Rhapsodic*, an adult paranormal romance novel that will be released in 2016. In addition, I have several other supernaturals who inhabit Gabrielle's world, and I'll be sharing their stories in the coming months and years.

If you enjoyed *The Unearthly* series, I ask that you consider joining **my mailing list** where I announce my new releases.

I'm so very humbled by your readership. If I could, I'd give you all big hugs. As it is, I'll have to settle for virtual ones.

Hugs and happy reading,
Laura

Be sure to check out Laura Thalassa's new adult
post-apocalyptic romance series

The Queen of All that Dies

Out now!

What if you had the power to become invisible for a price?
I did, . . . and I paid. Dearly.

Be sure to check out this new young adult series by Dan Rix

Translucent

Out now!

Be sure to check out Laura Thalassa's new adult science fiction series

The Vanishing Girl

Out now!

BORN AND RAISED in Fresno, California, Laura Thalassa spent her childhood reading and creating fantastic tales. She now spends her days penning everything from young adult paranormal romance to new-adult dystopian novels. Thalassa lives with her husband and partner in crime, Dan Rix, in Oakhurst, California. For more information, please visit laurathalassa.blogspot.com.